SEISMIC

SEISMIC

R. L. Roach

VANTAGE PRESS
New York

This is a work of fiction. Any similarity between the names, characters, and places in this book and any persons, living or dead, is purely coincidental.

FIRST EDITION

All rights reserved, including the right of reproduction in whole or in part in any form.

Copyright © 2005 by R. L. Roach

Published by Vantage Press, Inc.
419 Park Ave. South, New York, NY 10016

Manufactured in the United States of America
ISBN: 0-533-14967-3

Library of Congress Catalog Card No.: 2004094251

0 9 8 7 6 5 4 3 2 1

To my mother and father, whose spark gave
inspiration for this book

SEISMIC

Prologue

Bob Hoaglund was daydreaming that Friday morning as he drove down the I-15 to work in San Diego. It was his last day for two-plus weeks, he was going on vacation in central Oregon to do some fishing. The only thing to be done that morning was for the judge to instruct the jury in a burglary case they had been working on that week. It was a rather simple case; the guilt of the defendant was obvious. They could come to a verdict before noon, and he could get a head start. He hadn't had a vacation in a year. As a court reporter, that's a long time, and his nerves were frazzled and he needed some rest.

As he drove into the Hall of Justice and parked his car, he noticed his boss, Judge Robin Ruiz, across the way. He waved saying, "Hello." She said "Hi," and they both rode up the elevator together to the courtroom on the fifth floor. It was 8:30 and the only people there were Jeri, the clerk, and Bill, the bailiff.

Jeri said, "Well, this is the day you've been waiting for."

"Yes, indeed."

She asked where I was going and I told her: "A place that no one will find me."

"Well, that's smart."

The jury came in with a verdict at 2:00 in the afternoon, and after goodbyes, I was gone from the courthouse before 3:00. When I arrived home, there was a message on my answering machine to call Jim Elstein at the Old Mill Inn—that was the place I was staying at in Bend. He answered the phone and told me he had overbooked the inn, and that I had better be there at noon tomorrow to be sure to reserve the room. The Old Mill Inn is a bed-and-breakfast next to the refurbished Old Mill District, which is now a big mall complex. I told him I would be leaving Fallbrook by 5:00 and that I would drive non-stop, getting me there by ten in the morning tomorrow. I didn't want to lose that place for two weeks.

When I arrived in Bend mid-morning on the twenty-sixth of May, and immediately went over to the inn, Jim was there and told me how sorry he was, and that he appreciated my effort to help him out of a tight spot.

It looked like it was going to be a beautiful day. He told me it was the first nice day they'd had in a week. I was tired. I unpacked my things, lay down to take a nap and woke up at five in the afternoon. I was really hungry, so I got dressed and walked up Bond Street to *The Brewery*. It wasn't really crowded at the time, so I walked up to the bar and had a beer and hamburger.

After a couple more beers, I walked out the door. It was about 8:00 and the sun had not gone down yet, walked down by the river to relax a little more, and was just about run over by some young kids.

"Hey, watch where you're going," I said.

One of the kids replied, *"Fuck you, boy."*

Nice welcoming committee from the town. Decided not to go over to the river, so I got a *Bulletin* and walked on back to the inn. The paper was full of interesting small-town stories as I drifted off to sleep.

As I awoke in the morning, there was the smell of bacon drifting through the inn so I got dressed and sauntered out into the dining room for some breakfast. There were two other couples—one from Washington and one from North Dakota. We exchanged pleasantries and all. The couple from Washington was very familiar with Bend and had an itinerary to the tee. The couple from North Dakota didn't have a clue where to visit first, so I suggested they go see the lava at Newberry Crater, by Paulina Lake. They seemed keen on that, and that ended my tour guide advice for the day.

After breakfast, I went over to the fly shop to get a fishing license and trail pass for the next couple of weeks. The weather looked wonderful and I couldn't wait until the next day, when I would start my adventures.

1

The highway rose into the Ponderosa pines just as I remembered from the prior year. As I wound through the mountains, Mendelssohn's "Italian Symphony" seemed so appropriate and my excitement began to grow. Just two miles and I was at the bridge. As usual, there were but three or four cars . . . three to be exact parked there. It was about 8:00 A.M. and the sun was beginning to rise above the hills I had just traversed. As I exited my car, there were four people on the bridge peering into the river, probably looking for trout. Someone yelled, "There! Right there."

One of the girls said, "Nah, that's just a shadow."

"No, I *know,* a Brookie when I see one."

I exited the car to gather my fishing gear, the rod and reel, my waders and boots, and most of all: my flies . . . my dear little flies. The season had just opened on the upper Deschutes and it's always a guess as to what the weather is going to be, or what flies are hatched.

As I suited up, got my vest on, collected my rod, locked the car and started toward the bridge, I offered a good morning to the four, to which three of the four responded in kind. However, the fourth, a youngish-looking fellow, turned to look in my direction and at that moment I felt a chill the likes of which I've never felt before. His eyes seemed as though they turned bright red, with the most evil grin one could imagine. Moments like that are not only difficult to understand, but—well, why would someone—didn't make sense at all.

Should I go north or south of the bridge? Figured I'd go south, access is better. Walked about fifty yards in, saw a nice pool, saw no fish rising, and proceeded on down the path. There were some nice riffles, the river turned to my right with some moving water and another forty or fifty feet fed into a pond.

The thing about late May is there are very few people fishing during the week. In fact, you might not see any people at all.

I tied on a Pale Morning Dun and cast in the direction of the deep part of the pool. After about four or five casts, a brook trout struck my fly and the emotions of a year's wait of fly-fishing were spilled out. *"Yeah!"* I said. He was about seven or eight inches, but what the heck, he seemed like a pound at the time. There were three more little brookies in that pond and they all gave me the same thrill. It was time to move on.

As I moved on into the meadow, there was a crackle, as if someone stepped on a branch. It startled me. I looked over, and a young doe was staring at me from twenty-five yards away. She didn't seem overly startled, as I was, so she just ambled away into the forest.

I pulled out a leech and tied it on in hopes of getting a big brown trout. Made a few casts into the undercuts of the river. No hits. Made a cast down a few yards, felt a bump and something big was on the other end. He played me for a couple minutes, and just then I looked up, and on the other side saw something strange. I couldn't make out what it was. It distracted my attention to the fish and he worked the fly loose.

"Damn it!" I said.

There wasn't a place to cross the river, the pools were too deep, so I went downstream into the meadow and found a place to cross and approached what looked like a boot or something similar. There, to my astonishment, was indeed a boot. Not only that, but part of the leg, in a decaying state with dried blood.

In getting a closer look, there seemed to be some ceremonial artifacts and lines drawn in a square part of the dirt, maybe six-by-six. Four roundish jade pieces, they looked like they came from an American-Indian belt. They were facing north, east, south, and west.

I didn't have my cell phone with me, so I proceeded to make tracks to the car.

After traveling fifty or sixty feet, there was a swooshing sound and an arrow landed a foot above my head on an old burnt tree. The arrow quivered as I stood there breaking out in a cold sweat.

I immediately began to run, tripping and almost falling along the way. Upon reaching the car, I noticed that the two tires on the driver's side were slashed and it would be impossible to drive. I opened the door, reaching for my cell phone. It was not there.

A car approached. A woman was driving, and I hailed her down. She stopped.

"Can you give me a ride?"

She rolled down the window and said, "Who the hell are you?"

"Never mind," and I reached in and took the keys out of the ignition, opened the door and said, "Move over, I'm driving."

She looked stunned. Not knowing what was happening, she took out a flashlight from underneath the console and raised to hit me. I warded off the blow and said, "I'm not going to hurt you. I've got an emergency and I need to get down the mountain and get some help." It seemed to alleviate some of her concerns, but she still looked scared.

"No," she said. "Continue driving to the mountain east for about two miles, make a right turn to Crane Prairie Reservoir."

The engine turned over. We headed west toward the highway. There were no other cars in the area.

She said, "Turn here into the campground."

When we reached the store I said, "Is there a sheriff or forest ranger anywhere in these grounds?"

"I don't know."

"Wait here, Susan," I said, and I took the keys from the ignition and entered the store.

The clerk at the counter was a rugged-looking gentleman with a beard and floppy hat. He was engaged in conversation with two other men who were sitting on barrels. They were laughing and carrying on about some joke the clerk had made.

"Can I help you, sonny?"

"Yes, you can. Is there a peace officer on the grounds or anywhere close?"

"Well, maybe there is and maybe there isn't. Whatever would you need one for?"

"If you can direct me to the nearest person with law enforcement authority, I'd appreciate it," I said rather gruffly.

"Hold on, sonny. Just tell me the problem and we'll see what we can do."

At that moment, a forest ranger appeared in the front door. The clerk, looking very disappointed said, "Red, you're just the person we were looking for. This gentleman wants to speak to you."

Red Jensen is not a very imposing figure at just over six-foot-tall and maybe 170 pounds, but the way he moved, you knew he was all business.

"Thanks, Josh." He turned, "You want to see me about something?"

"Well, yes. Could we talk outside?"

"Sure."

Just as we stepped out the front door and onto the dirt, this voice from the Explorer, said, "This man forced his way into the car and tried to kidnap me."

"Is that true?" Red Jensen said.

"Not entirely," I said. "My car is disabled, I was in a bit of a panic, she was the only person that happened by and I commandeered her car. You'll understand when I explain the circumstances. I meant her no harm."

"What's this all about?"

"Let's just walk over here for a minute," and I proceeded to explain about the boot, the arrow, and everything that happened subsequently. He seemed to understand and went over to the SUV with the woman inside. She gave him a card, started the engine, and I said, "Sorry about the way things happened, and thank you for . . . " and she drove away.

Red Jensen came over to where I was standing, all the while the clerk and his two buddies were looking over my shoulder trying to discern what the fuss was all about, and he asked me, "You want to tell me what's going on here?"

I said, "Yes, I'll tell you, but I think we ought to get out to the river so you can see for yourself what I'm telling you about."

"Well, I mean, what's this all about with the woman? She was pretty upset and told me you tried to kidnap her and that . . . "

"Yeah, I know that's what it looked like, but I'll fill

you in on the way to the river. Did you call the sheriff or police?"

"No, I'll do that later."

It was about 1:00 when we arrived at the bridge and exited the car, and I showed him that I went south, and the path I took. When we arrived at the clearing I said, "It's right over here." To my astonishment, there was nothing there. *Nothing there.* The place was all smoothed out, small twigs and pine needles strewn upon the spot.

"Look, I don't understand this at all."

I turned around and went over to the tree where the arrow was embedded. No arrow. It was as if it hadn't happened at all.

"I know what you're thinking Red, but . . . "

"Maybe we just ought to forget about this whole thing. You better hope the woman doesn't want to press charges. I've got to make out a report, so let's go back to the store and you can use the phone to take care of your car, get a tow or whatever."

"All right," I said, "but don't you think we ought to inform the proper authorities about this?"

"I *am* the proper authority, mister. You just wasted a lot of my time, that girl's time, and you better give it a rest."

We arrived at the store, went inside, sat down at the table and he proceeded to write a report. At that point, he seemed pretty upset. I looked up at the counter and the clerk, Josh, was still there.

When I got up to go the restroom, I noticed the door to the backroom ajar, just enough to see what appeared to be a black bow and brown sheath with some arrows, black arrows. As I got back to the table, I said, "Red, there's something we should look at in the back." *No,* I thought, *this won't do any good.* "Are you about done with the report?"

"Here it is, right here. Read it over and sign it if you wish."

It read in part: "Subject alleges he was fishing when he came upon what he stated was a boot. Inside the boot was part of a leg bone. He stated there was what appeared to be ceremonial-type, jade-like trinkets facing 90 degree angles, with some lines drawn in the dirt. Subject stated he ran and an arrow was shot at him lodging in a tree just above his head. Subject and author of this report returned to the scene and saw no evidence in the area of what had been described by Subject."

I signed the report, reluctantly, and thanked him for everything. He said he was sorry the way things had gone and wished me good luck.

When I approached the counter, the clerk said, "What can I do for you, sonny?"

"Well, I'd like to use your phone if I could to call for a tow truck. My car is over . . . " Then I realized at that moment it was better if I said nothing further at all.

He said, "Maybe one of us could run you over there."

"No, I think I'll just have him meet me here."

"You have a tough day, sonny?"

"You could say that," I said.

The tow truck operator arrived, we went down to the bridge to retrieve my car, drove down to Bend to visit the Jeep dealership, had my tires replaced, and I went back to the inn.

The first thing I did when I got back was to call the service provider for my cell phone, Nationwide, to tell them my phone was stolen, and that they needed to cancel that service immediately and issue me a new phone. She told me to go to the nearest Nationwide store or provider and they would do just that.

2

Susan Woodson, still shaken from the events, drove down the mountain toward her office at Gibraltor Real Estate in Bend. She had been visiting a friend with an RV at a resort on Wickiup Reservoir over the weekend and had planned on stopping by the Sunriver office today when the incident took place. She wished that the gentleman had been arrested at the time, although she hadn't been physically assaulted or anything. She understood that Mr. Jensen was only a forest ranger and had to go through proper channels.

When she arrived at the office and parked her car, she entered the building, and hoping nobody noticed her entry, was almost to her office when she heard Joanne Behler say, "Susan, how are you? You've had some calls from—are you all right?"

"Oh, hi, Joanne. Yes, I'm . . ."

She approached and said, "Did you have an accident or anything? You look a bit shaken."

"Well, I did have an incident on the way from Wickiup this morning, but it's all resolved," and she gave a brief explanation of what had happened; the gentleman stopping and demanding her car, that it was an emergency, and that she was all right now.

"OK then. But you look like you need a drink or something."

As she entered her office, there were some twenty

messages on her answering machine, most of which related to real estate. One was from her friend at Wickiup, one from her boss saying he wanted to meet her for lunch at the restaurant at Broken Top Country Club. It was too late for that, so she started leafing through some listings for some clients, but finding her concentration waning, she told the staff she would be gone for the day. Joanne caught her going out the door and said, "Do you want to get some lunch somewhere or . . . ?"

"No, I think I'll just go home and rest. Thanks."

While driving home, she thought about how much better it would have been if she had gone and got her teaching certificate; that the stress level would be much less and maybe she'd be much happier. She was thirty-two years old and running around like a chicken with its head cut off and not getting anywhere. The money was good, but something was definitely missing. She thought of herself as somewhat good looking, but the men she met were either ski bums, or fitness freaks of some kind, with no plans or direction of any kind. Paradoxically, this may be the same path she's on; they may think of her as career-oriented and pigeon-holing her life. *Well, no matter right now. Get home, get the cat some food, get me some food, watch a movie, go to bed, get up tomorrow and start a new day.*

She parked in the garage, got the mail, said hello to her cat, Rebecca, noticed there were several messages on her machine and thought, *Won't anyone leave me alone?* Most of the messages were from friends, but the last one was from the forest ranger, Red Jensen. "Hello, Ms. Woodson, this is Red Jensen. I just wanted to inform you that Mr. Hoaglund directed me to the spot where he stated this incident took place and there was no evidence of anything. I think he's just some kook who became irrational, for whatever reason. However, if you still want to file charges against this gentleman, here is my number, give me a call and we'll proceed in some fashion."

Right then, she didn't want to make a decision on anything, only to get some food and sleep.

* * *

When she awoke in the morning, she felt refreshed and her head was a little clearer. Did yesterday happen or what? She got up, turned on Fox News, and began to make a little breakfast. Would she have some eggs and toast or a Slim Fast? She looked in the mirror and decided it was Slim Fast.

As she was driving to the office and listening to the local news, she noticed the newsman said, "This morning, at three thirty-two A.M., a temblor of 2.7, centered at Mt. Bachelor, shook the west side of Bend. It lasted for ten seconds and was noticeable by a few people."

Wow, she thought. *Didn't feel a thing.*

The office was abuzz, there was some big deal going on today. A two-million-dollar home in Sunriver was being sold and she wasn't a part of it.

Sam came around the corner, saw her and said, "Susan, glad you could grace us with your presence. Did you feel the earthquake this morning?"

Well, it was hardly an earthquake, she thought. "No, didn't feel a thing. Heard on the news it was very small and occurred up the hill."

"You must have tied one on last night not to feel that," he said.

Boy, he can really be a pain in the ass, she thought. *I'll just give it a rest and not respond. It could only get worse.* Joanne came into the office and said, "Feeling better today, are you?"

"Yeah, Joanne, everything is fine. Back on schedule. I've got a client at ten o' clock, I'm supposed to show something on the east side. Probably be back early afternoon."

"Well, how about going out later on, about six o' clock?"

She didn't really want to go. "Yeah, sure."

She checked her messages. There was one: "I know this is kind of awkward and all, but my name is Bob Hoaglund, the gentleman you were involved with on the highway with your car. I'd like to meet you and set things straight. If you could meet me at The Brewery at seven P.M. tomorrow." There was something muffled, " . . . sitting in the corner over by the window."

She bounced out of her chair, shaken again, and wondered how he found out where she worked. At that point, she remembered that he had used her name. *Where did he get that? This thing is starting to get out of hand.* She wondered if she shouldn't go to the police about all this. This was supposed to be all behind her after last night. *It's like a bad penny that won't go away,* she thought.

"See you later on, Susan."

"Yeah, OK, Joanne."

"Susan, the ten o' clock is here," the receptionist said.

"Be right there," and they went to look at property.

*   *   *

Bob Hoaglund figured he would go get a hamburger at the drive-in near Pilot Butte. He sat there in a trance as he mulled over the events of the day before. The ceremonial boot sitting in the middle of a square-like clearing, the four round silver adornments with jade, and the lines drawn around the boot. The lines seemed puzzling. There was a line directly through the boot—*that's it. That must be the place we're at.* The other lines were the directions of north, east, south and west. West could be anywhere: The McKenzie, Santiam, Willamette River. North is the Deschutes, East is the Crooked River, South would be the Williamson, the Rogue. The bone in the boot looked like it was cut with a serrated instrument, like a fishing knife. The silver pieces were obviously directional signs. *What else? What else? Facing north there was what?* It looked like two numbers,—a three and an eight? No. A three and a zero.

"Is there anything else, sir?" the waitress asked.

"Uh no. That's it. Thanks."

On the way back to the inn, he thought of something he had read in Saturday's paper—just a blurb about some people in Salem.

As he opened the door, he saw Jim Elstein and said, "Jim, do you have Saturday's paper anywhere around?"

"Probably not. We usually only keep them a day or two."

"Thanks," he said.

Well, what to do now? I'll probably have to go to the Bulletin's *office to get a copy.* He went over to their office and asked if he could see a copy of Saturday's paper. He was in luck, the girl said, "There's one on the back counter." She went and retrieved it and he opened it up to the front page and started leafing through. On page 4 there it was, a paragraph that read:

> *Salem*—a family of four has officially been reported as missing. Luis Chavez, 34; Ramona Chavez, 32; Enrique Chavez, 16; and Roberta Chavez, 15, left for a weekend

camping trip on Friday the 18th of May and have not been seen since. A friend said they were going down to the Rogue River and were to return late in the evening of the 20th.

Yes! I was right. There was an article about someone missing. God, could this have something to do with these missing people? Do I go to the police with this or—It was about eight o'clock the sun was getting low in the west. His mind was dizzy with possibilities. *Let's have a beer and maybe things will clear up a little.*

I went over to The Brewery and sat at the bar and tried to come up with some sort of plan. But what? There was a number 30. Did that mean the 30th . . . tomorrow? *Where?* It was right above the northern, what I determined to be, arm of the Deschutes River. If so, *where* on the river? *Well maybe Red took care and called the police, or sheriff. He never got back to me. Maybe I should call him. What about the girl from the real estate company, Susan? I called and left a message. Maybe I should leave well enough alone, but, you know, I really want to apologize for being such a jerk.*

He had enough for one day and retired to bed.

3

The aroma of hot cakes wafting through the inn woke Bob with a smile and pleasantness. He rolled over and saw his clock, which read 7:10 A.M. He put on some shorts, shirt, sandals and strolled out into the breakfast nook where he encountered Becky, Jim Elstein's wife, and stated he was going to take some coffee and the front page of the newspaper back to his room; but he'd be back for breakfast at quarter of eight. He sat down on the bed, looked at the front page, started leafing through the paper to see if there was any more news on the missing four people. Sure enough, on page 5 there was a blurb:

> Salem—Still no sign of the Chavez family. None of their neighbors have seen or heard from them since their departure on the 18th of May.

He sat on the bed beginning to wonder. *Is this pure coincidence? Am I just looking for something to hang my hat on?* The story is too ominous and foreboding to discount.

He took his coffee into the bathroom where he cleaned himself up a bit; shaved, brushed his teeth and entered the breakfast room once again.

"This morning, we're having blueberry pancakes and bacon with a side of fresh fruit," Becky said.

"That's great," I said.

Two people were sitting across from him, both in their thirties. He asked where they were from, and they both responded Missoula at the same time and laughed. He told them he had been fishing and enjoyed it a lot. They both finished their breakfast a few minutes later. He asked where they were off to, they stated Sisters and the surrounding area. He told them they'd enjoy that and they left. He finished his breakfast and returned to his room. Turning on the television, he heard: "The SUV, believed to have been owned by the Chavez family, was found last evening in a wooded area just south of Roseburg. None of the Chavez family were anywhere to be found."

This is getting too spooky, he thought. *I came up here to get away from the daily grind of criminal justice and I'm smack dab in the middle of a mystery. One thing that keeps coming to mind is that arrow quivering back and forth above my head. Was it fate I'm still alive or did he miss on purpose? Was it just to scare me? What about the bow and arrows hanging on the back wall of the store at Crane Prairie? They were black, weren't they. What link did the clerk with the beard have in this?*

He wondered whether Susan Woodson got his message. *Should I go over to her office and confront her?* No. He would leave it where it is.

* * *

The fly shop was across the street in the industrial complex of the Old Mill complex. He ventured in the front door to find out what flies were hot at the Crooked River, which was his destination today. The shop was adorned with rods, reels, waders, boots, etc. Over in the corner was an assortment of flies. A gentleman approached and asked, "Can I help you?"

"Yes, I'm going to the Crooked River today. What's hot?"

He answered, "Anything yellow. Comparaduns, Golden Stones, Yellow Sallys."

He scooped up two of each and went back to the inn to get his gear. The back way to the river by way of Prineville Reservoir was a shortcut and saved about fifteen minutes; that was the route he'd take.

Besides fishing, his greatest love was opera; specifically the Italians: Verdi, Rossini, Puccini, and most of all, Gaetano Donizetti. As he drove this back road, the radio blared Donizetti's *"Lucia di Lammermoor,"* the magnificent Von Karajan recording with the incomparable Maria Callas, life stood still. Every time the stress of life reared its ugly head, opera became his best friend. *I think I would give up ten years of my life to see Maria Callas. She was that most magical person; the greatest diva of all. Her performance in this opera clearly is on the top ten charts in heaven.*

As he arrived at the reservoir and swooped down to the river, it was late morning and the sun was on the water. The baetis would soon be on the water and he would see if the fly shop was right—*go yellow and make you a happy fellow.* The Crooked River was silt-colored water and usually nymphing is the best method of catching fish, with scud imitations (fresh water shrimp) the most popular. But dry fly was more of a challenge here and that's what he'd try. Those three flys attracted some fish and all went well for the two or three hours he was there. It was going on three o'clock when he decided he'd better get back to Bend for his seven o'clock date.

Driving to Redmond on my way to Bend, the sky was beginning to turn dark as a storm was approaching over the cascades. *Should I go to Bend, or should I take a right and go down to the lower bridge on the Deschutes River for a little while?* Instinct took over and he took the right on 97 to Terrebonne, made a left and it was five or six miles to the river. On top of the hill, just before the descent to the river, there was a little cut-out on the left side of the highway to cross over and park cars. It was just a walk of one hundred yards down to the river. He slowed down and noticed that someone had continued the barbed-wire fence and the entrance from the highway was closed. That meant he had to proceed down to the bridge, park his car in the parking lot, put on his fishing gear, grab his rod and hike about one half mile further than he would have had the cut-out been open. There was nobody else in the lot.

It was raining now, a clap of thunder in the distance, but he had come this far and it wasn't going to deter an hour or so of fishing. As he hiked along the path, the thought came to him: *The thirtieth. What if this is the place? The Deschutes is a long river, but there are not too many accesses to the public.* Just down and around the bend was a nice deep pool and an opportunity to catch some fish, hopefully. It was pouring and the sky lit up with a crackle and loud clap of thunder. Just as quick as it started, it let up. Approaching the pool, astonishingly there was the boot, with the bone protruding, standing upright in the middle of the clearing, with the silver piece facing towards him. It was rather dark and difficult to make out the surroundings.

As he turned around and looked up the hill in back of him, the sky lit up once again with a loud snap and a silhouette appeared. He took out his binoculars and honed in on the individual on top of the mesa, and there nodding with the same evil grin, was the gentleman he had seen on the bridge. The man appeared to bring up a rifle with a scope and aim it in his direction. At that point, he said, "*shit,*" dropped his rod and binoculars and dove towards the weeds. There was a report, surely in his direction, and he felt a hot, singe-like sensation in his left foot. He scrambled in the weeds, heard another report from the rifle which missed his head by no more than three feet, the bullet causing the water to spout several inches.

Then there was silence; dead silence. *Was he coming down the hill for me? Should I scramble along the river for a better place to hide? Yes.* He entered the river, the water was up to his chest, pushing him along. *Surely I'll hit a hole and submerge myself,* he thought. There was a bush hanging into the river. He grabbed hold and brought himself into some cover. He knew not where he was. In about ten minutes, there was a rustle among the bushes and weeds. It was still rather dark, but he dared not pick up his head to see what was going on. Pretty soon, there was silence once again and he scrambled amongst the bushes and weeds to the clearing. There, not to his surprise, the only items on the ground were his rod, reel and binoculars. The boot and silver piece were gone.

It was beginning to clear and his cover would not be as good. At that point he began to notice the pain his foot. He looked down and saw that the left heel of his boot was completely gone and there was stinging pain. There was no time to assess the damage to his heel as he needed to make his way back to his car. He crouched as he made his way along the path, looking up the hill to see if anyone was there. After a while, he reached where the car was parked. It still appeared to be the only car there. Waiting maybe ten or fifteen minutes, he surveyed the car to see if there was any damage. There appeared to be none. He opened the driver's door, tossed his rod in the back and made his way up the hill towards Terrebonne. As he reached the top of the hill and slowed, there was no evidence of anyone . . . not even a car. When he passed this way before, there were no cars parked anywhere to be seen, no evidence of anything.

He parked the car a few yards down, got out of the car and under the barbed wire to the cut-out. There was no evidence of any—*wait.* There was one continuous tire track. *Sure! A motorcycle. Is that what this guy used before? No wonder I didn't notice anyone or anything.* His foot was really stinging now, so he took out an emergency medical kit underneath the seat, took off his boot, saw the bullet creased the back of his heel, got some salve from the kit, put some on his heel, threw on a bandage, put his sock back on and was on his way.

It was six o'clock and time to get back to the inn, clean up and meet Susan . . . or not . . . at the Brewery.

* * *

There was a call on Susan's cell phone, it was Joanne wondering how much longer she was going to be showing property. This guy had run her all over town for the last three hours and didn't seem to be interested in anything.

"Well, I'm on my way in, Joanne. There's somewhere I'm supposed to . . ." *Never mind, she thought, she didn't need to know.* "Where do you want to go?"

"I'll leave it up to you, Susan."

"Let's meet at Broken Top at six-thirty for a drink, then."

"OK. Meet you there."

* * *

It was seven-thirty and Susan hadn't arrived. It was no surprise, Bob really didn't expect her to show. The episode has taken on a life of its own and she really didn't need to be involved.

"Can I get you anything else?"

"No. How much do I owe you?"

"Three fifty."

He laid down five dollars and started to make his way out the front door when it opened and there standing two feet in front of him . . . was "Susan?"

"Yes. How do you know?"

"Hey, you two. This really isn't the best place for you to be hanging out. It's right in the middle of the door."

"Sorry," I said, "Let's sit down here."

"Before you get too comfortable, whoever you are, let's get a couple of things straight. I don't know who you are and what your interest in me is, but it's going to stop, and it's going to stop right here and now. Besides, how did you know my name was Susan?"

"That's an easy one. The documents you had on the console had your name, Susan Woodson, and the company you work for on them. Look, I understand how you feel and, if I were in your shoes, I'd feel the same way. But, let me . . . but what happened yesterday was something I hadn't planned and I feel terrible about it. I want to explain that . . ."

"Look, you needn't explain anything, Mr. Jensen, the forest ranger, called me yesterday and asked me if I still wanted to file charges. I haven't returned his call yet."

"Are you?"

"Unless you can convince me otherwise. I don't even know why I'm having this conversation with you. I'm leaving."

As she began to rise, he grabbed hold of her sleeve and said, "Hear me out for a second, OK? I was fishing on the Deschutes by the bridge, I noticed what appeared to be some ceremonial-like marks showing in the dirt, a boot with the lower shin attached, some silver trinkets that looked like they belonged on a belt or something, and some drawings in the sand . . . some lines. I began to work my way to the car when someone shot an arrow at me into a dead tree just missing my head. At that point, I panicked, rushing toward my car. When I arrived, the tires were slashed, my cell phone was gone, I didn't know what was going to happen next. You arrived in your Explorer and you know the rest. Believe me, if there was any other alternative . . ."

"Why should I believe you?"

"I'm up here from the San Diego area. I have no friends here, and besides, you're kind of cute." He laughed. She didn't think it was all that humorous.

"Well, I'll accept your explanation and leave it at that."

He needed to do something to keep her here. "And here's the old line: can I buy you a drink? It's the least I could do."

She thought for a second and with a wry smile said, "Sure."

They sat there for a half hour, getting to know something about one another, and when they got up to leave, he said, "Can I call you again?"

She said, "Well, only if I drive," and they both laughed. They began walking to her car and she noticed he was walking with a slight limp on his left leg. "Is there anything wrong with your leg?"

"No, I just stepped on something."

She parked the car, and he got out and went in the front door, turned to his room and saw a note on the door. "Call Mrs. Hoaglund. Jim." *Think I'll wait until tomorrow.*

4

It was about midnight when the room began to shake. Bob bolted out of bed and said to himself "Earthquake." It lasted fifteen or twenty seconds, so it seemed. This is the second tremor in three days; odd for central Oregon.

He ambled out to the breakfast room about 7:30, the tables were full with people.

Jim said, "Good morning, Bob. We're having crépes with . . ."

"Could I just get some orange juice and a muffin of some kind?"

"Sure. Blueberry or Macadamia?"

"Um, Blueberry is fine."

The paper was sitting on the sofa so he grabbed some coffee, took the orange juice and muffin and returned to the room to read the news of the day. There in bold print was:

Roseburg—The bodies of Luis Chavcz, 34, and Enrique Chavez, 16, missing since May 18th, were located yesterday at the bottom of a pool in the Umpqua River. In retrieving the bodies, two things were noticed. The right leg of Luis, the father, was severed just below the knee and the left hand of Enrique was also missing.

Romana Chavez, 32, the wife of Luis, and Roberta, a daughter, have not been located.

My God, I was right! There is a connection. These

people have been murdered and maimed. The article went on to read:

> Authorities are skeptical as to the condition of the two females after discovering the condition of the two males.

The Umpqua River is north of the Rogue River by thirty or so miles; all in the same area. *Wow, I thought. What to do now?* It was apparent that Red Jensen would contact authorities, that he would be contacting Bob at anytime. This was officially not a vacation anymore, it was turning into a few days of hell. *I could contact Susan and . . . no, not right now. She needn't be involved. Whoever this guy is, he's one weird SOB. I've had cases of antisocial personalities, but I never thought I'd be involved with one of this magnitude. Plus, he's obviously psychotic. Yesterday's episode at the Deschutes River showed how cunning and dangerous this guy is.*

Bob walked out of his room toward the breakfast room, Becky Elstein approached and said, "Bob, this gentleman over here wants to go fishing today. You've gone out the last two days, maybe you can give him some tips?"

"Hi, I'm Bob Hoaglund. Becky said you're going fishing today and . . ."

"Yes. Joe Hammer from Pennsylvania. I went up Century Highway just about two or three miles yesterday and fished for a little while, but . . ."

"You're looking for something a little more provocative, I assume."

"Yes."

"Well, if you go up Century Highway and Mt. Bachelor, you will run into some lakes, and if you like stream or river fishing, the upper Deschutes is pretty nice, especially by the bridge on 40. There's some nice browns and brook trout there."

"Thanks a lot," he said. "I'll let you know how I do."

*   *   *

Nationwide Communications has a kiosk right across the street in the Old Mill District, so he made his way over there around 10:00 A.M. Bob inquired about the same phone that was stolen and was told they'd give the same deal, with a $100 rebate, so he purchased the phone. The salesman there was a young man, asking if he wanted a few more bells and whistles, to which he stated, *No, just the same as I had before.* He contacted the company, they activated the phone and Bob was in business. The mall wasn't too busy, so he looked around a little and made his way back to the inn. Becky greeted, "You have a message to call Judge Robin Ruiz."

"Thanks, Becky." *Well, that's two messages so I better get to them.* He dialed up his mother's number and when she answered, he said, "Hi Mom, this is Bob."

"Robert." She always called him *Robert*. "I hope this is not your idea of a joke, but . . . "

"What are you talking about?"

"Well, this is a message I received Monday evening, you tell me. 'Mrs. Hoaglund, your husband's ashes will be scattered amongst the Lonesome Pines soon.' "

"My God, what time did you receive that message?"

"It was about seven in the evening."

He didn't want to get into the specifics, but he had to figure out something to say and quick. "Mom, it's just some prank call. The person obviously thinks you're my wife and is trying to scare you."

"Yeah, well they've done a pretty good job, I'd say. You take care of yourself up there."

"OK, Mom. Bye."

Bob's mother and him are not estranged, so to speak, but they're not very close. She blamed him for everything bad that happened to her. Something like this didn't help. Hopefully, that's the end of it and there will be no more calls. Bob decided he better see what the judge wants.

"Hello, Bill, this is Bob. I understand the judge wants to speak to me."

"You're right. Something happened and she's worried about you. Let me put you through."

There is a click.

"Bob? This is Judge Ruiz."

"I got your message that . . ."

"Yes. I'll let you listen to this message: 'Bob Hoaglund's ashes will be scattered among the Lonesome Pines soon.'"

"That's basically the same message my mother received, the only difference being . . . Judge, could you call me back on your private line? This is pretty sensitive stuff." He gave her his new cell number and she called back. Bob told her about the encounter in the meadow, the boot, the near death experience with the bow and arrow, how his tires were slashed and cell phone stolen; and that apparently the thief had used it until it was deactivated. Bob didn't tell her about the day before incident.

"Did you tell the authorities about any of this?"

"Oh yes. I contacted a forest ranger and told him of the incident, but when we returned to the scene, there was no sign of anything. It was as if it hadn't happened at all."

"Are you coming home?"

She knew nothing of the Chavez family, at least I don't think she did, there was no mention of it.

"Not right now. I've got some decisions to make and I'll be in touch."

"Take care of yourself, Bob."

"Thanks."

That was the focus of the moment, some decisions to make. Maybe a ride up to Sisters would clear the air, which was becoming extremely foul right now. On the way, he might well surprise Susan Woodson.

* * *

Joanne Behler was busy with a client in her office when Susan walked in the door. She noticed that Susan had an extra little spring in her step since she left her at Broken Top. Susan's life, like hers, lacked that little something; that *something* a man might bring. Did she have that little something on the side that she didn't know about? Well, if she did, she sure hid it well.

Susan Woodson got a cup of coffee and sat down at her desk to retrieve her messages and see what new listings were out. It was Wednesday and Wednesday was new listings day. She would have to review all the new properties the agency had received. After doing all of the aforementioned, she told the receptionist she was going downtown for awhile, she would be back for the 10:30 A.M. caravan.

* * *

Sam Rossetti was an irascible sort; someone whose divorce two years before turned him topsy-turvy. Although he had a penchant to fool around, he never thought of it as a big deal. After all, he kept his wife happy with all the things she needed and wanted. One day, she had enough and filed for divorce. Sam pleaded with his wife, for he knew he had a lot to lose, that although in the past he had stepped out—which, she knew all about it—this last affair was the last straw and she became entrenched in her thinking and this was it.

It was 10:20 when Susan arrived back at the office. She had ten minutes to get things together before the caravan. She pulled out her briefcase, began collecting the new listings, looked up and saw Bob Hoaglund enter the office with some flowers. *Not now,* she thought. Just then, Sam entered her office and said, "Susan, after the caravan, I want you and I to go over some figures from your last two sales, and maybe we can have dinner together."

"Uh, Sam, I've got a date tonight around five P.M. In fact, he's here right now, I want . . ."

"I didn't know you were dating any . . ."

"Come on, I'll introduce you."

She walked hurriedly with Sam out to where Bob was standing, talking to the receptionist. He was handing the flowers to her when Susan said, "Oh Bob, how nice. You didn't have to do that. Are we still on for tonight at five P.M.?"

What's going on here? Bob thought. *Is* what *still on for five?* She winked at Bob and he sort of smiled and said, "Well, yes. Sure."

Susan introduced Sam to Bob, they exchanged a few pleasantries, and Sam said, "I'll meet you outside in a couple minutes."

"OK. Be just a couple minutes. Look, Bob, I know this caught you by surprise, but I have to go and . . ."

Bob looked at her quizzically and said, "I don't know what just happened, but these flowers are for you and you can do what you want with them."

"I know how this looks, but I'll call you later on and let you . . ."

"Here's my telephone number." He threw it down on the desk and was gone.

* * *

On the way up to Sisters, Bob's thoughts were about the events of yesterday and today. If form held true, another ceremonial act will occur today, somewhere, maybe on the Crooked River. The silver piece was facing east, which is the Crooked River out near Prineville. *What about the messages to my mother and Judge Ruiz? What do the terms ashes and lonesome pines mean? What was that scene about at the Gibraltor Real Estate office?*

He drove on past Sisters to the Metolius River, a secluded spot near Black Butte. Bob bought a sandwich and apple at the general store in Camp Sherman and relaxed by the river to the slurps of trout rising and feeding. It was about seventy degrees with a hint of breeze. Summer was around the corner. After a while, he drove on back to Sisters and stopped in the fly shop to see how fishing was on the lower Deschutes. The owners were an energetic young couple who, in a very short time, were an institution in the area. As he exited, his cell phone rang. "Hello?"

"Bob, this is Susan Woodson."

"Yes. I'm glad you called. What was that scene all about in . . ."

"I'm very sorry about what happened in the office. It's an internal problem within the office, that's all I can say about it. But I shouldn't have used you as a pawn. The yellow roses are very nice and I appreciate it very much. But what I said about being *still on for tonight,* well I can't. . . ."

"Whoa, whoa. You made a date tonight . . . voluntary or involuntary . . . and I'm not letting you wiggle out of it so easily. Whether you wanted to or not, you picked door number two and you're going to stick with it. You don't seem the type to break too many promises. Besides, as a pawn I'm not so bad. As a stalker, I might be. So what'll it be; a pawn or stalker?"

"Well, Mr. Hoaglund, I owe you one for this and we'll make it a date. Pick me up at the office at . . ."

"No dice, girl. Your place at what time?"

"OK, OK. Seven o'clock at 2422 Dunhill Road just off Reed Market Road."

"See you there. Bye."

* * *

Red Jensen was perplexed by what had happened, and at around 10:00 A.M. on the thirtieth he returned to the scene of Bob Hoaglund's crime. He surveyed the area for about fifteen to twenty minutes. Finding no more than he had two days before, he started to return to his truck when he noticed something on the ground. It had the logo CRANE PRAIRIE GENERAL STORE and had the name JOSH ROLLINS on it. It appeared to be a cloth patch of some kind. He bent down to pick it up and that was the last thing he remembered . . . when he awoke he was tied to a tree and a man with a bow and arrow was standing thirty feet in front of him.

"What do you want? Why am I here? What are you going to do?"

The man raised the bow and delivered an arrow into his right shoulder. The pain was excruciating and he yelled out "Who are you? Why are you doing this?" The man leveled another arrow at Red's leg and shot one clean through the thigh. Red yelled out with loud gasp. He sagged with intolerable pain. As he raised his head he saw the man with a rifle leveled at his head. That was the last thing Red Jensen saw or remembered.

* * *

The radio was tuned to the news and Bob Hoaglund heard the announcer state: "This morning at twelve-o-four A.M. the City of Bend was shaken by another earthquake 2.7 in magnitude. The tremor lasted for about seventeen seconds. This is the second such tremor in three days. Scientists believe there may be some activity below Mt. Bachelor." *I thought so. Activity below Mt. Bachelor could only mean magma is accumulating. There's a chance of eruption, such as Mount St. Helens. This time it could be real serious and there is a sizeable population in the city and its surroundings.*

He thought about his date tonight and where they were going, what to wear, all that good stuff. He felt like a school kid again. He hadn't really had a date in a long time. He decided to make it dressy casual, for that seemed to fit most of Bend anyway.

5

Bob arrived at seven o'clock on the dot, walked up the sidewalk to the front door, rang the doorbell, the door opened there stood Susan Woodson. *Wow* he thought. "Hi, Bob. Come on in, I'll be ready in a moment," Susan said. He stood there in a trance with his mouth open. She took a couple steps away, turned around and with a wry grin said, "Come on in, have a seat, I'll just be a moment."

"Uh yeah . . . sure." *Was he that much of a geek? Did it show that much?* She looked lovely in all black, a silk camisole, matching slacks and shoes, wearing pearls. He noticed a baby grand Steinway in the corner of the living room. She came in the room trying to attach an earring.

"Do you play?"

"A little. It's been a while since I sat down to play anything serious. Been listening to too much country, I guess."

After seeing the way she was dressed, Bob wondered if maybe he was underdressed. "Do I need a jacket or anything?"

"No, no, you look nice. You're fine."

"Do you have a place in mind?"

"Well, if you like Italian, there's a new place in the Old Mill that I like pretty well, named Lucia's."

"*Quando rapita in estasi,*" Bob mumbled.

"*Lucia di Lammermoor,*" she said.

"You're right," I said. "How in the world did you know that?"

"That's for me to know and you to find out."

This girl is a little too quick for me, I better catch up real fast. They drove over to the restaurant and walked in. The maitre d' greeted, "Hello, Susan. Your usual table?"

"Yes," she answered.

Boy, we've been together less than fifteen minutes and I'm impressed. The waiter, whose name was Vincent, came over to the table and asked if they wished a wine list, to which Bob responded yes.

Bob looked at Susan and said, "You're very familiar with the menu, I'll take care of the wine. Give us a couple seconds, if you might."

The waiter said, "I'll be back momentarily."

Bob glanced over the wine list. When the waiter returned, he told him, "We'll have a bottle of *Castellano di Fonterutoli Chianti.*"

"Good choice," he said.

Right after the waiter left, Bob realized how that must have sounded and said, "Listen, Susan, I apologize for that. I should have asked if you wanted white or . . ."

"No, that's fine. Besides anyone who likes *Donizetti* knows what wine to order in an Italian restaurant."

Whew, Bob thought. *I've got to turn this around. I'm not a client, I'm her date.* They sat for a few awkward seconds, it seemed like a minute, and just as Bob was about to broach the subject of her piano, the waiter came back, opened the bottle of wine, and poured a taste in Bob's glass. It was wonderful. "Excellent," Bob said.

Bob noticed Susan appeared to be looking at him with amusement so he stated, "Now, about that beautiful Steinway in the corner. What's the history on that?" Her look of amusement swiftly turned to concern with the question. She paused for a second, not knowing if she should answer or not. Finally, she said, "Well, that's got a long history that would take too long over dinner. Why don't we save it for another time."

"How about a brief overview? A short synopsis, if you would."

He felt like a newspaper reporter then, not a court reporter, but it seemed to change the atmosphere. He wasn't sure if it was for the better or, hopefully not, the worse. She seemed to be fumbling with her glass, looking down all the while, looked up with pleading eyes: "What do you want to know?"

"When did you start playing?"

"I was four when I started. My mother, who was a soprano, sang with many opera companies, and wanted me to start early. I progressed really fast and by the time I was ten, was written up in the *Portland Oregonian* as the next up-and-coming American star. By fourteen, my mother wanted me to go to Dallas and school under Van Clibern. He said he didn't have the time right then but would recommend someone my mother would be happy with, which she wasn't. By the time I was sixteen, I was accepted at Julliard in New York where I spent a couple of years and totally burnt out. I just wasn't interested in a career as a classical pianist. My mother did not take to this at all; she told me to go live with my father on the East Coast."

"Were they separated?"

"No, not really. He was a rep for European wines and cheeses and so he had to stay on the East Coast. My mother didn't like the East Coast, she's an Oregonian at heart, and so they saw each other maybe three or four months out of the year."

"Did you move to the East Coast to be with your father?"

"No, I went off to the University of Washington, wanting to be a teacher rather got involved with real estate. Here I am."

"You said you're interested in country music now. Does that really take the place of . . ."

"No, of course not. Maybe at some point the fires will burn and I'll get back to it. What about you? You are interested in opera, I assume."

"Yes. That's my musical passion. By the way, when you mentioned your mother's career, I understood why you were able to grasp the aria from *Lucia* so fast. I've been a court reporter for a number of years, living down in San Diego. I come up here to fish because I love the area."

At that point the waiter arrived and said, "Are you ready to order?"

Susan looked Bob's way and said, "Is there anything you don't like?"

"No, be my guest."

"We'll each have the asparagus salad with beets, new potatoes and mustard vinegrette; follow that up with one order of basil risotto with shrimp and roasted garlic, one order of veal medallions sauteed baby artichokes, white wine potato puree and truffle oil."

"Very good," the waiter said. "Is everything all right?"

"Yes," she said.

All the time she was ordering, Bob couldn't take his eyes off of her. She was gorgeous. Obviously, she could tell he was staring at her all through dinner. The dinner was wonderful, the wine magnificent. By the time they were done, she had lost her edge and seemed very relaxed. They haggled over who should pay the bill, and after a few minutes, agreed to split it. As they walked out of the restaurant, she said, "Care to take a walk?"

"I'd be delighted."

It was a rather warm night for the end of May and as they walked on down by the river, it was rather balmy. As Susan clasped Bob's hand and moved a little closer, the scent of her perfume roused his sensations. She turned and said, "Why did you pursue this date on the phone after I tried to brush you off?"

"Why? You mean after dinner, you don't know?"

"Well, you know, I've got an idea but . . ."

At that moment, Bob stopped, turned and kissed her. She responded in kind.

"Does that give you any idea now as to . . ."

With a sparkle in her eyes, she put two fingers to his mouth and quietly nodded. They continued to walk, saying nothing and soaking up the moment. When they got back to the car she commented on his taste in wine. Bob told her it was one of the best Italian dinners he'd had. They drove back to her house, walked up to the door and she said, "You're in luck, Mr. Hoaglund. I'm going to play you a nightcap."

She walked over to the piano, sat down and said, "What would you like to hear?"

"Are you sure you want to do this, Susan? I mean, really, we can do this another time when . . ."

"No, I'm ready now."

She seemed a little *tipsy* to him, he didn't think this was really the time to be . . . "Come on, now, Mr. Hoaglund. You want to hear me play and here I am."

The more time passed, the more agitated she became, so I said, "How about a Schubert *Impromptu?*"

"In C minor or G flat or what?"

"In G flat."

As she started to play, you could see it had been a while and she was struggling, but she had great facility and sensitivity. After a minute or so, she dropped her head and her hands came crashing down on the piano and she broke down and started sobbing. Bob walked over and tried to comfort her, bringing her over to the sofa. He put his arms around her and told her "Susan, it's all right. It's all right."

She continued to cry stating, "I can't do it. I just *can't* do it." He told her that it was his fault, he goaded her into playing. She said, "No, I just wanted to play for someone who I knew would appreciate the music."

At that point they didn't say anything for ten minutes or so when she said, "Turn on the radio." He walked over and turned the radio on and *Moonlight Serenade* began to play. He walked back to Susan and said, "Do you want to dance?"

She wiped her eyes, smiled and said, "I'd love to." They swayed back and forth for the two and half minutes and he looked at her, winked and said, "You're really something, Susan."

She said, "Thank you." At that point he kissed her again, she put both arms around his neck, sighed, and said in a low tone, "I think you'd better go now or . . ."

He thought a moment and responded, "You're absolutely right." Neither one of them wanted to ruin anything; it was time to go. "Can I call you tomorrow?"

"Well, I don't know where I'll be." She smiled once again and said, "But you can try."

He kissed her again and said, "Good night, Ms. Woodson."

"Good night, Mr. Hoaglund."

* * *

When he awoke in the morning, the sun was shining through the curtains, the birds sounded a lot chirpier. It was a wonderful morning. He propped himself up, smiled to himself, and thought, *That's the best evening I've had in, well—it's been a long, long time. She's marvelous.*

He arose, washed himself up, and strode into the breakfast room where he spotted Joe Hammer all by himself at one table. He walked over and said, "Excuse me. I'm Bob, the person you were talking to about fishing yesterday. How'd it go?"

Joe looked up with this frightful look and said, "Oh, not too well."

"Fishing wasn't too good?"

"No. I took your advice and stopped by Davis Lake. I was the only one there. I walked along the shore about one hundred yards and there right in front of me was a body of a young girl with her hand cut off. God, it was awful."

"Well, I'm really sorry."

"She looked like she was dead a while."

He looked away and began to eat his breakfast. Bob sat down and began to think, *there wasn't supposed to be . . .*

Becky entered the room and said, "Bob, what would you like this morning?"

"Just give me some oatmeal and a muffin of some kind. Joe, could I see the front page, if you don't mind? Are you through?"

"Yes."

At that moment, it was enough to knock him off his chair. There in the headlines read:

The body of John Jensen, a local forest ranger, known fondly as Red, was found near the bridge on Route 40 yesterday. He was found tied to a tree at 10:30 in the morning by two fishermen. The cause of death is an apparent homicide.

Right below that, in the right-hand corner was a story:

A young woman in her teens was retrieved from Davis Lake in the early morning hours. An investigation is being undertaken. However, the body is believed to be that of Roberta Chavez, missing since the 18th of May.

He checked the rest of the front page to see if there was any further news that could ruin his day. There was none. *Red was my cover for this whole episode. There surely would be an investigation by the homicide team of the Deschutes County Sheriff's Office, and they would uncover my name. But what was he doing out by the bridge anyway? And why, if he didn't believe my story? This is going too fast for me, I've got to sit down and sift through all of this. Is Susan Woodson now going to be brought into it? Not if I can help it. Every day this maniacal killer has harassed us; every day something new. What will it be today? The sign for yesterday was to be the east. No story about anything unusual, I wonder if anything happened.*

His foot was feeling a lot better today and he thought he would go on down the Deschutes River past Madras to Warm Springs where the fishing can be exciting. A good hour's drive. As he entered his room his thoughts were on his date with Susan the night before. It was the first time in a long time, that he felt and had to deal with so many emotions. *It's too bad the night had to end. I'm thirty-four years old and it's time that—well, I can't get ahead of myself.*

6

Lieutenant Al Santorini sat at his desk in a trance as he recalled the phone call from Deputy Wally Berger informing him there had been a homicide by the Deschutes River and that the body was that of John Jensen, one of his best friends. He drove to the site just off Route 40 and observed the ghastly image of Red tied to the tree with two arrows in his body and a bullet to the forehead. He remembered kneeling beside his friend and saying *"Why you, Red, why you?"* He was one of the nicest people he had ever met. Not an enemy in the world—until now. Whoever it was will wish every day they had not made an enemy of Al Santorini. Red's car had been towed to the Sheriff's Department in Bend. Al had received a call from Deputy Berger that the forensics team was about to do a search of the interior. Al had requested to be at the search.

He went out to the garage, the forensics team was swabbing the outside of the car. He put on some surgical gloves and booties and, with the keys, opened the door. There weren't many items in the car. A flashlight, a clipboard with some notes attached, a forest ranger jacket, a map of the general area, a couple bats and a glove. He loved softball. They had played for twenty years. There was a cell phone and phone book of the area. The glove compartment was nearly empty except for a registration slip and some batteries for the flashlight as well as some paperclips. He was about to exit the car when he noticed a small slip of paper scrunched up halfway underneath the passenger mat. He retrieved the paper, smoothed it out, and a message read: CALL SUSAN WOODSON IN REGARD REPORT. Instead of leaving it for inventory, he put the piece of paper in his pocket and exited the car.

"Thanks, Wally. There's a clipboard with some notes. Let me know if any of them are relevant in any way."

"I will, Skip."

He went back to his office and immediately scoured the phone book for a Susan Woodson. Having found none, he called over to the phone company to see if they could help. There was one Susan Woodson found, she worked for Gilbraltor Realty. He was about to call over to Gilbraltor when he thought, *Uh uh. I'm going over there and see her personally.*

On his way over, he thought about Red's wife, Jennifer, and their three kids . . . how it felt when he had to tell her what had happened. It had been the lowest moment in his life.

* * *

Susan had stopped by Starbucks on her way in to get a café au lait. Although coffee made most people jittery without any food in their stomachs, it had the opposite effect on her. When she arrived at the office, she immediately looked around to see where Sam was. She was in luck, he wouldn't be in until early afternoon. The receptionist said there was a message from Carole Chapman to call her ASAP. *How could I forget? The concert tonight at Sisters!* Carole and two other sorority sisters were coming down from Seattle to see Cade McHenry, the country's newest sensation, perform in concert.

She got to her office and immediately called Carole. "Hello Carole, this is Susan."

"Hi Susan! Are you ready for tonight?"

"Sure am. What time you coming down?"

"Well, there's only going to be two of us. Janie can't make it, so we'll have an extra ticket. Do you have anyone in mind?"

"Don't worry, it'll be gone in two shakes of a lamb's tail."

"Our flight lands at Redmond about four-thirty. We're staying at the Hampton Inn in Bend, should be there about five-thirty or so. We'll be ready to go about six o'clock."

"Good enough, I'll see you there."

Susan asked the receptionist if Joanne was in the office yet and she replied, "Yes, but she's on the phone."

"Well, tell her that I want to . . . no, never mind." Susan decided to call Bob Hoaglund.

"Hello. Is this Bob?"

"What a surprise. Hello Ms. Woodson."

"Look, I know this is kind of short notice and all, but would you be interested in going to a country-western concert tonight? I know this isn't your first love, but we couldn't get Beverly Sutherland."

"It's not Johnny Cash, is it?"

Susan laughed. "No, his name is Cade McHenry. You just might enjoy him."

"I'd love to."

"Two of my sorority sisters are down from Seattle and we have an extra ticket. We'd love to have you join us."

"What time and where?"

"Meet us at the Hampton Inn in Bend around five forty-five. Is that all right?"

"Sure. See you later, Susan. And thanks."

"Bye."

Right then Joanne showed up in front of Susan's office. "Did you want to see me?" she asked.

"No, not really. I was looking for advice but I solved the problem myself. Thanks."

*   *   *

Susan and Joanne arrived back from lunch at 1:30. As Susan was walking to her office, the receptionist said, "Susan, this gentleman wants to see you."

"Oh, hello! Did we have an appointment?"

"No, my name is Lieutenant Al Santorini, I'm from the Deschutes County Sheriff's office. I wonder if I could ask you a few questions."

"Sure. Come with me into my office."

As they were walking, she introduced herself and as they entered the office she said, "What can I do for you."

He responded, "Do you know a gentleman by the name of John Jensen, also known as Red?"

She thought for a brief moment. *How do I answer this question?* "I don't believe I do. Should I?" *Whoops, that was a little cavalier.*

"I have a slip of paper with your name on it that indicates he was to call you."

"About what?"

"I was hoping you could give me an answer to that."

"Well, I don't remember a call of any kind from Mr. Jensen."

"He was calling you about a report."

"In the real estate business, we have all kinds of reports. I don't recall one from Mr. Jensen."

She was looking at him the whole time and was getting the impression he didn't believe her.

"Ms. Woodson, thank you for your time. If something jogs your memory, here is my card. You can call me at that number."

As he left the building she began thinking. *Why was he asking her those questions? Did something happen to Mr. Jensen? Is Bob somehow involved?* She walked into the front lobby to look for a newspaper of some kind. There on the table was this morning's *Bulletin,* the sports page on top. She began rummaging through the different sections. To her shock, there on the front page was the headlines: FOREST RANGER FOUND MURDERED.

She immediately sat down to gather her wits and thought, *No wonder he was here questioning me.* She wanted to call Bob but thought better of it; she would see him that night. *I wonder if his name and number were on there?*

* * *

Lieutenant Santorini left the realty office, got in his car, and sat there thinking to himself. *She's not telling the truth; she's definitely hiding something.* Nonetheless, he had to go over to Red's office and see if he could find out what this report was all about. Red was not in the market for another home at the time, so he knew it was something other than an escrow report or anything of that sort. *He came across her in some venue different than real estate,* he thought.

When he got to his office, he called Wally Berger. "Wally, has there been any investigation of Red's office yet?"

"Not yet. We had a deputy go over and lock up his office and put tape on the door."

"I might go over there this afternoon and see if I can find anything."

"Did you want me to accompany you over there?"

"No, Wally. I can handle it myself."

* * *

It was the end of May. That meant the salmonflies were out in abundance along the river. Each year at the end of May and beginning of June, these terrestrials which measure about three to four inches in length, are the main delicacy of the rainbow trout on the lower Deschutes River. It was a bit cloudy down at Warm Springs. Bob turned off the highway and took a dirt road back into Mecca, which was about two miles away. There were only three other cars there when he parked his Jeep and took out his gear: rod and reel, boots, waders and vest. He began a trek down the river. He wouldn't be able to go far because it was twelve thirty and he had to be back in Bend at five o'clock. He was the only one on the trail and he had this queasy feeling in his stomach at every turn there would be some ceremonial display, for the Indian reservation was right across the river. He walked about a half mile where he waded out to an island, tied on an adult salmonfly and cast it up and across. On the third cast the fish took off, the reel singing, "*z-z-z-z-z;*" the line going all the way to the backing of the reel. He fought this rainbow, also known to the locals as a "Redside" because of its markings, for a good fifteen to twenty minutes. The current in the river was strong and these fish were very strong swimmers. When he landed, the fish was fourteen to fifteen inches. Bob unhooked him, said, "Good day you beautiful thing," and released him. After three more fish, he decided to call it a day and made his way back to the car. After a sandwich and cola, it was back to Bend.

On the way back to Bend, Bob thought it was a good idea to put on some of his music for he knew not what the night would bring. He opened the windows, put on *La Traviata* and sang arias all the way back to Bend.

* * *

Lieutenant Santorini walked into the Bureau of Land Management offices, sought out the person in charge, and told him he was there to do an investigation into John Jensen's office. His office was covered with yellow tape. He opened the door, ducked under the tape, turned on the light, and began to explore the office. The desk was right in front of him when he noticed a picture of Red's wife Jennifer and their kids and a tear ran down his cheek. *Dirty bastard, I'll get you.*

After sifting through everything he could find, there were no clues as to any motive anyone may have, nor any reason at all to kill John, especially the manner in which it was done. He looked for any record or report that may give any clues, and there were none. After an hour or so, there was nothing else to be done, so he closed the door and went back to his office, a confused and beaten down man.

There must be something, he thought. *Something.*

7

Susan left work a little late and she had to scurry to get to the Hampton Inn by a quarter to six. She hadn't seen her sorority sisters for four or five years and was greatly anticipating the reunion. She wasn't sure why she called Bob to join them but . . . well, yes she was. There was something about him that interested her. She was smitten. She arrived in the parking lot at a quarter of, parked her car and made her way toward the lobby. Carole and Joyce were sitting there, dressed in their country dress, as Susan was—boots and hats.

Susan said, "U of W," to which both turned and smiled. They greeted each other, exchanged pleasantries, said they were so glad to see each other, how they were looking forward to the concert. At that moment, Bob came through the front door. He wasn't dressed appropriately for the evening. Susan walked forward and greeted him. He said, "Susan, you look smashing."

"Well, you look like . . . like a dude."

He stepped back and said, "You know, I doubt if Aaron Copeland, when he wrote *Rodeo,* was wearing boots, a hat, and an oh-so-smart suede jacket."

Carole said, "Bravo, Señór. Touche."

Joyce said, "Ditto."

"I guess I asked for that, didn't I?"

Carole approached Bob, stuck out her hand and said,

"You must be Bob. Nice to meet you. I'm Carole Chapman."

"Hello, I'm Bob Hoaglund."

Joyce approached Bob and introduced herself. "Hi, I'm Joyce Gilmore. I can't tell you how terrific what you did just now was. We stay up long and late to put it to Susan like that."

"Well, I'm not sure what I did, but I'll take your word for it."

Carole Chapman was an attractive blonde, a CPA with the firm of Ashworth & Deems, a prominent accounting firm in Seattle. Joyce Gilmore was a tall, angular African-American who owned a boutique and also did some modeling work in Seattle.

Susan thought they'd better get on the road, the concert started at 7:00.

Joyce asked Bob what his line of work was, and he told her he was a court reporter, worked in San Diego, and was up here on vacation for a couple weeks.

Carole asked, "Well, how did you and Susan meet?"

Susan said, "It's a long story and . . ."

Bob interrupted and said, "We met in The Brewery in Bend one night early this week. She was with a girlfriend, I strolled over to their table and asked if I could join them. They allowed me to and here I am."

"Sounds terribly romantic, Susan," Joyce said.

"Sure," Susan said.

"What other reason could there be for me getting an invite?"

"Don't press your luck, Robert."

Why did I call him Robert? Sometimes he brings out the best and the worst in me.

They pulled into the rodeo grounds for the concert outside the town of Sisters around six-thirty. Inside, they grabbed a table and had some hamburgers and drinks. *Bob is a charming guy, he has my two friends eating right out of his palm. It's as if I wasn't here.* Bob leaned over and whispered in Susan's ear, "I don't care what you think, you look downright smashing."

She looked at him and said, "I'll bet you say that to all the girls you meet."

"Only if their name is Susan Woodson."

I must say, it makes me feel—well, warm inside, Susan thought.

After they ate they sallied up to the stage to listen to some warm-up acts, in the entertainment vernacular, is the best way to put it. They were local and decent. Then came the main event. "And now straight from Memphis and the Grand Ole Opry, Cade McHenry." He didn't disappoint. He sang some old standards and wound up his show singing an old Willie Nelson song *"On the Road Again,"* and a couple Patsy Cline songs, *"San Antonio Rose"* and *"Walkin' After Midnight."* The crowd went wild. Everyone was all hootin' and hollerin', tossing up their hats and all.

At that point, the ground started shaking, the lights on the stage started flickering for about twenty to thirty seconds, and the whole place became dead quiet. Everyone knew what it meant.

*   *   *

Bob thought Susan's friends were a lot of fun. *Must have been quite a sorority house. I must say, they like their country music almost as much as I like my opera.*

As Cade McHenry was singing his last song, *"Walkin' After Midnight,"* and looking around the audience, seeing how happy they all were, Bob noticed two men walking toward the gate. One of them had a beard and floppy hat, the other a cowboy hat. The one with the floppy hat was the one Bob had seen at the store with Red Jensen and the other looked familiar but he just couldn't get a good enough look. They were up in the front and Bob wanted to get closer so he said, "Excuse me, Susan, I'll be right back." As he was trying to force his way through the crowd, he bumped with his beer into a gentleman, which spilled all over him. The man was gruff, "Why don't you watch out what you're doing, you little flake." He hit Bob upside the head, knocking him sideways. Bob got up and scrambled through the crowd toward the gate. As he got out into the lot, it was dark . . . real dark . . . and he could just make out—it looked like a pick-up truck with something on it—an attachable shell of some type.

As Bob walked back inside, he spotted Susan, Carole and Joyce. "What happened to you?" she said. Bob told her he bumped into someone's elbow on the way.

On the way out, the girls were all talking about the concert and all the different songs. Bob was beginning to get a little dizzy from the punch, so when they got back to the Hampton Inn he told them how much fun he had but that he was feeling a bit under the weather and thought he'd call it a night. As he exited the car, he leaned over to Susan and whispered, "Call you tomorrow, Ms. Woodson."

"I'll be looking forward to it, Mr. Hoaglund."

*   *   *

Charles Warren arrived in Portland at 9:30 A.M. from Los Angeles. He was a professor and Seismologist from Cal Tech. He had been summoned to Portland by the governor the morning before to ferret out the details of the tremors under Mt. Bachelor.

Ken Bailey, the governor's aide, met Mr. Warren at the gate. "Hello, Mr. Warren. My name is Ken Bailey, I'm an aide to Governor Thomas. I want to welcome you to Portland."

"Thank you, Mr. Bailey. I'm glad to be here."

"After we grab your bags, we'll go the hotel and go over your itinerary."

"All right, that would be nice."

As they drove to the Benson Hotel in Portland, Ken Bailey told Charles Warren that Governor Thomas was very interested in what was happening this week at Mt. Bachelor.

They arrived at the hotel, exited the car and went to Mr. Warren's room. Ken Bailey told him they would meet him downstairs at 11:30. Mr. Warren agreed.

When they all met at 11:30 down in the lobby, Governor Thomas was introduced and said, "If we can get right to it, Mr. Warren, right over here in the conference room."

Charles Warren brought out his briefcase, put it on the table and brought out some graphs and notes. He began to inform the governor and Mr. Bailey about what an earthquake was, then pulled out the graph, one a personal graph and one a Richter scale graph. He showed them that May 29 at 3:32 A.M. a 2.7 tremor was felt under Mt. Bachelor for ten seconds, and explained that was a very low level earthquake, and one that could normally be discounted as anything serious. The next tremor was May 30 at 12:04 A.M. and was 2.7 for seventeen seconds. That by itself was nothing serious, but coupled with the May 29 tremor was a little more cause for concern. Last night, at 10:30 P.M. there was 4.3 tremor which lasted for twenty-six seconds, and that brought this whole thing into a different ballpark. No longer were they thinking about the earthquake, but they had to consider the possibility of magma massing under Mt. Bachelor, which was an inactive volcano.

Governor Thomas asked, "Is this analogous to what happened with Mount St. Helens a few years ago?"

"Well, it could be. The cascade range is made up of inactive volcanos and we never know at what time anyone of them could activate. The magma may be a thousand feet down, it may be a mile down, we just don't know."

The governor then asked, "Well, Professor Warren, put on your speculation cap, if you would. What's your best guess as to where we are now?"

The professor responded, "Your guess is as good as mine. This is current activity in Mt. Bachelor; we don't have a good record to rely on. We just have to watch it and see."

"*If,* and I use the word reservedly, *if* this volcano were to blow, what would be the consequences to the cities of Sisters—especially—Bend?"

"Well now, you are asking a very pointed question for which there are few answers, and I would be guarded in my speculation. Bend is what, twenty miles from Mt. Bachelor?"

"Give or take."

"Depending on the size of the discharge, the amount of ash and debris in what is it, Deschutes River?"

"Yes."

"Everyone would have to be evacuated from Mt. Bachelor to the City of Bend, which is what, 50,000 people?"

"Yes. A little more."

"So, there, you see? I can extrapolate a little more,

but the scenario is not a pretty one. But let's just wait and see what happens."

"Thank you, Professor Warren. Mr. Bailey will take care of your needs. Enjoy your stay tonight in Portland."

"Thank you, Governor Thomas."

* * *

Lieutenant Santorini arrived at his office at eight-thirty in the morning. He said to his secretary, "Did you feel that shaker last night? It was bigger than the two before." She said she had felt very uneasy afterward. The first thing he did when he got to the office was to try and get hold of Wally Berger.

"Hello, Wally?"

"Yes."

"This is Al here. Have you gotten hold of Red's computer yet?"

"Not yet."

"Well, I want you to get that computer and get an expert to get into the hard drive, especially anything for the last two or three weeks, any notes, reports; anything. I want his telephone logs for the last month, anything that will shed light on where he was and what he was doing."

"Yeah, Skip. Will do."

"Thanks, Wally. Bye."

He knew that sooner or later he was going to have to tackle the FBI on this since it was under their jurisdiction. He hoped he would have some answers before that time.

* * *

Bob strolled into the breakfast room early that morning, 7:10 A.M. He grabbed the front page of the *Bulletin* and there was a headline that read: QUAKE of 4.3 ROCKS BEND.

At 10:30 P.M. an earthquake registering 4.3 on the Richter scale and centered at Mount Bachelor rocked Bend for the third time in three days. Experts are scratching their heads as to what to make of this since there have been no earthquakes in the last seventy years in this area.

The registration on the Richter scale has to be worrisome because of the location of these tremors. Sounds like magma activity to me. On the third page was the blurb:

Sisters—The body of Ramona Chavez, thirty four, was found near the McKenzie Bridge trail on the McKenzie River. She and her family had been missing since May 18th. As with the other victims, Mrs. Chavez's right hand was missing.

Well, the circle is now closed on the Chavez family. It seems obvious that two of the bodies were transported from the Rogue/Umpqua sections to the Deschutes County area. There have been five killings and no hint or sign of a suspect. There has to be some tie-in with this Josh fellow at the Crane Prairie store. If I could have only caught up with them last night. Someone out there is doing some investigating and it only will be a matter of time until they came upon that report.

After breakfast, he went downtown for a walk. Wall Street was abuzz with activity so early in the morning. He began to think of Susan and how much fun they had together and when he would see her again. He walked down by the pond and saw the swans defending their territory against any and all intruders. It was going to be a warm day. He sat down in the park and called Susan on his cell.

"Susan, how are you this morning?"

"Fine. And you?"

"Couldn't be better. I want to tell you how much fun it was last night with Carole and Joyce. You're lucky to have friends like that."

"I know. We're going out tonight to the new country-and-western club that opened in Bend, The Roundup. Should be a lot of fun. Haven't done the two-step, let alone any line dancing, in a couple years so it should be fun."

"Can I see you Saturday then?"

"I've got to show some property in the early afternoon, but I'm free after that. Oh, by the way, I forgot to tell you last night with the excitement and all, but a Lieutenant Santorini from the sheriff's office dropped into the office. He was asking questions regarding the forest ranger who was killed near the bridge, asking about some report that was written, that there was a slip of paper with my name on it, did I know him, and why there was a slip of paper with my name on it. I told him I didn't know a Mr. Jensen, that I didn't know anything about a report of any kind. I got the impression he didn't believe me, but . . ."

"Well, there was a report written and I don't think he'll give up so easily. You gave the right answers, but I'm not sure it was the right thing to do. Anyway, have a good time tonight and tell the girls hello for me. Talk to you tomorrow."

"Will do. Have a nice time today, Bob."

It seems obvious that the lieutenant hasn't come across the report or he would have contacted me by now. There are so many details I could give to this investigation but my participation in all these events won't serve me well in the eyes of the law right now. Better to lie low.

* * *

The girls were waiting for her at the hotel when she arrived just before eight o'clock. They were going over to The Roundup that evening. It was the first time she would have been there. Everyone was dressed in their Sunday best country clothes. Joyce had bought some new boots and they seemed to be a little tight on her.

"You're going to have to get out and dance tonight to get those broke in, Joyce," Carole said.

"I don't know, I could use a little more room."

"Maybe you'll just take them off," Susan said.

"After I spent as much as I did on these things! Are you kidding?"

They all laughed and took off over to the club. The club was packed; bodies all over the floor, whoopin' it up. The first number up was a line dance.

"Get out there, Carole," Joyce said.

"Only if you two join me."

They all three got up and strolled onto the floor, basically just trying to learn the steps. After the song was done, Susan's legs felt like jelly. The girls staggered off the floor. After two-stepping through a few songs, a young fellow in a cowboy hat came over and asked Susan if she wanted to dance. He was about six-foot, rather on the lean side, but had a peculiar way about him. "Think I'll sit this one out," she said.

"I've seen you out there, you're pretty good. Just a trip around the floor."

"Oh . . . all right."

He was a pretty good dancer, she had to admit. But

when he asked her for a date and she told him she didn't think so, his demeanor turned sour, his eyes lit up and he had this scary grin on his face. Her skin began to crawl and she broke out in a sweat. As he turned away Susan heard him say to himself, *"She'll be sorry for that."*

When the girls came off the floor they looked at Susan and said, "What happened to you, Susan? You look like you've seen a ghost."

"Maybe I have. Look, could we maybe go somewhere else? My thighs and calves are screaming."

Carole said, "Sure. Where to?"

"Let's go down to The Brewery for a quick beer." She was secretly hoping Bob might be there. They got there, no Bob. They had a couple of beers, reminisced, and then Susan dropped the girls off at the Hampton Inn after hugging and saying their goodbyes. Susan said that she would be in touch for the next get-together and left for home. On the way she was thinking about that man at The Roundup and his evil eyes and smile. It affected her all the way home.

8

The day before had been a nice day for Bob Hoaglund, nothing extraordinary happened. He came home early, read some, and listened to music. He went out for breakfast, it was seven-thirty and there was no one in the room. This was Saturday, wasn't it? Both Jim and Becky greeted him and said he had the whole room to himself, they were at his service. He laughed about that, and asked them what was for breakfast. Becky said, "Orange juice, bacon and eggs with sourdough or wheat toast." He said that was fine.

He was almost afraid to look at the front page of the *Bulletin,* every day there had been some shocking news. Today was a quiet day. He went to the sports page to see if there was any fishing news. There was.

> Fishing great at Lake Paulina. The month of June has produced some big fish at the lake and more is expected in July. A better than average winter runoff is cited as the reason.

He had never been to Lake Paulina. Maybe that afternoon he and Susan could run over there. He didn't even know if she was a fisher (wo)man or not. He decided to ask. *Got to make a run to Costco this morning to pick up some nourishment; sports bars and Gatorade.*

After breakfast, he went back to his room, walked

over to the fly shop and picked up some flys for the Fall River, looked at the merchandise and came back to the inn. The clouds were beginning to accumulate to the west, as they called for thundershowers today and tomorrow. He got in his car and made his way to Costco.

* * *

Lieutenant Santorini called Jennifer Jensen around nine in the morning to see how she was doing. She answered the phone and in a weak voice said, "Hello, this is Jennifer."

"Hi, Jennifer. This is Al. How are you doing this morning?"

"As well as can be expected, I suppose. The kids have been very upset, my interest has been with them and it has kept my mind off Red a little."

"You know you can call me anytime, Jennifer. You and Red were my closest friends and . . ."

"I know, Al. I know."

"Are you up for a few questions, Jennifer?"

"Yes."

"Did you and Red have any discussions about buying property or a new house, anything of that sort?"

"No."

"Do you know of any reports such as a title report, real estate appraisal, anything?"

"No. Why do you ask?"

"We came across a piece of paper for Red to ask a real estate lady about a *report*. And we don't know what it refers to."

"We hadn't discussed anything of that sort."

"Well, my love to you and the kids. If you need anything, be sure to call and ask."

"I will, Al. Thanks for calling."

He felt terrible for asking those questions, but he needed to know, and now. The next week, the FBI is surely going to be involved.

* * *

It was about 1:30 and the phone rang. It was Susan.

"Hi, Bob. Listen, my afternoon appointment fell through so I'm free from two o'clock on."

"Great. You know, I never asked, but do you fish?"

"Not really. It's been a long, long time. My uncle used to take me out on the lake once in a while, but it never amounted to much. Do you want to go fishing?"

"Not without you, I don't. I thought we might go up to Lake Paulina this afternoon and slum around in a boat and chum for some fish."

"Hey, that sounds great. What time?"

"I'll pick you up around three."

"Means I gotta hustle then. I'll make some sandwiches and bring some beer."

"See you then."

Bob rang the doorbell, she opened the door. He kissed her on the cheek and said, "You know, with that wonderful perfume you're wearing, you're going to scare the fish."

She laughed and said, "As long as I don't scare you." They both laughed.

He stared into her eyes, deep pools of blue that seemed to carry on a conversation all of their own.

"Are we just going to stand here or are you going to help me with the ice chest?"

"Sorry, I forgot myself."

They drove over to 97 and headed south. The clouds were dark over Mt. Bachelor and they could see the mountain was getting some weather. As they got to the turnoff to Sunriver, Bob asked about the girls, The Roundup and if they all had a good time. She told him she was sore this morning from line dancing—and dancing period. She said they left and went over to The Brewery, had a couple of beers, and then she took them back to the inn and went home.

"You know, there was one thing odd that happened, though. This guy came up and asked me to dance. I didn't want to, but eventually agreed. We were dancing and he asked me for a date. I refused and his whole demeanor changed. He had these really light eyes that glowed and a grin that gave me the shivers."

At that point Bob almost ran off the road.

"Watch out where you're going, Bob."

Bob found a turnout, stopped the car and put both hands on Susan and said, "Do you remember the story I told you about being shot at and all?"

"Yes."

"Well, I'm afraid you just ran into that person."

"How do you know? I mean . . ."

"Susan, that's the only person I've ever seen with eyes like that and that God-awful grin."

Her whole demeanor changed, she became sullen and worried.

"I'm sure he has no idea who you are so let's not worry about it."

She looked at me with pleading eyes and said softly, "OK. Let's go fishing."

They arrived at the lake and went to the restaurant and store. There they got a one-day license for Susan and rented a motor boat. They only had one left and it had a small two-and-a-half engine. They asked the best place to fly fish for browns and the store clerk told them the moss beds near Big Bay or the moss beds near Little Crater Camp. He showed them a map, and they went down to load the boat with the ice chest and fishing gear and took off for the moss beds. It seemed like forever to get there in that little twelve-footer, but eventually they found it on the east shore and anchored in.

Bob hooked up Susan's line with a leech, showed her a few casts and she gave it a try. At first, she had a little trouble with the rhythm of the cast, especially sitting down, but on the ninth or tenth cast she made a beauty. He was holding her rod, showing her how to strip the leech with little twitches. They had stripped about twenty feet or so and boom, she got a strike.

"I've got a fish, I've got a fish!" she said.

"Indeed you do. Just let him take the line. Hold your rod up. Don't let the line get too loose. That's it. Now reel him in slowly. Let him run a little. Reel again."

As the fish approached the boat. Bob told her to hold the rod up as high as she could, and he netted the fish. A beautiful twelve-inch brown one. They looked at each other and smiled.

"Can you believe I caught that fish? You're not going to let him go, are you?"

"Yes, so he can give someone as much pleasure as you got."

"Well, bye Mr. Brownie."

They sat there awhile, no more fish. Timing was the master of fate.

"How about a beer and some food?" she said.

"Sounds good to me."

They sat there in the boat, feet on the edge, heads on

the pillows, eating their sandwiches and drinking their beer, wondering if anything could be more perfect.

They moved down a little and out, still there were no more fish. The sun was beginning to set and Bob said, "You know, I think we better get back. It's a good ways and we don't want to be out here in the dark."

"Fine," she said. "I'm ready. Too bad we didn't have a camera to show *who* caught the only fish."

"How did I know that would come up." They both laughed.

As Bob was preparing to lift anchor, off in the distance, there was a boat coming toward them at breakneck speed. He was a couple hundred yards away and didn't seem to be slowing down at all. Bob had just got the anchor up when he shouted, "Jump, Susan! He's going to hit us!" Bob looked over his shoulder and saw that he was fifty feet away and veered off. The wake was a good four to five feet and as they jumped, swamping the boat. The wave submerged both of them. He could feel the weight of the boots making it difficult to rise. When he did surface, he gasped, looking around. "Susan? Where are you?" She rose a few seconds later, spewing water. He grabbed her and held her head up above the surface. Grabbing hold of the boat he peered over the top to see what was there and saw the boat preparing to make its way back. Bob told Susan to hang on. "We're going to try and make shore." It was about fifty to seventy-five feet to shore through the moss beds, but they had to try. Bob held her head to his chest and started a one-armed backstroke. At that moment, he could see a shadow on the bow of the boat with a rifle leveled at them. It was getting darker and more difficult to see. He told Susan they had to separate, that she'd have to make it alone or they'd be in trouble. "Swim underwater for about ten feet and stay about ten or fifteen feet apart. It's our only chance." At that moment, there was a crack and zing a few feet away. "Let's go under. Now." They did that about three times. Bob could hear the results of the shots on the water. One close, two not so close. They hit the moss beds at about the same time. "Susan, wade and keep low. Crawl if you have to."

They finally made it to shore and scrambled to the nearest tree. They huddled together and comforted one another for a few seconds. Bob peered out and heard the boat start up and go away. At that moment, someone came running and saw them huddled together. He said, "You all right? What happened?"

"Yes, we're all right," Bob said.

"I thought I heard shots," he said.

"No, that was just our motor sputtering. We stood up and swamped our boat, panicked, and made our way to shore." Bob didn't want the law involved in this in any way.

"Are you all right, Miss?" the gentleman said.

"Yes, I'll be all right. Thanks."

"Well, come on up to the house and we'll get you back to the store."

"Thank you," Bob said.

They stood outside the garage while the man got his car out. Susan looked at Bob and said, "It's that guy, isn't it?" He nodded his head in agreement. "He's out to kill us, isn't he?" Again, he nodded his head in agreement.

"Come on people, let's get you up to the store."

They arrived at the store, thanked him for everything, and went inside. The clerk looked at them and said, "You're a sight for sore eyes. How did this happen?"

Bob stated, "We stood up and fell overboard. The boat turned over and was swamped. We made our way to shore and here we are. It's over near the moss beds on the east side."

"We'll get someone out to retrieve it in the morning. Did you lose any gear?"

"Just a couple of rods and reels and an ice chest. We can come up tomorrow and settle up."

"Oh, that's all right, folks. It happens all the time."

They hurried out of the store and over to the Jeep. Bob checked if everything was okay with the car, it appeared that it was. He opened the door, they both jumped in, and took off for Bend. They were both soaked and Susan was taking off her boots as Bob was looking in the rearview mirror to see if anyone was tailing them. There was no sign of any cars.

"Who is this guy, Bob? Why is he doing this?"

"Somehow, some way, he knows I have information. How much, he doesn't know. I'm really sorry you're involved in this, Susan. I'd give anything if . . ."

She put her two fingers to his lips, smiled. "Ssh."

He leaned over and took her hand, raised it and kissed it. "Thank you."

The radio was on a country station, the announcer said, "That was Alan Jackson on Country Radio, KCON." They both smiled.

*   *   *

When they arrived at Susan's house, she told him to put the Jeep in the garage so it wouldn't be visible. They went in the house and she said, "You can take a shower down the hall. Just leave your clothes outside. I've got an old robe that you can wear while they're drying."

Bob went down the hall and jumped in the shower.

He heard her come in the door to collect the clothes. "My whole body is green with moss."

As the hot water ran over his body, he thought, *I'm not going back to collect the equipment I lost, not in a New York minute. We're just lucky to be alive.*

After the shower, he dried off and donned the robe which, surprisingly, fit pretty well. Susan was about 5′6″ and it fit fine. He cracked the door while she was taking a shower and said, "You know, I'm glad you're tall. This robe fits."

"Hey, just leave it at that, okay?"

"That's all I have to say."

He made his way out into the living room and turned on the classical station. Arturo Rubenstein was playing a Chopin ballad. Susan, sporting a nifty lavender robe, strode into the room.

"Look, I can change the station. It's just an automatic . . ."

She looked at him, smiled and said, "No, that's perfect. Do you want some water, a soda, beer, wine?

"I'll have a beer."

She went into the kitchen and returned with two Brewery Pale Ales.

"Good choice," he said. "I feel very bad about this."

"No, not now." She curled up next to him with her feet on the couch. She looked up at him, her eyes darting back and forth, took her two fingers, kissed them and pressed them to his lips. She moved closer, inviting him to kiss her. He moved his head down and kissed her, and then kissed her again. The belt was undone on her robe and his hand moved on her thigh. She sighed and stiffened. He realized she had nothing on underneath her robe. His hand moved up her waist to her breasts, fondling them. She felt so warm. Her hand moved on his thigh, so warm and soft.

They stood up, swaying back and forth to the rhythm of their bodies. She took off her robe, took off his robe and dropped them on the floor. He laid her down, kissed her breast, kissed her neck. She looked into his eyes and said, "It's been a long time, Bob." "Me too," he said. All of a sudden the world was a wonderful place.

"You were wonderful," she said. "In fact, there isn't a thing about you that isn't wonderful."

"*Pshaw,*" he said. "You're the first person to say that."

She reached up, took his head down to hers and kissed him. "And hopefully, for some time."

* * *

They sat up in bed, she in the cradle of his arm, their bodies as one. She leaned over, looked at him and said, "What are we going to do, Bob? I'm scared."

"So am I. We need to do something, and something fast. Trust me, Susan?"

"You know I do."

"Well, here's what I think we ought to do. I don't know whether he knows where I'm staying or you reside, but we can't take the chance. Tomorrow morning, I want you to call your friend, Joanne, and ask her if you can stay there tomorrow and tomorrow night. We'll get you a ticket out of Redmond to San Francisco the first thing Monday morning."

"What about my business . . . my clients?"

"You're more important to me than any of your clients, or your business."

"How come San Francisco?" she asked.

"Because I'll pick you up in San Francisco and we'll drive down to San Diego for a few days. Tell your boss you've got a sick aunt in San Francisco. We don't want anyone tracing our whereabouts."

"Then what?"

"We'll figure something out in the meantime. Okay?"

"Wherever you want to go, dear."

He hadn't had anybody call him *dear* in a long time. It sounded good. He rolled over, kissed her once and said, "You feel wonderful, Ms. Woodson." They made love again.

9

When he awoke, the smell of bacon permeated the air. He rolled over and knew she was fixing breakfast. He looked at her clock: it said 7:26. He yelled out, "Hey, we slept in this morning." She responded, "I wonder why!" He laughed.

She came into the bedroom with that same lovely robe and asked, "How do you like your eggs? Over easy or scrambled?" He reached up and pulled her down to him, knowing that all he had to do was pull that draw around her waist and they would start again. "Anyway your *dear* heart desires. Although I would prefer them scrambled." She kissed him and pulled away. "That's the way you'll get them then."

In a few minutes, she brought in some juice and tossed the paper on the bed. She asked, "Are we going to make reservations this morning?"

"I think we better if you're going to get out of Redmond on a Monday. Is Joanne working or at home this morning?"

"She should be at home until nine-thirty or ten on Sundays."

"You better give her a call as soon as possible to set up your schedule."

"*Yes sir,*" she said.

"I don't mean to be bossy, but this is very serious, Susan. We could be in real danger."

"Yes, I know. And I don't mean to be flip, but it's happening real fast and—well, my eggs; I've got to tend to my eggs."

He laughed and said, "You'll do anything to get away from me."

"Don't be—do you always keep your cool in times like this?"

"Not always. Only when you're around." They both laughed.

He knew he had to get in touch with Jim or Becky and tell them he had an emergency and was going to have to leave this morning. He hoped to be out of here by noon and on his way south. He asked if they were having breakfast in bed or out at the counter. She said it was out in the kitchen. "Do I wear the robe again or . . ."

"Your clothes are in the washer and should be dry in a half hour. You're stuck with that same robe again. It served you well last night."

"Yes, it sure did."

They had breakfast and then Bob asked if she had a laptop so he could make some reservations. She said she had one in her office. She logged on and brought up a travel server. There was a 7:50 A.M. flight out of Redmond to Portland, and then from Portland arriving in San Francisco at 12:30 P.M. She said that would be fine. He made reservations with Alaska Air and they were set.

"I'll call Joanne. She should be home." She dialed. "Hi, Joanne? I was wondering if I could stay at your place today and tonight and if you could take me to the Redmond airport early tomorrow morning? I know it sounds bizarre, but I'll explain everything to you tonight. . . . Oh, you're not working this afternoon? . . . Your appointments have cancelled? Well, I'll . . . if you could leave your key in the regular spot. Would that be all right? Thanks, Joanne. I'll see you later on. Bye."

"I really feel bad about all this, Bob. She's such a good friend."

"That's what real friends are for. We will have to leave this morning in as surreptitious manner as we can. Everything will be fine."

"What'll I tell her?"

"Tell her that you will explain everything in due course; that it's very important that she not press you on this."

"Well, I'm not one to misrepresent . . ."

"You did for me."

"You're right. And what for? Look what it got me."

"That's all the thanks I get for this last week?"

She reached over and they kissed. "You got a *lot* of thanks last night."

Bob shook his head back and forth and said, "I know."

"What time did you want to leave here?" she said.

"By eleven or before, I would think."

"OK. I'll have to take some of my laundry over to Joanne's then."

"Is there anything I can help you with?" Bob said.

"Make this all go away."

"Sorry."

"How long are we going to be gone?"

"Pack enough for a week or ten days."

Bob felt helpless and in the way. She picked up the phone and called the realty company.

"Hello, Sandy? This is Susan. I won't be in today. I believe I have one appointment at two this afternoon, if you could cancel it for me? Thanks."

* * *

"Well, Susan, have a nice day today and call me this afternoon when I'm on the road."

"You know I will."

Bob helped her with her luggage downstairs to the car. She locked the house, opened the garage and got in her car. He strolled around to the driver's door, reached his head in and said, "Susan, I . . . I . . . have a safe trip. I'll see you in San Francisco." He kissed her. She appeared to have tears in her eyes and she said, "Don't let anything happen to you, Bob."

"Are you kidding? I've got a date in San Francisco tomorrow at noon."

They waved, left her garage, and went their separate ways.

*   *   *

Bob arrived around 11:00 at the Old Mill Inn. Standing around the breakfast table was a young lady he hadn't seen before. She looked up when he approached and he asked, "Is Jim or Becky here?"

"No, they've taken the day off and won't be back until later tonight. Can I help you? I'm Fran."

"Hello. I'm Bob Hoaglund, I've been staying here a little over a week. There's been an emergency and I will have to be leaving. I will write a note that you can give them and I'll be in touch with them later."

"Sure," she said.

He asked if there were any messages for him and she said there weren't. When he returned to the room he wrote out a note that he was sorry to leave so suddenly, but there was an emergency down home that needed his full attention. He gathered all his stuff and began to ferry it out to the car when the thought arose that maybe he should be in contact with the sheriff. *No, that wouldn't be wise. I'll do the same thing, write a note with some information.*

When the Jeep was packed, he went back inside and gave the note to Fran. He told her to tell them how sorry he was to have to leave so suddenly. On the way over to the sheriff's office, he pondered the best way to leave so as to not attract attention to himself. It was Sunday, there wasn't much activity anyway, so he strolled up to the front door, looked around, there was no one in sight, and put an envelope under the door addressed to LIEUTENANT SANTORINI. CLASSIFIED INFORMATION. Hopefully nobody would bother to open the envelope, it would be disastrous if they did. He scurried around the corner to his car and quietly slipped away.

*   *   *

Sundays were usually slow days at the office so Lieutenant Santorini didn't think it was necessary to go in. None of the reports would probably be ready, and besides, he had to get ready for the funeral tomorrow morning at 9:00 A.M. Giving a eulogy is never easy, and this one would be extremely difficult, with Jennifer and the kids sitting in the front row. He puttered around the house for a few hours and decided he would give Susan Woodson a call to see if she could recall any information about that note of Red's.

He called the realty office. A voice answered, "Gibraltor Realty. How may I direct your call?"

He said, "Susan Woodson, please."

The person on the other end of the phone said, "Could I take a message? Susan Woodson has cancelled all of her appointments today and won't be in the office."

"No, that's all right, I'll get in touch with her later. Thank you."

*   *   *

Susan was doing some laundry and ironing when Joanne came in the house.

"Joanne, is that you?"

"Yes, Susan. What a surprise this is. What's going on?"

"Yesterday I was fishing up at Paulina Lake and there was an incident. I believe I'm being stalked."

"You, fishing? Did you notify the authorities?"

"No, not yet, and I don't know that I will."

"Well, how . . . what . . . you went fishing? *When is* the last time you did that?"

"I was out there with another person, who I don't care to identify, who liked to fish. That's all the further I'll go."

"This isn't like you, Susan. I think you need . . ."

"Trust me on this, Joanne. I'm going to San Francisco early tomorrow morning to visit my aunt who's ill and needs my help, and I'll be there for a few days."

Joanne looked at her quizzically but then said, "I'll go along with this, Susan, but just for a little while and then . . ."

"Thank you, dear friend."

They sat around talking about Gibraltor and Sam, and Joanne said, "It wasn't Sam, was it?" They both laughed. Susan went about getting everything ready to go when Joanne came in and said, "How about some Mexican food? I'll pick some up down the street."

"That'd be great."

She went into the living room and dialed up Bob on her cell.

"Hello, Susan."

"Where are you?"

"I'm just outside of Redding coming down the mountain from Mount Shasta. How ya doing?"

"Pretty well, I guess. Joanne's a bit skeptical about this whole thing, but she's a good friend and will go along with it. Where are you staying tonight?"

"At the Hampton Inn in Fairfield, which is not far from San Francisco. I wish there was some other way of doing this, Susan, but there isn't without taking a big gamble."

"I understand."

"One other thing. I don't think you should use your cell unless it's an emergency. We don't want anyone tracing our calls."

"All right."

"Miss you, Susan."

"And I you, Bob."

"See you at the airport tomorrow at twelve-thirty."

"Good night."

She sat there feeling like this was all a dream and wondering where it would end, like Bonnie and Clyde on the lam.

* * *

Susan and Joanne arrived at the airport at 6:00 A.M. There weren't many people there at that hour. As Susan was exiting the passenger seat, Joanne said, "Well, have a good trip. You look like you're going to stay week or two."

"Thanks for everything yesterday, Joanne. I'll be in touch. I hope my SUV is not going to cause a problem for you."

"Don't worry about that, it'll be fine."

The skycap took her bags and she asked if she could check them in curbside. He said she couldn't unless she had a ticket. She went and found a trolley and hauled them in to the ticket counter, got her ticket, checked her baggage, got a paper, and went upstairs until they could board the plane.

On the way to Portland, she mulled over the events of the last two days in her mind. *If you told any of your friends about all this, Bob, the incident on the lake and all, they wouldn't believe it.* She sat back and awaited her fate in San Francisco.

* * *

The funeral of John "Red" Jensen was a spectacular affair. There were over a thousand people who attended, four hundred of whom were law enforcement officers from all over central Oregon. Al Santorini gave a very sensitive eulogy for his friend, one that was a testament to one of the most popular people in the community. "Everyone knew Red," he said. "We will all miss his warm smile, his honesty, the way he dealt with all of us. Good-bye, good friend. I felt honored to know you."

After the ceremony and burial at the cemetery, Al hugged Jennifer and told her if he could help out at all with her and the kids, he would be at her beck and call.

It was 10:45 when he arrived at the sheriff's office. He went into his office and called down to Wally Berger. "Has anything come in yet, Wally?"

"Yeah, Skip. I've got some info right here."

At that moment, he noticed an envelope with the words: LIEUTENANT SANTORINI. CLASSIFIED INFORMA-

TION. Wally stepped into his office, closed the door and began to recite what he had. The final autopsy results found that the cause of death was a .308 Winchester bullet; that the two arrows found in his body were a Beman carbon shaft, 6.0 Ulrafast 5500. The diameter was 7.0, 28 3/4 inches. It had a carbon tech razor tip. Toxicology showed no remarkable results.

"Does it state what kind of rifle was used?"

"The only thing it said was possible Los . . . 7 or 7.1."

"Anything else?"

"We had the hardware specialist go over the computer for the last two or three weeks and there were no signs of messages the preceding days before his death."

"Thanks, Wally."

He looked down at the envelope and opened it. Inside was a note that read:

> Lieutenant Santorini. This concerns the death of Red Jensen. It concerns an incident that occurred one day prior. If I were you I would run a rap sheet on a clerk at the Crane Prairie Store. His name is Josh. He may have some valuable information you need to go forward with your investigation.

Lieutenant Santorini sat the note down, stepped out and asked Wally to return to the office. "Wally, was there any information on the computer about a Josh?"

"Here's the report, Skip."

He scanned the report for any—lo and behold, there, on Wednesday, May 23rd, was the last note in Red's computer. "Investigated ruckus at Crane Prairie Store with C.J. Josh Rollins and customers. Rollins became verbally abusive toward customers. Author was there on grounds and questioned Rollins. No further action was taken."

"Thanks, Wally."

"OK, Skip."

He sat there for a moment trying to decipher what it all meant. *Maybe there was a report of an incident after all. Maybe Ms. Woodson knows more than she's willing to convey to us.* He got in his car and made his way over to Gibraltor Realty.

"Hi, I'm Lieutenant Al Santorini. Could I speak with Ms. Woodson, please?"

"Ms. Woodson is not in the office today."

"When do you expect her back?"

"I'm not sure."

"Is there anyone here that might know her whereabouts?"

"Well, Sam Rossetti is the broker in the office and he might be able to help you. . . . Sam, there's a gentleman out here to see you."

"Hi, I'm Sam Rossetti, what can I do for you?"

"Yes. Lieutenant Al Santorini from the Deschutes County Sheriff's Office. Can you tell me how I might contact Susan Woodson?"

"Well, she's not here right now. I haven't talked to her myself, but was informed by an employee that she is out of town."

"Who might that employee be?"

"Joanne Behler, right over there."

"Thank you." He crossed the room. "Ms. Behler; Joanne Behler?"

"Yes?"

"I was told by Mr. Rossetti you might know the whereabouts of Susan Woodson."

"Yes, I do. I took Susan to the airport this morning to catch a flight to San Francisco to visit a sick aunt."

"What time was her flight, do you know?"

"I think it was seven-thirty or seven-forty-five, I don't know exactly."

"Did she say when she would return?"

"No, she didn't."

"Thank you very much."

Something very strange is going on here and I'm going to get to the bottom of it. He went back to the office, got on the computer and checked flights from Redmond to San Francisco. *Bingo, Alaska Airlines, flight 210 from Redmond to Portland, Portland to San Francisco arriving 12:30 P.M.*

While shuffling through Red's old acquaintances, he came across the name Jim Smith, a detective with the San Francisco Police Department. It was 12:10 P.M. and he had to call someone now in order to get . . . "Hello, Detective Smith?"

"Yes."

"My name is Al Santorini, I'm a lieutenant with the Deschutes County Sheriff's Office in Bend, Oregon. I've got a problem that needs immediate attention."

"What's that, Lieutenant?"

"I've got a woman who may be a percipient witness in a homicide up here in Bend who is landing in San Francisco on Alaska Airlines, Flight 210, at twelve-thirty. I wonder if you could hold and detain her and give me a call back."

"Will do, Lieutenant."

10

It was 12:00 as Bob pulled into the parking lot for the terminal of Alaska Airlines. He drove around for about five minutes and when someone pulled out right in front, he nudged in, thinking, *This is my lucky day.*

He walked across the street to the terminal. It would be twenty minutes before Susan's plane touched down. It was the usual cloudy and cool day for the bay area, probably in the high fifties or so. He had a sweater on and felt comfortable.

They wouldn't allow greeters to enter and greet people as they are deplaning anymore, security was a lot more vigorous, so he thought he'd meet her down by where the luggage accumulates. It was 12:35 when he spotted Susan coming in to collect her luggage. She spotted him and they waved at each other. She came over, he asked her if she had a good flight and all, she said she did. The luggage began to arrive on the conveyor belt. A woman knelt down to retrieve her luggage, took it off the belt and Bob heard a gentleman say, "Are you Susan Woodson?"

"No, I'm not. Who are you?"

He pulled something out of his coat and said, "Could I see some identification?"

"Sure," she said.

Bob looked at Susan and told her, "Move on over here

next to this other conveyor belt." There was a conveyor belt for another airline, it said, "United, Flight 324."

He told her to stay over here out of sight, that he was going to attempt to get into the baggage area. While looking around he noticed there were two people checking people's luggage tags, it would be impossible to enter there. Just then, an Alaska Air employee wearing blue overalls was about to enter twenty feet down through a gate with a crossbar. He hurried past the two security personnel, he looked back and noticed they were checking someone's luggage. As the employee opened the gate, he slid furtively behind him, and as he turned to close the gate, he sidled off to one side into the crowd.

He walked around and in back of the people at the conveyor belt and over to Susan. "Look, we have to act fast. There is a plain-clothes detective who is looking for you. Let me have your ticket and baggage stubs and I will collect your baggage. When I have bags in hand, you join me at the check-out with security."

He went over to the belt, looked over and noticed the detective, or whoever he was, scanning around the belt to see if anyone fit the description of the girl. He grabbed the bags, and proceeded toward the security personnel. Once he arrived, he kept the back of the ticket closed and only showed the baggage tickets. As he approached, he noticed Susan had nestled up against him with her head down.

"Baggage ticket, please," the gentleman said. Right next to him was a woman assisting. He showed the tickets to the gentleman and at that moment he dropped his keys and loose change from his pockets on the floor. "*Oh God,*" he said.

At that moment he noticed Susan wasn't next to him any longer. "Thank you very much for helping me," he said. He heard the woman say, "Miss. Miss." He looked over and his heart was in his throat. She had stopped someone else. He stopped to get his breath and proceeded to the exit. She was huddled next to a newsstand. She saw him and smiled, "You are smooth, Mr. Hoaglund."

"Let's get out of here," he said.

They crossed the street, got to his car, hugged and kissed each other, and got in the car. He paid the parking fee and they were out of there. They got on the Bayshore Freeway and headed west to pick up Highway 5 south.

"Somehow Lieutenant Santorini is on to you, Susan."

"How?"

"He found out you were on that flight and sent a detective to detain you. He still doesn't have the forest ranger's report, though, or I would be involved also."

"Do you think he knows where we're going?"

"No. But I doubt he thinks it's San Francisco because—well, because he's a bright guy and he'll make the right deduction."

"Do you think we're safe then?"

"For the time being."

*   *   *

"There's a call for you on line two lieutenant."

"Thanks. Lieutenant Santorini here."

"Lieutenant, this is Jim Smith."

"Yes, Jim."

"I've got some bad news for you. We went down to San Francisco International. We got there too late for the offloading of the plane. We went to the baggage area and stayed until everyone had left and no Susan Woodson. Sorry."

"That's all right, Jim. Thank you for everything."

He called over to Gibraltor Realty to talk with Joanne Behler once again.

"Joanne, this is Lieutenant Santorini once again. Sorry to bother you, but did Ms. Woodson have any baggage when you dropped her off this morning?"

"Yes, she had two bags: one medium, I'd say, and one medium-large."

"Thank you very much. Bye."

Exactly what I thought, she has help. Someone finessed their way right through security. So, there was a report after all. John must have had it on his person the day that he died and the person who killed him removed it from him. Susan Woodson may not have a sick aunt, and she may not be staying in San Francisco at all.

He walked down the hall and hailed Wally once again.

"Wally, could you run a rap sheet on a person, initial C, initial J, Rollins, using a nickname of Josh, and let me know when you get something back?"

"OK, Skip."

*   *   *

It was 6:00 and the traffic in the Pasadena area was frightful. Everyone and their brother must have gone out today.

"Did you want to stop for something to eat, Susan?"

"Whatever you want to do. I am kind of hungry, though."

"We'll get off up here on Rosemead and find a little restaurant you'll like. It's not *Lucia's,* but you'll like it."

They got off the freeway and drove for a couple miles and turned into The Black Forest Inn. It was a big restaurant made out of logs. They entered and the place was busy. They had a honky-tonk piano player and wooden tables with peanuts on the floor.

"Give us two draughts, please."

The waitress brought the beers and they asked if they could eat in the bar. The waitress said they could. They ordered two corned beef sandwiches and some tasty red cabbage salad.

"Wow, this is really good. How do you know about this place?" she said.

"I lived in this area for a few years."

"Good choice."

"Nothing but the best for a beautiful woman on the lam."

"I don't think that's funny."

They drove on down toward San Diego. It was 9:30 when Bob drove up the hill and parked the car in the garage.

"Here we are."

"*Where?*"

"Where *I* live."

"I figured that. *Where* is it that you live?"

"Just this side of heaven, my dear."

"You're impossible."

"They gathered their luggage and toted it into the house. He turned on the lights and took the bags into the bedroom.

"The bathroom is over there if you want to use it."

He went out in the kitchen and turned on the answering machine to see if there were any messages. There were about ten. Most were solicitations but one was from Judge Ruiz following up the message she received. She said Bob should call her when he returned. That he would do tomorrow.

When he got back into the bedroom, Susan was in the

shower. It was all he could do not to join her. He got on the computer to see if there was any news from Bend. There wasn't. She exited from the bathroom in her lavender robe.

"You made a good choice in bringing that robe."

"Thank you."

"He went over to the bedroom window and opened the curtains.

"*Wow,* it's like we're on top of the world," she said. "Can I go out on the veranda?"

"Sure."

"I'm going to take a shower and I'll join you. Did you want something to drink? Wine, beer, a soda?"

"How about a glass of wine?"

"Burgundy or chardonnay?"

"Chardonnay."

"At your service, madam."

When he stepped out of the shower and onto the mat, there was Susan with her wine. She said, "You've got one sexy pad, sir," and she kissed him. "Come join me."

"Let me shave and get a beer and I shall."

After putting on his robe he went into the living room, put on some music, got a beer and strolled onto the veranda.

"That's *Brahms 2nd* piano concerto with Emil Gilels?"

"You're *so* right, Ms. Woodson."

"What am I looking at our there?"

"We sit on top of a hill and about half a mile away is Highway 15 running north and south."

They sat down on a chaise lounge, cuddled up together, because it was rather cool. She looked at him with pleading eyes and asked, "What are we going to do, Bob? I mean, they're going to start putting this thing together pretty soon."

"You're right, they will. But we have to buy some time. In the meantime we're safe here so long as that report doesn't show up."

They sat there for—it seemed like an hour. She looked at him and said, "Come on, let's go try your bed."

"The best idea you've had all day."

* * *

It was 8:30 and Al Santorini was sitting at his desk drinking some coffee and eating a donut. Wally Berger came in and said, "Here's the rap sheet on Rollins, Lieutenant."

"Thanks Wally."

C.J. Rollins, also known as Josh Rollins, also known as Bear Rollins.
   Two years assault with a deadly weapon, Huntsville, Alabama; five years, armed robbery, Vacaville, California; seven years, assault with intent to kill, San Quentin, California.

"He looks like a pretty bad dude, Skip."

"Yeah, he is. We've got to go out and see this gentleman."

Wally went and got the car and they drove out to the Crane Prairie Store. They walked in, there was a woman behind the counter. He asked, "Is Josh Rollins here today?"

"Yes, he is. He's in the backroom. I'll get him."

Mr. Rollins entered the room, saw the two gentlemen, looked at them and said, "What can I do for you, sonny?"

"Well, first of all my name is not *sonny,* it's Lieutenant Al Santorini, I'm from the Deschutes County Sheriff's Office. I wonder if I could ask you some questions."

"Well, you can ask, I don't know that you'll get any answers."

"Maybe you can come outside for a few minutes."

They walked outside and Al said, "Look, Mr. Rollins, we're well aware of your past record so we can make this easy on you or . . ."

"Make what easy on me? I haven't done anything for you to be here."

"Did you know Red Jensen?"

"Sure, I knew Red. Everybody did. What's this all about?"

"We had a report that there was a ruckus around the store a couple days before Red was killed, that you were involved, and that he broke it up."

"Yes, that's true. But what does that have to do with . . . ?"

"Do you have any weapons on the premises, Mr. Rollins?"

"You know I'm not allowed to have any weapons."

"Any rifles or hunting accessories, such as bow and arrows?"

He thought for a moment and remembered that the bow and arrows were not hanging on the back wall, and wondered what happened to them.

"None."

Lieutenant Santorini glanced around the premises and noticed nothing out of the ordinary and told Mr. Rollins, "Well, thank you for your time, Mr. Rollins. Here's my card. If you hear of anything, give me a call."

"Is that it?"

"That's all."

*   *   *

Susan rolled over and Bob wasn't there. She felt something roll across the back of her neck that tickled. "Bob, is that you? She turned around and staring her in the face was a cat; a beautiful tabby, rust and white.

"That's *Cimaron,* he's the king of the house. He's got good taste, I see. Are you ready to eat some breakfast?"

"Yes." She put on her robe and went over to the window and out onto the verarnda. "This is beautiful, Bob. Are these orange trees?"

"And lemon trees, also. Over there on the hill are some avocado trees."

"So you wake up to the sunrise every morning?"

"I do, but obviously you don't." They both laughed. "Do you like figs in the morning?"

"*Figs*? I don't think I've ever had *figs.*"

"OK, you'll try them then?"

"Sure."

He went in the kitchen and fixed some figs, toast, and coffee and they ate out on the veranda.

"I'm going to call Judge Ruiz this morning and see if we can meet tonight and get some counsel. You'll like her."

After he did the dishes, he went in and called the courthouse. It was 8:45, court usually started at 9:00 and she would be in by then.

"Judge Ruiz?"

"Is this Bob?"

"Yes. I'm back in town. Listen, I've got a problem and I need to seek your counsel on what to do."

"Well, I've got a few minutes before court starts so . . ."

"*No, no.* It's a lot more complicated than that. Are you free after work for an hour or so?"

"Let me check my calendar. Yes, I am."

"Well, how about meeting at the top of the Marriott by Seaport Village at five-thirty. Is that all right?"

"Sure."

She sounded somewhat uneasy and skeptical.

"I'll be bringing a friend along from Bend. I'll see you there."

"OK, Bob. Have a good day."

* * *

Sam Rossetti approached Joanne Behler and asked, "Joanne, I know Susan is in San Francisco. I've got a problem. My car is at the dealership, they don't know what's wrong with it. Do you suppose she would mind if I borrowed her car for a couple of days?"

"Well, Sam, I don't know. It's at her house in the garage and . . ."

"Do you have an extra key to her house?"

"Yes, I do, but . . ."

"I don't think she'd mind." *Besides,* he thought, *it's a company vehicle anyway.*

11

Lieutenant Santorini scanned for breaking news of any kind in Oregon. He noticed in the state section a blurb about a ceremony honoring the Chavez family in Kaiser that night. He made a note to call Douglas County about the ballistics on the two bodies found there, and also the body found in Davis Lake; to follow up on Susan Woodson and a would-be accomplice, the person who sent the note, and to check on the parole officer for Josh Rollins.

He entered his office and exchanged pleasantries with his coworkers. He passed his secretary and as he went by she stood up and said, "Oh Lieutenant, there's a man in your . . ." Too late. As he entered there was Bud Olsen with his feet up on his desk with a half-baked grin. "Well, *Al,* glad to see you again."

"It's *Lieutenant* to you, Agent Olsen. Get your damn feet off my desk. Were you born in a barn? What the hell are you doing here?"

"Well, my boy, I think you very well know what I'm doing here. You've been putting your foot in doors that shouldn't be opened. Ranger Jensen was not, and I repeat, *not* a state agent, he was employed by the federal government and hence, *voilá,* here I am. So don't get smart with me, *Lieutenant.* I've got some questions and I think you've got some answers."

As he moved over to his desk he said, "What do you want?"

"First of all, I want to know what you've got. You've been through his office, what did you find?"

"We took his computer and have examined his disks and the hard drive."

"I want that. What else?"

"Look, Agent Olsen, we can do this civilly or we can do this with a lot of difficulty. What'll it be?"

"Go ahead."

He showed him a note that he had gotten regarding Josh Rollins. He did not show him the note about Susan Woodson. "Here is the rap sheet on Mr. Rollins. We went to see him yesterday but found nothing that . . . " At that moment the room started shaking violently.

"What the hell was that?" Olsen said.

"We're having some earthquake activity in Bend and each one seems to be more severe."

It lasted twenty or thirty seconds and then abated.

"You were telling me about Mr. Rollins."

"Yes. There was nothing, after brief questioning, that appeared to be of an incriminating nature. He's very institutionalized and very distrustful of law enforcement."

"Anything else?"

"Not that I can think of."

"Well, Lieutenant Santorini, here's my card. If you can think of anything else, you be sure and call me. From now on, this is *not* your jurisdiction so your time in this play is over."

He stomped out of the office, leaving Lieutenant Santorini fuming, although he knew there was nothing further he could do officially. *Officially,* he said to himself and went about his business.

"Hello, Mr. Benson. I'm Lieutenant Santorini of the DCSO. Are you C.J. Rollins's parole officer?"

"Hi, Lieutenant. We met a few years ago at some

function in Bend, I can't remember what it was. Yes, I am his parole officer and have been for a couple years. What can I do for you?"

"What kind of parolee has Mr. Rollins been?"

"Considering the amount of institutionalization he's undergone, he's been no problem. Has kept himself employed and no complaints from the citizenry."

"Does he have any relatives in the area?"

"Not that I know of. He's from back somewhere in the midwest. Let me check . . . from Ohio. Toledo, Ohio. Says, 'No contact with living relatives.'"

"Thank you, Mr. Benson, for all your help."

"Good to talk to you again, Lieutenant."

"Bye."

Another dead end, what else is new. He thought he'd call the Douglas County Sheriff's Office about their ballistics on the two bodies.

"Hello, this is Lieutenant Al Santorini from the Deschutes County Sheriff's Office. Could you put me in touch with the officer in charge?

"Hello, this is Lieutenant Thomas Whitehead. Can I help you?"

"Yes, Hi, Tom. Al Santorini from the DCSO office in Bend. I'm calling about the two bodies that were found last week in what was it, the Umpqua River?"

"That's right."

"I'm calling with regard to any ballistic evidence with regard to those bodies."

There was a pause on the other line and Lieutenant Whitehead said, "Well, Lieutenant Santorini, we're not quite through with that yet, and the person in charge, Larry Krautheimer, is otherwise engaged today. I'll leave him a message to call regarding ballistics."

"Thanks, Tom. How's the fishing on the Umpqua this year?"

"It's going to be a good summer Steelhead year. Maybe you can get down."

"Sounds good. Talk to you later."

Doesn't anyone want to help the lieutenant? he thought.

He roused up a paper and found that the ceremony was not in Kaiser, as he had first read, but was in Mt. Angel at the Catholic church at 7:00 P.M.

* * *

On the way up through Sisters on Highway 20, he was thinking about the puzzle and the missing links. *Who was this other person involved with Susan? Why hasn't there been any identification at all? Someone must have met him. I mean, she's . . . Joanne. Joanne knows more than she's letting on, she must. What does Rollins know? My fault. I should have pressed Susan more when I had the chance.*

He went through Sisters and onto Highway 22 on his way to Salem when, on the top of a hill and turning to the right on a blind curve, was a motorcycle parked partly in the road. He swerved to miss it. He screeched to a halt and noticed a gentleman looking at the engine. He looked rather young. "Son, you've got to get this bike off the road." The boy looked at him rather odd with piercing eyes and a funny smile. "Oh, you may be right."

Al jumped on the motorcycle, told the kid to get out of the way, released the emergency brake, coasted around his car and down onto the shoulder two hundred feet or so down the road. As Al got off the bike, the kid came running down the hill and said, "Thanks a lot for that. Maybe I panicked, I don't know."

"Well, you're safe now. But you could have been killed with some big rig coming around the corner."

"Yeah, you're . . . you're right."

"What's the problem?"

"The bike just quit on me. I coasted to the top of the hill but it wouldn't go any further. I should have . . ."

"Well, let's look at it and see what's the matter."

Al wasn't able to identify anything.

"I can give you a ride to Detroit Lake just down the mountain and they can help you out."

"That'd be fine, I'd appreciate it."

As Al stepped away from the motorcycle, he noticed a rifle sheath attached to the motorcycle with a rifle. It had blond stock, looked to be a carbine of some sort.

There wasn't much conversation as they traversed the ten or so miles to Detroit Lake. There was a certain uneasiness on Al's part. The kid seemed to stare at him a lot, with piercing, penetrating eyes.

"Is this a police car?"

Al said it was.

"Are you a detective or something?"

That was as far as he was going with this. "There's a truck stop in Detroit, I can let you off there and they can help you."

"Fine. I appreciate it, Detective. . . ."

"There it is right there." Al waited for him to exit and made his way on to Mount Angel. It was six—and he had an hour to spare. Mount Angel was an old German town settled by descendants of the Oregon Trail. They had a festival once a year that drew from all over the state.

It seemed like the whole town turned out for a candlelight vigil for the Chavez family. There was a eulogy by the priest of the church, and some kind words by friends of the family. All the while this was taking place, Al was scanning the area to see if he could spot any sign, discern anything out of the ordinary. After the service, he approached some close family members, introduced himself, and attempted to ask some delicate questions. "Do you know anyone who would want to do this to the family? Was Mr. Chavez extremely popular in the Latino community, or unpopular?" No one could fathom any reason.

As Al walked back to the car after the ceremony, he thought about how lucky that boy on the highway with his motorcycle had been. *You know, sometimes you're in the right place at the right time to help somebody out—and I was.*

* * *

"Boy that dress looks great on you, Susan."

"I don't like it," she proclaimed.

As they proceeded from Fallbrook down to San Diego, some forty-five miles away, they were listening to some Beethoven on the radio and Bob asked, "Greatest Beethoven interpreter?"

"Twentieth century or prior?"

"Twentieth century, that's good."

"Josef Hoffman."

"Arthur Schnabel," Bob said. "But Hoffman's good."

"Tie on that one."

"How about Franz Schubert?"

"Vladimir Horowitz."

"Arturo Rubenstein," Bob said.

"You know your music, Robert. Obviously, I'm the more restless music critic."

Bob smiled and said, "I think you're right, but you have to show me sometime."

"You remember what happened last time? It'll be a little while."

They arrived in San Diego about 3:00 P.M. He showed her the new ballpark, the Gaslamp District and said, "We've got an hour or so to kill, let's go over to the mall."

He parked the car in the garage and they walked around the downtown mall, which was done in a renaissance motif. She came upon a nice boutique and said, "Let's go in here for a sec." She grabbed his sleeve and pulled him in. "Whoa, girl. You see something you like?"

"Possibly."

Bob browsed at some of their cocktail and evening gowns, which were very sexy, turned around and there she was. "What do you think?"

"*Wow.* Good choice. You look . . . " and he walked over and whispered in her ear, "sumptuous."

It was a lavender floral shift that was *her*. They walked out of the store, got in the car, and Bob said, "Well, I guess you really didn't like what you had on before."

She looked over at him with a wry smile, and in a soft tone said, "Something I can put my robe over, don't you think?" They both laughed.

The top of the Marriott had a spectacular view of San Diego Bay. Susan was impressed. At about quarter of six, Judge Ruiz came to the table and said, "Hi Bob. Sorry I'm late, but you know how the judiciary is."

"How well I do. Judge Robin Ruiz, this is Susan Woodson."

"Glad to know you, Susan. What a nice dress that is!"

Susan looked over at Bob and winked, "Nice to meet you, Judge. And thank you."

"Well, you're back in town early. What's up?"

They ordered some drinks: Judge Ruiz had a martini, Susan, a scotch on the rocks, and Bob, a Crown Royal on the rocks.

"It's a long story, Judge. We'll try to make it as short and succinct as possible without leaving out too many details."

"Before you start, Bob, how do you two know each other?"

"That's part of the story, Judge."

"Oh, sorry. Go ahead."

"The third day in Bend, I went fishing. While on the river, I came upon some ceremonial display, a boot that looked like it was severed from a leg, with some jewelry pieces surrounding it. It looked bizarre. I was going back to get some law enforcement personnel to look at this when I was shot at with a bow and arrow, which missed just above my head."

"Did you get a look at who shot at you?"

"No. When I got to the car, my tires were slashed and my cell phone was gone. I didn't know what was going to happen next, so I flagged Susan down, commandeered her car and found a forest ranger. Later, we went to the scene and there was no sign of anything at all. I looked at Susan and asked if *she* was going to press charges, but she thought me so nice and charming that . . ."

She glanced at Bob with that perturbed look. "Get on with it, Bob."

"So that's where he got the number down here in San Diego. Off your phone! Hence the message about your ashes in the Lonesome Pines," the judge said.

"*My God, that's it!*" Bob yelled out. They looked around and the whole place was looking at them. Sheepishly he said, "Sorry, but that message was a code. It's not

Lonesome Pines at all." He looked over at Susan. "But *Lake Paulina.*"

Susan smiled and said, "You're right."

"The next day I had another incident on the river where the same scenario happened once again and I was almost killed."

Susan looked shocked. She said, "You didn't tell me about that."

"I know I didn't, but—then, later on—and I will spare you the details—we had an incident on Lake Paulina where this same individual tried to kill us again. Meanwhile, there is a whole family, four people, the Chavez family that were killed, plus the forest ranger I told you about, he was killed also. There is a lieutenant at the Deschutes Sheriff's Office that is tracking Susan. I don't think he knows who I am yet, but he's very persistent and it's probably only a matter of time."

"You two really have yourselves in a pickle, don't you? Neither one of you are charged with anything, so you still have some options open. He knows about you, Susan, because of what?"

"He found a note that Mr. Jensen, the forest ranger, wrote about a report."

Bob broke in and said, "Mr. Jensen wrote a report about my description of the first incident and apparently wrote a note to himself to contact Susan to see if she wanted to follow through with any charges of kidnapping or anything of that sort."

"You told the lieutenant you didn't want to what?"

"I told the lieutenant I knew nothing about any report."

"So, the lieutenant has deduced that you know something about a report—of which he knows nothing about—and that you exist because . . ."

"Because I helped her get away at the San Francisco Airport, which is another story."

"It is a complicated web, isn't it?"

"Yes, it is, Judge. Do you have any advice for us?"

"Well, you both have a few bargaining chips because he doesn't know very many of the facts. However, the more investigation he does regarding the murders, ballistics and all, the more he'll need you as witnesses, the more agitated he'll become and—well, I think you know where I'm going. You're probably best to go back up and see if you can work this thing out. You don't want to turn into false fugitives."

"You're probably right, Judge. It's just that . . ."

Susan put her hand on Bob and said, "Thanks for the advice, Judge Ruiz. You're a good friend."

They finished their drinks and Bob told Judge Ruiz that they would be in touch about their decision, and inform her when they would be returning to Bend.

On the return trip to Fallbrook they discussed the different possibilities and they both came to the same conclusion . . . they had to return and clear this matter up.

* * *

Sam Rossetti saw Joanne in the office and told her that he had borrowed Susan's car, that he expected his car to be ready tomorrow afternoon and he would return it then.

It was 1:30 in the morning and no one was in the Blue Bird bar in Bend except Sam Rossetti, Marjorie, the waitress, and Ted, the bartender. Marjorie had dated Sam for a while and knew that he drank too much. Ted nodded at

Marjorie and she nudged Sam and said, "Sam . . . Sam . . . It's time to go, don't you think?"

Sam looked up at Marjorie and mumbled something that was inaudible. He was quite inebriated and could hardly speak.

Marjorie looked at Ted and said, "Is it all right if we leave early, Ted? There's nothing going on and hasn't been for the last hour."

"Sure, Marjorie. You take Sam home and we'll close up shop for the day."

Marjorie got Sam's keys, went to get his car and noticed that he had a company vehicle, an SUV. She tried the keys and they seemed to fit, so she brought the SUV to the front door, went in, got Sam and put him in the passenger seat. She told Ted she would see him tomorrow night.

As they proceeded through the town toward Century Drive, she noticed only one car on the road, a red pickup, which turned the corner and followed behind her. As she drove up Century Drive toward Mt. Bachelor, she noticed that the faster she drove, the faster the red pickup drove, that when she slowed down to let the pickup pass, it did not. *Go ahead and pass me,* she thought. As she sped up, the pickup did also. All the sudden it was alongside her. She looked up and said, "What the hell are you doing, you *SOB*?" At that moment, the pickup veered toward the passenger side, Marjorie panicked and overcorrected her turn to the left and the SUV ran off the road into a ditch, up the ditch and square into a tree. The SUV bucked sideways and rolled onto its side, the horn blaring and both driver's side wheels spinning.

* * *

The sheriff's office, an ambulance, and a reporter who had just arrived were all standing around the SUV awaiting the coroner. The reporter from the *Bulletin* approached one of the officers there and asked, "Does anyone know who is in there?"

One of the officers looked at him and said, "It's Sam. Sam Rossetti."

12

Brian McCartney, the mayor of Bend, deplaned at the Salem airport at 9:00 A.M. in the morning and was immediately met by Ken Bailey, the governor's aide. They greeted each other and Ken said, "Glad you could come, Brian. The governor looks forward to seeing you."

"I wish I was here under better circumstances, Ken, but I look forward to seeing you all."

They drove from the airport to the capitol building and Brian said, "It's getting a little scary up there; the last one shook pretty hard yesterday."

"Well, I think the governor can fill us all in."

They arrived at the governor's office and Governor Thomas rose to meet Brian McCartney. "Brian, good to see you again. It's been a while. About six months ago in Eugene, wasn't it?"

"You've got a good memory, Governor." *That's why he's governor,* Brian thought.

"Well, I think we all know why we're here. I will get Mr. Charles Warren on the speaker phone and he can fill us in on the latest information. Mr. Warren is a seismologist, a professor at Cal Tech; one of the preeminent minds on volcanic activity in the United States." He paused, "Is he on the phone yet?"

The secretary said, "Yes, he is, Governor."

"Mr. Warren, this is Governor Thomas. Good to speak to you again."

"Thank you, Governor."

"For the record, we should identify everyone in the office. I'm Governor Thomas. With me is my aide, Ken Bailey, and the mayor of Bend, Brian McCartney. On the speaker phone is Charles Warren, a seismologist and professor from Cal Tech in southern California. Professor Warren, could you update us on the activity to date at Mt. Bachelor."

"Yes. We've had three tremors: One on May 29, measured at 2.7; one on May 30, measured at 2.7; one on May 31, measured at 4.3, and finally, one yesterday measured at 4.2."

"And Mr. Warren, could you tell us what you make of all this?"

"Well, maybe a little history might be in order before we jump into this. The Cascade mountain range is made up of many static volcanoes, ranging from the northern volcanoes in Washington: Mount Rainer, Mount Baker, Mount Adams, all of which are over 10,000 feet, to the most recent activity, Mount St. Helens, 9,677 before the eruption, 8,364 after the eruption. The Oregon volcanoes, the northern and the central reaches, which we're concerned with here, consist of Mt. Hood, near the Columbia River basin, and Mt. Jefferson, working our way down to the Three Sisters, north Sister, middle Sister and south Sister, all over 10,000 feet, to Three Fingered Jack, Broken Top and finally Mt. Bachelor, the volcano we're most concerned with now.

"Mt. Bachelor, which is 11,000 to 15,000 years old, is the youngest in the chain of volcanoes in the Cascades. It has a scoria cone, which are fragments of burnt, crust-like lava, lava flows, and a few step-sided cones of basalt and basaltic andesite, which is a fine-grained volcanic rock. The last eruption was around 2,000 years ago."

"Mr. Warren, we met with you a few days ago in Portland. Could you repeat a little of what you told us so that Mr. McCartney might have a better understanding?"

"Yes. I told you that I thought this might not be earthquake activity at all, but to consider the possibility of magma massing and becoming active, that we're not sure as to the depth of such magma."

"Mr. McCartney, do you have any questions of the professor?"

"Yes, I do. Professor, consider for a moment the possibility of magma becoming active and that we may well have some volcanic activity, do you have an opinion as to when that might occur?"

"Well, we know that the magma, if there is magma, has not produced any bulges in the earth's crust, so we're not sure as to the depth. It would take further study."

"One more question. If there were to be some sort of eruption from this volcano, and it were to occur on the east side—meaning the side facing the city of Bend—some twenty miles away—what do you think the consequences might be?"

"That's hard to say, because we don't know the size of the eruption and the volume involved. However, I can state one thing very clearly—because I have done a little research as to the terrain involved—and that is the Deschutes River would be clogged with large amounts of debris from an eruption and there would be serious flooding in and through the city of Bend. That we can be sure of."

"This is Governor Thomas again. Thank you very much for your time and thoughtfulness, Mr. Warren. We appreciate it."

"Thank you, Governor."

"Well, Brian, there you have it. We don't know the seriousness of the matter at this time, but we know there well could be a catastrophe."

"Yes, Governor. Do you have any thoughts as to what we should do?"

"Putting me on the spot, aren't you. We probably ought to hold off on any emergency measures; although it wouldn't hurt to look into what to do and when to do it. As I recall they had a little time in the Mount St. Helens situation to evacuate; the difference being the area was isolated and Bend is not. The public probably has some idea since all this tremulous activity is located under Mt. Bachelor. There's plenty of time, let's not alarm the general public unduly."

"It's not a pretty scenario, Governor. You're probably right, let's not alarm anyone any further."

"I've got a meeting at eleven but—when's your flight back?"

"Two-thirty."

"We can have lunch at around noon then."

"Fine, Governor."

On the flight back to Bend, a whole lot of thoughts went through Brian McCartney's head as to what action he would take, the severity of damage that might occur, the displacement of people. He also thought of his good friend, Red Jensen, and how he would miss him.

* * *

As he passed by Sandy, his secretary, Lieutenant Santorini asked if there was any news this morning—because there had been every day. He went into his office and immediately began mapping the crime scene. Two bodies found in the Umpqua River, one body found in Davis Lake, one body found in the McKenzie River, and Red's body found in the upper Deschutes River. Sandy came in and said, "Have you heard the news?"

The lieutenant said, "No. *What else?*"

"A local couple were killed this morning on the Century Highway."

"Anybody we know?"

"Sam Rossetti and a Marjorie Yeakel."

"Where do we know these people from?"

"Sam Rossetti ran a real estate agency here in Bend."

Of course, Al thought. *He's the gentleman from Gibraltor where Susan works.* "Sandy, can you get Lieutenant Rivers from the Bend Police Department on the phone?"

"Right away, Lieutenant."

"Hello, Randy? This is Al Santorini."

"Good to hear from you, Al. What's up?"

"You know that accident you had on Century Highway this morning?"

"Yes."

"Can you give me a little info on the events prior to and the accident itself?"

"Yes. We got a call this morning from a Mr. Ted Lyons, a bartender at the Blue Bird bar and he told us that Marjorie Yeakcl was an employee there, a waitress, and that she was a girlfriend of Sam Rossetti, who ran Gibraltor Realty, that he was quite inebriated, and that at closing time, Marjorie took Sam out to the car and that was the last Ted Lyons saw of them.

"As far as the accident itself, we're not sure as to exactly what happened. The skid marks show that the car made an abrupt turn to the left and ran off the highway into a tree and that death appeared to be instantaneous."

"Well, Randy, I sure appreciate that. How's things going otherwise?"

"Great, other than these shakers that are happening every day, it seems."

"I agree. They're a little unsettling. Thanks again."

He set the phone down and thought to himself, *Another coincidence?* "Sandy, can you get the Blue Bird bar on the phone?"

"*Blue Bird,* you say?"

"I know it's a little early in the morning, but . . ."

"A woman named Jean is on the phone."

"Hello. I'm Lieutenant Al Santorini from the Deschutes County Sheriff's Office."

"Yes. My name is Jean Whitherspoon, I'm the owner of the Blue Bird."

"Do you have an employee named Ted Lyons at your place?"

"Yes, I do."

"Is he available?"

"No, he works from six P.M. until two A.M."

"Is he working tonight?"

"Yes, he is."

"Well, I'll get in touch with him later then. Thank you."

He looked back at his map with the pins in it and tried to get some visual aid as to a pattern, but could not. *I need more information, and Susan Woodson is the best place to start.*

* * *

Susan woke up and recognized a familiar aroma in

the kitchen. *My, this man does get up early in the morning.* Bob entered the bedroom, looked at her and said, "Are you ready for something to eat?"

She sat up and smiled and said, "Yes. I'll have some orange juice, a cheese blintz with some fruit and . . ."

"No, you won't," he said. "You'll have what I'm having, which is nowhere near that order."

"OK. But you do have some orange juice?"

He walked in and came back with a tray with some coffee and some oatmeal. "Oatmeal?"

"Right on, Susan."

She bent down and smelled it and said, "What's it got on it?"

"Taste it and you'll find out."

She took a bite and said, "You're feeding me booze in the morning. But it's good."

"It's Irish oatmeal with some Baileys Irish Cream, some brown sugar, and a few raisins."

"You know, you are spoiling me, young man. I may not want to go back to work."

"That wouldn't be so bad, would it?"

"I must warn you, I'm pretty expensive."

"I'll take that into consideration."

They ate their oatmeal, read some of the paper and retired to the veranda to have their coffee.

"I've got to call Joanne this morning and see what's going on in the office."

"Yes, I know."

He leaned over, kissed her and started to say something but thought better of it. "I'll clean up the dishes then."

It was a bit foggy this morning, but the fog was lifting and she could start to see the outline of the groves to the east as the glint of the sun gave an orange glow. *This is paradise,* she thought.

After she cleaned herself up and got dressed, she took out her cell phone and dialed Gilbrator Realty. It was a little after 9:00 in the morning and Joanne would be there. "Hello, Joanne?"

"Susan? *Oh, God,* you haven't heard the news, I'm sure."

"*What news?*"

"Well, it happened early this morning and *oh, God!*"

She seemed to be becoming hysterical and crying and Susan said, "*What news,* Joanne?"

"Sam Rossetti was killed this morning in an automobile accident."

"*Sam? Where? How?*"

"He and a cocktail waitress on the Century Highway at around two in the morning."

I can't believe it, she told herself. *How is this all happening?* All she could think about was a funeral. "Listen, Joanne, I think I better get back to Bend. I'll try to get a flight in today or tonight."

Joanne had composed herself and said, "One further thing. He was driving *your* Explorer."

"My Explorer? How could that be, Joanne?"

"His car was in the shop, he knew you were gone and so he thought you wouldn't mind if he borrowed it for a couple days."

Swell, she thought. *That's all I need.* "I'll let you know when I'm coming in. Can you pick me up, Joanne?"

"Yes, I can."

She turned off the phone, walked over to the window and thought, *Why is this happening to me? What else can go wrong?*

Just then Bob entered the room and said, "Did you get hold of Joanne?"

In a low whisper Susan responded, "Yes, I did."

"I'm sorry. You *did* or *didn't*?"

Susan whirled around, looked at Bob and said, "*I did. And you know what?* Sam Rossetti is *dead.*"

"He's dead?"

"That's right, he's dead! And you know what? Ever since you came into my life, bad things have and are happening."

Bob could see a drastic change in Susan's demeanor. She was extremely angry. Susan came over and said, "Why did you have to stop *me* that day on the road?" She started crying and further stated, "You've turned my life upside down." She began hitting at his chest with both fists. "I can't take it anymore. When will it end?" He began to try and calm her down. "Susan, I'm sorry. I know that . . ."

"You *know* what? You know that if you just sit here in your ivory tower things will fix themselves and everything will be all right. But you've ruined my life."

She was ranting and raving, throwing her hands and arms in different directions and pacing the floor.

"What do you want to do?"

"What do I *want* to do? It's what I have to do, and that's go back to Bend today and see if I can get my life in some semblance of order."

"Let's see if we can get a flight back to Bend today."

"Not, *we,* dear Robert. *Me.*"

This was no time to argue or even try to reason with her, she was hysterical. He told her she could use the computer in the other room and make her reservations.

"Hello, Joanne. This is Susan again."

"Hi."

"I've got a flight that gets in at eight tonight in Redmond. Can you pick me up?"

"See you there, Susan."

She exited the room, calmed herself down, and walked into the bedroom. With her head down, she said, "I've got a flight that leaves San Diego at two today so I've got to get packed. What time should I leave to get down to San Diego?"

"We have to leave by eleven A.M."

"You don't have to go, I'll get a shuttle."

"Wait a minute, Susan. What's going on here? I've just had the greatest five days of my life and you're going to throw this all out the window? I care for you deeply, Susan, and I think you . . ."

"I'm sorry for the way I acted in there, but . . ."

"*But* what?"

As tears started streaming down her face, she looked up and said, "*But* I need some time to figure out what to do. I can't handle this as well as you can."

"Look, we'll go see Lieutenant Santorini and get this all straightened out."

"No, Bob. You're not involved, and . . ."

"Not *involved*? I'm more involved than anyone—except that psychopath out there—and mostly, I'm *involved* with you."

She picked her head up, grabbed his face and kissed him tenderly. "That's the problem, Bob, we're both *involved*." They both smiled at each other and hugged.

"You better get ready, Susan."

They drove on down to the airport. Bob started to park the car, she grabbed his arm and said, "No, Bob, just let me off here in front of the terminal."

"I'll talk to you later then?"

She sort of cocked her head sideways and nodded up

and down. He grabbed her head, kissed her and said, "Don't throw this away yet, Susan." She opened the door, grabbed her bags, waved and was gone.

*   *   *

13

It was late morning when Lieutenant Santorini approached Mt. Bachelor on his way to Crane Prairie. As he started around the mountain he thought, *What mysteries are you hiding, you beautiful creature?* When he arrived at the store at Crane Prairie, it was 11:30. He walked in and saw no one. "Is anybody home?" No answer. He walked out of the store, went around back and there sitting in the same place was the red pickup with the white camper shell. *Not moved a bit,* he thought. He started looking over toward the lake when it hit him. *No, it's been moved because it's facing the other way.* He started walking toward the vehicle, and upon reaching it began to move around the back. At that moment, he heard a voice. "Hey, what the hell you doing back there?" He looked down toward the store and there was Josh Rollins walking at a brisk pace toward the truck. Josh walked around the truck, face to face with Lieutenant Santorini and said, "Oh, it's you, *Lieutenant.* If Agent Olsen knew you were here then . . ."

"Well, he doesn't."

Rollins walked toward the lieutenant and gave him a soft push. "*But* if he did . . ."

At that moment Lieutenant Santorini pulled out his .44, turned Rollins around, and put the gun up to his head, cocked it and said, "Listen, you *piece of shit,* where in the hell were you last night?"

Josh Rollins broke out in a cold sweat and said, "OK, OK, lieutenant. Just funnin' with you."

"Well, Mr. Rollins, I don't have much of a sense of humor this morning, so let's cease with this *bullshit* and you answer my question."

"I was over at my sister's in Bend."

"Where does she live?"

"Over near the 97."

"Until how late?"

"Ten, eleven o'clock."

If that's true, then his alibi still falls short by two to three hours. "You go stand over there for a few minutes." Rollins went over about fifty feet and the Lieutenant said, "That's far enough. Just so I can see you." He skirted the truck, knelt down and saw some white paint on the front bumper. He scraped some fresh white paint off into a little vial he carried with him. He popped back up and said, "Who has access to this vehicle, Josh?"

"Well, really nobody except myself. The boat mechanic sometimes drives it, but not very often."

"Where might I see this mechanic?"

"He's only here three, four days a week. Won't be here until tomorrow, I suspect."

"What's his name?"

"Jerry McCrory."

"How can I get in touch with him?"

"I don't know where he lives and he doesn't have a phone so . . ."

"Well, when he comes in tomorrow, you have him give me a call—here's my phone number. And listen, Josh, if you breathe a word of this to Agent Olsen, *your ass is mud.* You understand? Because I'll find some way to get your *ass* back in the pen. You know it wouldn't be hard."

"Is that a threat, *oh holy Lieutenant?*"

"Call it what you will, Rollins. I'm sure you get the message."

*   *   *

The plane was ready to land at Portland and Susan was thinking about what happened between she and Bob. It wasn't his fault. After all, the fate that brought them together was a strange occurrence. She really cared for him—a lot. She had about an hour and a half layover in Portland so she thought she'd better give him a call. This morning they were happy lovebirds, this evening—*this.*

His phone rang a few times and then a message came on saying, "This is Bob. I'm unavailable now. If you'd leave your name and a message, I'll return your call." She elected not to leave a message. For someone so—so creative in his music—he could have said *Caruso* or something. She laughed. *Should I use the cell?* she thought. *No, I don't want him brought into this, if possible.*

She boarded the plane for the forty-minute flight to Redmond. They landed, she deplaned and walked toward her luggage. There was Joanne. "Susan, over here!" They grabbed her luggage and proceeded to the car. While driving towards Bend, Joanne said, "Where were you? You left no forwarding address or phone number and everyone was worried about you."

"That part is over now. Can you promise you won't question me about this again?"

"I guess so. I mean . . ."

"Over and done with, all right? All right, Joanne?"

"All right, Susan. Over and done with."

"Is there any further news on Sam?"

"No. Only that apparently he wasn't driving when the accident took place."

"Who was this other party?"

"Her name was . . . I can't think of it right now, but it's in the paper."

"Has anyone said anything about when the funeral might be?"

"I think it's this Saturday, but I'm not positive."

They drove to Joanne's house and parked the car, unloaded the luggage and sat down for a cold one. "Joanne, would you mind if I stayed here tonight?"

"Oh, no. I thought you would want to, being late and all."

"Is my Explorer demolished?"

"They didn't say, but I imagine so being the severity of the accident and all. The truck hit a tree."

They sat there enjoying their beers, talking about the future of the office and who would take it over. Joanne had heard from an old boyfriend and had a couple dates. *She seems enthused again,* Susan thought.

*　　*　　*

"Ted Lyons?"

"Yes?"

"I'm Lieutenant Santorini from the Deschutes County Sheriff's Office."

"I already gave a statement to the police department."

"Yes, I know. I just want to follow up on a few things, if I might. Did Sam Rossetti frequent the Blue Bird quite often?"

"Well, ever since he started seeing Marjorie Yeakel. Probably two, three times a week, I would guess."

"Last night, early morning, what was the sobriety of Mr. Rossetti?"

"He started off pretty loud, then as he began to consume alcohol pretty heavily, he quieted down . . . he was almost in a stupor, you might say."

"Did you notice anything unusual in the parking lot?

"As a matter of fact, I did. I went out about eleven to set some empty bottles on the back stoop and I didn't see his car. He usually parks it back there. The only vehicle back there was an Explorer with the lettering *Gibraltor Realty* on it."

"Had you ever seen that vehicle there prior?"

"No, never did."

"In your opinion, would Mr. Rossetti have been able to drive that morning?"

"No, not at all."

"One last question. What color hair did Ms. Yeakel have?"

"Brown, mousy brown, I would say."

"Thanks, Mr. Lyons, you've been a big help."

* * *

Jake Hanson was dancing at The Roundup to a Travis Tritt tune, and was prancing around the floor like a show pony. His partner said, "Hey, you're holding me a little rough, wouldn't you say?" He whispered under his breath, "Little bitch. I'll show you what *rough* is." Just then the girl stopped, turned and looked at him and said, "Let go of me, *asshole.*" She ripped her body away and stomped back to her girlfriends. He looked at her and thought, *If she was alone I'd rip her tits off.* He finished his beer, went outside, got on his motorcycle and went on his way to La Pine, where he was sharing a room with another gentleman.

*   *   *

Bob was approaching Stockton and thought to himself, *I've made this trip too many times lately.* It was 8:00 and he thought he could make Redding by 11:00 for the night. His thoughts kept coming back to the mess he was in, and looming was the likelihood that someone would put two and two together, that Susan would be made the scapegoat because of his selfish desires. When would they catch this psycho? He had to get to Bend to lend of himself in whatever way he could to straighten this thing out. The ride would be much easier listening to Donizetti's *"L 'Elisir d'Amore"* (The Elixir of Love).

*   *   *

The first thing in the morning when Lieutenant Santorini got in, he had a message to call Agent Olsen. He knew what this was all about, that *slimeball* Rollins had called over and told him what happened yesterday. First he had to contact Jim Fazio in forensics about the vial and its contents.

"Hello, Jimmy, this is Al Santorini."

"Yeah, Al. What can I do for you?"

"I've got a vial here I want analyzed. It contains a paint sample. I'll see if I can get you a known exemplar for comparison."

"Just drop it off in my office with a note and we'll get right on it."

Getting an exemplar was going to be a difficult task. He couldn't call Randy Rivers because he had jurisdiction, and he couldn't ask. *I'll approach this task when the times comes; think maybe of a better way.*

"Lieutenant, Ben Olsen is on line two."

Oh great, he thought.

"Agent Olsen, nice to hear from you."

"Oh, you think so, huh? Let me tell you something, Lieutenant. I'm a pretty patient man, and this is the second strike, so let me tell you *what's going to happen.*"

"I take it Rollins called you yesterday."

"You know damned well he did. He told me you were out there harassing him. Now, I don't know whether you were or weren't, but—let me tell you this. One more incident like this and you're going to join civilian life real soon. What the hell were you doing out there anyway?"

"Admiring the scenery, I suppose."

"Waving a forty-four in this man's face? What did you want with him?

"He seems a part of the puzzle but it's like putting a square peg in a round hole."

"Well, you let us worry about that. And keep your *ass* out of our business, because the third time's the charm."

"Right, Mr. Olsen."

Now I'm going to have to walk on egg shells. This guy means it, I think.

Sandy came in and said, "Lieutenant, I forgot to give you this message this morning."

"Thanks, Sandy."

The message read: "Jerry McCrory called at nine-ten A.M., and gave a phone number. *Well, I have to take a different tact now, use different investigative tools.*

"Hello?"

"Is this Jerry McCrory?"

"Yes."

"I'm Lieutenant Al Santorini from the Deschutes

County Sheriff's Office. I wanted to ask you a few questions about that red truck with the white camper shell if I could."

"Sure, go ahead."

"Do you drive that truck?"

"No, never have."

"Does anyone drive it?"

"Well, Josh drives it and, well, I've only seen one other person drive it, who I'm not familiar with; probably two or three times."

"Do you know his name?"

"No, no. Just seen him around a few times. Never met him."

"Could you describe him?"

"Well, probably late twenties, six feet tall, 160–170 pounds."

"Did you notice anything distinctive about him?"

"No, not really. No scars or—well, yes, as a matter of fact I did. He's got an odd—weird look about him. A very impish, mischievous-looking grin."

"What color hair, eyes?"

"The eyes were sort of yellowish—no, orange-looking. The hair was brownish."

"Thank you very much, Mr. McCrory, you've been very helpful."

Very helpful, indeed. That's our man.

* * *

Susan and Joanne decided to stop at Starbucks in Bend for some coffee before venturing into the office.

"A little high-octane this morning hits the spot," Joanne said.

"The best fortification for the morning." They both laughed.

When they arrived in the office, the only people there was the receptionist, Jane, and David Long, another real estate agent. Jane saw Susan and said, "This is terrible. I knew his drinking would get the best of him."

Susan said, "Has anyone heard anything further?"

David responded, "Only that *Sam* wasn't driving."

"How do you know that?"

"I talked to a reporter from the newspaper this morning who was there and he told me a woman was driving at the time of the accident."

Susan thought, *For him not to be driving at the time of the accident, he must have been really drunk.*

Jane asked, "Does anyone know anything about who will be handling the funeral arrangements and when the funeral will be?"

They all looked at each other and shook their heads.

David said, "Probably this weekend, I would guess."

Susan and Joanne proceeded to their offices. On the way, Susan stopped and turned to Jane and asked, "Any written messages of any kind, Jane?"

"Just a couple."

She went in her office and thought about calling Bob and apologizing for yesterday and the way she acted, but thought, *not today, not right now.*

There were numerous messages on her machine, most relating to property she was showing. She came upon one that said: "I read your ad in the *Bulletin* about a piece of property on the north side of Bend on Cardwell Road. Could you meet me there tomorrow at two P.M.? Thank you." I've *never* received a message like that before. The message was two days old so the message wouldn't apply anyway. But that voice. I've heard that voice before. Thank God I wasn't here to receive it. There was a message to call Lieutenant Al Santorini. We'll, I'll get to that in due course. No message from Bob. I didn't think so.

"Hello? Irene? I'm so sorry about your father. He was . . . the funeral is Saturday? I know it's hard. If you need anything, just holler. Okay? Bye, Irene."

That poor girl, the difficult times he's put her through shouldn't happen to anyone. And now this.

"Joanne, the funeral is Saturday at one in the afternoon."

Joanne came by and said they had a meeting of all the agents and brokers at eleven that morning. It would be a doozy trying to pick up the pieces while the business was in limbo.

The meeting was called to order by David Long. He reminded everyone that they still had a business to run, that there were a number of properties in escrow and that they ought to try and preserve the integrity of the business in the meantime. He stated that the funeral for Sam was at one o'clock at the mortuary downtown, and that there would be a gathering there at the office immediately afterwards. Irene got up and spoke about what a wonderful bunch of people worked for her dad, that she knew it would be in good hands in the future.

Susan didn't feel like going out so she told Joanne to pick her up a salad or sandwich down the street. Having no car, she didn't know whether she wanted to go home that night or not. *We'll figure it out this afternoon.*

14

"Lieutenant, line one is for you."

"Thanks, Sandy. Hello?"

"Hello. My name is Larry Krautheimer, I work for the Douglas County Sheriff's Office. I had a message that you called."

"Yes, Mr. Krautheimer. Thank you for returning the call. Have you done any ballistics work on the two bodies found on the Umpqua River, Luis and Enrique Chavez?"

"Yes. Both the autopsy and ballistics are completed."

"Can you tell me what they show?"

"Well, both subjects were shot in the back of the head, at close range, with a twenty-two-caliber projectile. Death was instantaneous. The body of Luis Chavez showed a detachment below the knee on the right leg. It appeared to be caused by some serrated instrument, possibly a large deer knife of some sort. The body of Enrique showed a detachment right at the left hand, also by a serrated instrument, possibly a large deer knife."

"Was there anything more remarkable about the bodies, such as bruising or any evidence of rope burns? Anything of that nature?"

"No. The autopsy report was pretty short, as autopsy reports go, and those were the main findings."

"Well, thank you, Mr. Krautheimer. You've been most helpful."

A .22 caliber, huh? That's the first introduction of an-

other weapon into the equation. However, a deer knife is interesting because if you couple that with the Los-7 and .308 cartridge, he's obviously a deer hunter—amongst thousands of others in this state. But maybe we can hook up a name to that face.

"I'm going out, Sandy, I'll return hopefully by five today."

"All right, Lieutenant."

He drove over to Highway 97 to a used car lot looking for a 2001 white Ford Explorer. At the first lot, he had no luck. He drove down a block and saw an Explorer sitting near the rear of the lot. He had changed into civilian clothes so as not to give away an identity. He parked the car on the street and was immediately approached by a salesman. "Can I help you find a car today?"

"No. I think I will look around and if I find something, I'll let you know."

"Okay. Feel free."

He walked over to the Explorer, which was in the back row, and had a 2001 sticker on it. He opened the driver's door, looked around, there was no one in sight, bent down and, underneath the driver's door, scraped some paint into a vial, and shut the door. The salesman again approached him and said, "How's that little beauty look? Can I get you into that today?"

"No, I don't think so. I'm just shopping, don't know what I'm looking for."

As he approached his office, he walked over to Wally Berger and said, "Wally, could you get this vial over to Jimmy Fazio in forensics and tell him it's from Lieutenant Santorini. He'll know what it's in regard to."

"Sure, Skip. Just leave it there."

Lieutenant Santorini sat there perplexed and wondering, *I wonder what's in that white camper shell.*

*   *   *

Joanne approached Susan's office and asked, "Do you know what you're going to do tonight?"

"No. But Irene is familiar with my predicament and she has rented a car for me until we can get this straightened out."

"So do you want to stay the night?"

"Would you mind?"

"No, not at all. How about if we go over to Jenny's in the Old Mill Mall and get a salad or something, and maybe go home, get our togs and hop over to The Roundup?"

"NO!"

"Well, that was rather emphatic."

"I'm sorry, I'm not up to a night on the town tonight. How about we pick up some Mexican food and take it back to your place?"

"Sure, that's fine."

I probably should have said at least yes to Jenny's because Joanne is always watching her weight and Mexican food is probably the last thing she wants or needs.

"On second thought, I think I'm up for Jenny's, Joanne. That sounds great."

At that moment Jane, the receptionist, said, "Call for you, Susan."

"Hello, this is Susan Woodson."

"Hi, Ms. Woodson. This is Mr. Hoaglund."

She said in a soft tone, "Bob, how are you?"

"I'm doing well. I'm back in Bend."

"*You're what?*"

"I'm back in Bend at the Old Mill Inn. I got my room back. When can I see you?"

"Not tonight, Bob. It's a little—why did you come back up here?"

"Because I didn't catch enough fish, I miss the Italian food, and I miss *you,* dear girl."

"Well, I don't know what to say. I'll have to give you a call tomorrow."

"Until then. Bye."

Sometimes I want to—but how can I? He's everything that's . . .

"Susan, you want to go home first?" Joanne asked.

"Yeah, why don't we?"

* * *

Bob arrived about noon and checked into the Old Mill Inn. Becky said they had not rented the room, that it was available, and he took it. He read in the paper about the earthquake they had under Mt. Bachelor, the fourth such one. He still thought that the possibility of volcanic activity was great; with the proximity of Mt. Bachelor to Bend and the Deschutes River, it was a disaster waiting to happen.

He decided to lay down and take a nap; the activity of the last two days had worn him out. He awoke about 4:00 and took a walk and decided to call Susan. She was surprised to hear he was in Bend. She said she was busy tonight—he didn't press her—he didn't know what he was going to do next. He walked into The Pump House for a beer and sandwich. *The food's good,* he thought, *but the beer's not up to The Brewery.*

Just then, on the news, the reporter was talking about a funeral to occur Saturday at 1:00 P.M. The man's name was Sam Rossetti.

* * *

Agent Bud Olsen was stuck; he didn't know where to turn. He was trying to do an investigation and the person with the most knowledge was Al Santorini. One thing was clear, though, Lieutenant Santorini would *not* stop his investigation because Red Jensen was one of his very best friends. *Should he join in his search or? No, that wouldn't work. He'd just go on doing so in a covert fashion. Should he tap his phone or put a tail on him? If he found out, there would be a complaint to the FBI and his ass would be in a sling. There must be some clue out there with Josh Rollins at the store that Agent Olsen was missing. Josh was very evasive in his last conversation and it was evident the truth would not be forthcoming.* He decided to go out once again and see if he could uncover something; anything to hang his hat on.

"Hello Josh."

"Agent Olsen, good to see you again."

"Maybe so, we'll find out. What was Lieutenant Santorini out here for the other day?"

"Oh, nothing much. Just asking some questions about Red and did I know anything about his murder; things of that sort."

"That's it? Nothing more?"

"Yeah, that's about it."

Agent Olsen was a pretty big man. He walked over to Josh, put his hands on his shoulders and started to squeeze, each few seconds a little harder, saying, "Rollins, I don't believe you. You've got a few seconds and you're going to the hospital and have your shoulders put back in place."

"Okay, Okay. When I saw him he was over by the red pickup over there."

"Doing what?"

"I don't know. I swear, I don't know. Just looking at the pickup. I surprised him and he got pretty angry."

"Let's take a walk over to the pickup and see what he may have been looking at."

"Man, Olsen, you've got pretty strong hands."

Agent Olsen just smiled at Josh Rollins. They walked over to the truck and Agent Olsen asked him, "What the hell was he looking at, Rollins?"

"He was over on the driver's side. I approached him and that's when he put the gun to my head and told me to get over on the other side of the truck."

They both walked over to the driver's side of the truck. Agent Olsen looked at the truck from one end to the other and saw some white paint on the bumper. He looked at Josh and said, "How long has that paint been on there, Rollins?"

"A week or so, I think."

"How'd it get there?"

"I ran into a white building over near Wickiup Reservoir."

He bent down and scraped some off the bumper. "It looks pretty fresh."

"About a week," he repeated.

"What's in the back end here; in the camper shell?"

"After Lieutenant Santorini had been there," Josh explained he went through the cab and bed and found nothing. "There's nothing in there."

Agent Olsen looked through the cab and then opened the rear end. There were two sleeping bags, a small stove—something alongside the wall of the bed. He put his hand in a small hole and retrieved two small .22 shell casings. "What's this?"

Josh Rollins was stupefied. *How'd he miss that?* "I don't know. What is it?"

"Two small casings, look like twenty-twos I'd say. Do you own a twenty-two?"

"You know I can't own a weapon of any kind. I don't know how they got there."

He looked through the bed more carefully and could find nothing more. "Let's go back to the store and get me a little plastic bag." They walked back to the store and he got a Ziploc baggie and put the two casings in the baggie.

"I don't know what's going on here, Rollins, but you better hope we can't connect these to you or you know the consequences."

"Yes, I do, Mr. Olsen."

"I'll be in touch, Rollins."

As he left the store for Bend he thought, *This might be the straw that broke the camel's back.*

* * *

Joanne and Susan returned from a nice time at Jenny's, especially since they both had at least two glasses of wine; Susan three. As they entered the house, Susan said, "Joanne, have you got some good wine we could try?"

"Are you sure, Susan? I mean, we had . . ."

"Aw, com' on, Joanne. We can put on a little country and—the night's still young, don't you think? Com' on, whatta ya got?"

"Well, I've got a nice bottle of chardonnay."

"Great, open it up."

They put on some George Straitt, and Susan started hootin' and hollerin'. All the sudden, Susan's cell phone rang. She answered, *"Hi,* this is *Susan here."*

"Are you sure that's *you* Susan? You been tippin', youngin'?"

"Well, who . . . who is this?"

"This is Joyce, *Joyce Gilmore.*"

"Oh, hi, Joyce! What do you know, girl?"

"Boy, you really are having a good time."

"Yeah. Sure am."

Susan tried to compose herself a little, but obviously she was beyond control. But she tried.

"Listen, Susan, I'm going to be in Bend tomorrow, so . . . well, are you alone?"

"No-o-o. Joanne is here."

"Could you put Joanne on then."

"Yeah. Sure. You don't want to talk to little-o-me?"

"Just put Joanne on."

"Hello Joyce, this is Joanne. I've heard a lot about you."

"Hopefully all good," and they both laughed. "Listen, I would tell Susan but I'm afraid she would forget. I'm going to be in Bend tomorrow and I'd like to get together with Susan, I'll call her later in the day. But could you tell her tomorrow morning—assuming she's up to it—sounds dubious to me—that I'll call her later when I'm free."

"Sure, Joyce. She'll look forward to seeing you, I'll see to that. Bye."

Joanne got Susan to bed, she was singing all the way into the bedroom. Then Joanne crashed.

* * *

Josh Rollins had his flashlight as he moved around the store toward the pickup truck. He opened the rear end and began to dig through the bed of the truck. He moved the sleeping bags and stove around looking for any tell-tale signs that would get him in trouble. He knew that obviously someone had driven this truck last night, either Jerry McCrory or Jake. He knew that the rifle was missing and the bow and arrows, and the sheath, but he knew nothing about a .22. He kept rummaging through the truck looking for anything. Suddenly he came upon some—looked like putrid, dead skin. *It's been there awhile,* he thought. *I can't let them find anything in this truck. They'll hang me.* He went back to the store and got a swab and some ammonia and returned to the truck and began swabbing the bed.

When he finished and returned to the store, he sat down with a beer and began to try and put things together. *Dead skin? Whose?* He had an eerie feeling that something bad had happened and he didn't want to know about it. *Who had this truck and when?* The truck had only been used for any period of time within the last two months by one person, and that person was his nephew, Jake Hanson.

15

The mayor, Brian McCartney, had called a meeting for 9:00 that morning. Most of the important people in the city were there: the fire chief, the police chief, all the city council, the city treasurer, the city planner, the gas and electric company. Mayor McCartney opened the meeting with an overview of what he had learned in his meeting with Governor Thomas and discussions with the seismologist from California. He stressed there was no need to panic at this time, that a team was coming from Seattle to set up some sensors to track the activity and what exactly was going on at Mt. Bachelor. Kevin Quinn, the City Planner, spoke up and asked what exactly the mayor wanted them to do. Mayor McCartney said, "Kevin, I understand your concern, and I'm with you on this. We don't know the severity of the activity, and until we do, there is no need for grave concern. *However,* and I used that word advisedly, I thought it prudent to give you all a heads up on this potential problem that could engulf our city, so that the various departments might look into emergency measures to make things run smoother in the event of the worst-case scenario."

The mayor further alluded to the vast problem of the Deschutes River running amok through the city and causing an untold catastrophe. "We all know about the rivers after the Mount St. Helens eruption, and that was through a mostly unoccupied area. Think what would happen if the Deschutes crested twenty to thirty feet rumbling through town." He delegated differing responsibilities to the differing agencies and the meeting was adjourned.

*   *   *

When Lieutenant Santorini arrived, there sitting in his office was, "*Guess who?*" Agent Olsen greeted. "Lieutenant Santorini, you and I have to talk. There's a lot of information that *you have and I need.* Now, what were you looking for in that red pickup out there in Crane Prairie?"

"I was just looking around to see if I could . . ."

"Cut the *bullshit,* Lieutenant. I was out there yesterday and I have something in my pocket you may need. Now, what did you find out there?"

"Well, everything looked okay except some paint on the front bumper; I'm sure you saw that."

"Yes, I sure did. What do you think it was?"

"I don't know. Could be paint from a garbage can, or some building. I don't know."

"Now, you really don't believe that, do you, Lieutenant Santorini? It looked like an enamel of some sort to me. Didn't it look like that to you?"

"Could be, I don't know."

"You're not holding anything out on me, are you?"

"It wouldn't do any of us any good if I was."

"Well, I think I'll just hold on to what I have here in my pocket, because frankly, Lieutenant, *I don't believe you.* Furthermore, if I find out you are holding out on me, I'll make sure you're charged as an accessory after the fact."

"You do what you have to do, Olsen."

"Good day, Lieutenant."

As he left, Lieutenant Santorini began to think about what evidence he claimed from that truck. It wouldn't hurt to let him know what the forensics showed on that paint. However, it probably wouldn't end there and he'd continue to pester him further. "No, I'll just hang onto that for the time being."

Later on, Jimmy Fazio called confirming a match between the Explorer in the accident and the Explorer in the used car lot. He also said that the bodies found in Davis Lake and the McKenzie River showed a single gunshot to the back of the head, .22 caliber. They were probably killed at the same spot as the other two. And *that* red pickup was involved in the accident. Maybe Josh did have something to hide.

* * *

Josh Rollins dialed the number, it rang, and a voice on the other end said, "Hello?"

"Hello. Jake?"

"Yeah."

"This is Josh. Have you been driving that pickup in back?"

"Only a couple of weeks ago."

"Well, the law's been snoopin' around here the last couple of days. Even the FBI has been here. I don't know what they're lookin' fer, do you?"

"Naw, don't worry about anything, Josh. Probably somebody missing or something."

"Well, you stay away from that truck from now on, ya hear?"

"Yeah, sure, Josh, whatever you say."

*　*　*

Joyce Gilmore touched down mid-morning, rented a car, and made her way toward Bend. She really liked Bend and wouldn't mind settling there for a while. Bend had become a little progressive lately and she thought a young, forward-looking black woman in the business industry would be a benefit. She was there to look at Mary's Boutique, which she noticed in the *Western Commercial Newsletter* was for sale. She checked into her motel and drove over to the store, which was on the main drag of Bend. Having been in the modeling industry for a number of years, Joyce was very familiar with the garment industry. The inventory was strikingly beautiful, she was very impressed. After discussing the details of the sale, they agreed in principle and a deal was struck. Joyce and Mary needed to discuss things with their lawyers and would meet later to wrap things up. Joyce walked outside, looked around, took a deep breath and thought, *Some days are definitely better than others.*

She sat down on a bench and called Susan on her cell phone. "Susan?"

"Yes, Joyce?"

"Hello, Susan! I'm in Bend and . . ."

"I know. Joanne told me you were coming today. Sorry about last night."

"Are you feeling OK today?"

"It's all relative, Joyce. But, yes, OK."

"You'll never guess what I did."

"What?"

"I just bought Mary's Boutique."

"*You what*?"

"Yes, I did."

"*Wow,* that's the best news I've heard in—I can't believe it. Well, we're going to celebrate—sort of. I mean, you don't mind if I temper it a little."

"Not at all." She laughed.

"Give me a call around five o'clock. You don't mind if Joanne comes along, do you?"

"No. The more the merrier. You can even bring Bob, if you like."

"Well, let's just leave it with the three of us."

"Bye, Susan."

* * *

Susan figured that Bob had his cell phone off so she left a message on his voice mail saying that she was sorry that she wouldn't be able to see him tonight, but that she would be in touch later on.

She wondered what would happen to the company and all. Irene didn't seem like she would want, or, as a matter of fact, *could* run the business. It was just the right size and the location was premier. She didn't want to look for another job. *I hope Bob understands. But, damn it, what's he doing up here anyway?* She figured that she should go home tonight, although she didn't really want to. Joanne has been real nice about it and all, what a true friend.

* * *

Bob turned on his cell phone and got the message from Susan that she wouldn't be able to get together tonight. *Has she lost all interest?* he thought. *Well, I'll do a little fishing this evening maybe up on Tumalo Creek. There's not much fishing in this little creek, some nice little brook trout, a few browns, but it's nice and handy.*

It was still light at 8:00 and the mosquitos were

starting to get feisty when he decided to call it a day. He packed up his gear and headed down the highway toward Bend, planning on a visit to The Brewery and then home.

* * *

Joyce saw Susan in the parking lot of Gibraltor Realty. She got out of the car and said, "What do you think?"

"Looks mighty nice, girl."

Joyce was showing off her new cowgirl hat and boots. "These are from my new store."

"Joyce, when it comes to clothes, you always were on the right track. I guess I know where you want to go."

"*Really?* That *obvious,* huh?"

Joanne came out and joined them in the parking lot. They decided they would go over to Joanne's first and then go over from there. During the conversation while they were getting ready to go, Susan said, "You know, I guess I'm going to be dressed down, what with no togs for The Roundup."

Joanne said, "Susan, you'll look right at home with anything you wear, you know that."

"I didn't Joanne, but that makes me feel better."

Joyce said, "Say, Susan, whatever happened to that dude, Bob Hoaglund?"

Susan lifted her eyes upward, raised her hand shoulder high, waved it back and forth as if to say, *Cool it, Joyce.* "Well, I think we ought to take one car over there, don't you?"

"Hold on," Joanne said. "Who's this *dude* Bob Hoaglund?"

"He's just someone I had a couple of dates with." She looked over at Joyce and Joyce was smiling as if she was *the cat that got the canary.* Joyce loved it when she could get Susan on something.

"I'm not talking about any of my dates tonight. Let's celebrate Joyce's new store."

They drove over to The Roundup, parked the car, and went inside. The place was jumping, it always was. A Trisha Yearwood piece came up and Joyce said, "Come on girls, let's dance." Joanne went out with Joyce. She turned around and said, "Susan, aren't you going to dance?"

"No, I don't feel like it." She was really uncomfortable and scanned the room to see if that man was anywhere in sight. She slumped in her seat to make herself less recognizable. When the girls came back they looked real proud that they were able to keep up with the line dance. Joyce said, "Susan, it's not like you to miss a dance like that. Are you all right?"

She turned her head and said, "Huh? Yeah, sure. Just didn't feel like it."

They had been there for an hour and a half, two hours. Suddenly Susan remembered she hadn't locked the car when she came in. She told the girls she was going outside to lock it and she would be right back. The parking lot was dark and the car was parked in the rear of The Roundup. She turned the corner, looking warily all the while, then suddenly she felt a person behind her and a cold shiver on her neck. "I told you I'd get you, *bitch. Don't scream or you'll never see another thing.*"

Right then, she knew that voice . . . that voice over the phone to meet her at the North Bend property. She had to do something—and fast. Instinctively, she whirled around to her right, surprising him, and scratched the left side of his face, he dropped the knife and yelled out, "You piece of shit! I'm going to carve your *ass* into little pieces." As he reached for the knife, holding the side of his face, she kicked the knife away and ran into The Roundup. The door was open and she turned and saw him run to his motorcycle and speed away—where, she didn't know.

As she walked up to Joyce and Joanne, they looked at her and asked what happened. She told them she was jostled by a couple guys out in the parking lot, but that she was all right.

"Let's get security," Joanne said.

"*No, no,* Joanne. I'm all right, I am. But do you mind if we go?"

Joyce said it was a good idea and they left. On the way home, they were questioning her as to exactly what happened and Susan said, "Look, girls. I'm all right. It wasn't that big of a deal." She realized she was probably about a second or two from being dead.

When they arrived at Joanne's house, they went inside and toasted Joyce's new venture. Joyce said, "Well, Susan and Joanne, it's been a nice day, and I thank you all for it. I think I'll get along." She hugged Susan and told her she'd see her real soon—and maybe bring some of the girls down for an open house.

Joanne said, "Susan, you're going to spend the night, aren't you?"

"No, Joanne. I think it's time to go home. Thank you ever so much."

She dragged all of her luggage and clothing out of the house into the car and told Joanne she'd see her in the morning; if not, at the funeral. As she was driving away, she kept one eye on the road and one eye in her rearview mirror. She thought she saw a motorcycle behind her and slowed down to let it pass. She turned off on Franklin Avenue. At that moment, she stopped the car off the side of the street and began crying uncontrollably. *I can't do this,* she told herself. *I've got to get control of myself.* She got her cell phone out and pushed in the number.

"Hello."

"Bob, it's *me.*"

"Susan, you sound like you're crying. What's the matter? Where are you?"

"I'm on Franklin just off 97. I don't know what to do."

"You drive over to the inn right now. It'll take you about two or three minutes. I'll be waiting outside."

He looked at the clock and it was around 10:30. He frantically put on some clothes and went into the little parking lot to wait for her. He stood on the sidewalk and was looking for her Explorer when a Ford Focus pulled in behind him. He looked and there was Susan. She jumped out of the car and into his arms.

"Susan, what's wrong?"

"Oh Bob, I'm so scared."

"Let's get you inside and we'll . . ."

He opened the front door, looked inside and no one was in the downstairs portion. He took her hand and led her up the stairs and into his room. They sat on the bed, she looked at him and started crying again. "Susan, Susan. It's all right, you're safe now. What's wrong?"

She began to tell him the whole story about this man who called her agency and wanted to meet her at some property, that she recognized the voice, but couldn't place the face; that she went with Joyce and Joanne to The Roundup, and that he assaulted her with a knife in the parking lot, that she hadn't been home since she got back to Bend, and that she was going home tonight when she couldn't go any farther.

"It was *him,* Bob. *Why? Why do I turn to you in times like this?*"

At that moment, it was exactly what he wanted to hear, but he needn't show—he should act surprised. "I don't know, Susan."

She smiled and said, "Yes, you do. And you love it. But I don't like the feeling."

"That's the way the cookie crumbles, sometimes, you adorable woman."

That's not the way it goes, Sir Robert." They both laughed.

They kissed and he said, "There's an extra towel in there, you can take a shower."

She went in and took a shower, came out and slid between the sheets. She looked up at him and whispered, "Mr. Hoaglund, I think I love you."

He smiled and said, "And I you, Ms. Woodson. What's next?"

They both knew.

16

Bob leaned over and kissed Susan on the cheek and asked, "What would you like for breakfast this morning, Ms. Woodson?"

"Do I get a choice?"

"Probably not, but I thought I'd ask anyway. I'll go down and get us some juice, coffee, and maybe a muffin of some kind."

"That's *exactly* what I wanted!" They both laughed.

He made himself as inconspicuous as possible as he tip-toed into the breakfast room. *Good, no one is there.* He grabbed a tray and put two glasses of orange juice, two coffees, and grabbed four blueberry muffins. As he was about halfway to the stairs a voice said, "Are you getting breakfast for the person next door, perhaps?" He looked back and there was Becky with a smile and a wink.

"That's a brilliant deduction, Becky. Good morning."

He entered the door and Susan, who had sat up in bed, said, "Did everything go all right?"

"Perfect timing," he said.

They sat and ate their breakfast and Bob looked at Susan and said, "You're probably going to want to go home and get freshened up, get something to wear."

"Yes, I'll need to do that. The funeral is at one P.M. at the Valley Memorial Chapel so I need to get home and see how things are."

"Do you want me to accompany you home?"

"Would you?"

"You know I would."

"After last night, I don't know what this guy will do. I scratched his face pretty hard. There obviously is going to be some damage, and he'll be pretty upset. If he knows where I live . . ."

"Now, Susan, we don't know what he knows. But I think it's a good idea anyway."

They got themselves together and made their way out to the car. "Susan, I'll follow you." On the way to her house, they both kept a wary eye out for a motorcycle and that familiar face. Neither was forthcoming. They parked both their cars in the garage and took her luggage inside.

"The place smells *musty*. Or is it me? We haven't been gone all that long, have we?"

"No. Six days."

She took her luggage into the bedroom and went back to the living room where they contemplated the upcoming day's events. She said that after the funeral they were all going back to the realty company for a while, and she'd call him after it was over. He was walking into the garage when he heard a loud scream. He rushed into the living room, looking around, and said, *"Susan? Where are you?"*

"In the bathroom," she said.

He rushed into the bathroom and on the outside of the window were the words: YOU DIE, CUNT. He grabbed her, held her, and said, "I'm not going anywhere." He went outside and erased the words, which were written in lipstick, he expected, to simulate blood.

She showered and put on a black dress. They left her place at 11:30 A.M., he in his car, she in hers.

*   *   *

It was early Saturday morning and Lieutenant Santorini, although he did not know Sam Rossetti, was certainly going to the funeral, for he thought that Susan Woodson would be there and he had to get in touch with her, they had to talk. She had valuable information and he didn't want this trail to get cold. He had to learn about this other party, he felt sure that was the key to this whole case.

* * *

Jake Hanson arrived at his place in La Pine. It was a secluded little two-bedroom, almost shack-like residence. It had water and power, but no heat. He opened the door and rushed into the bathroom to see what his face looked like. He gasped as he saw three scratch lines running from above his left eye, halfway down his cheek. *That little bitch is gonna die.* Just then his roommate came through the door, Allen Jeffcoat. Allen was a little guy, maybe 5'4"–5'5", 145–150 pounds. He was cocky and always needling Jake. He yelled out, "*Jake? You here?*" No response. He walked around the corner and there in the bathroom was Jake. He had a towel up on the left side of his face. Allen asked, "What happened to you?"

"None of your business, Jeffcoat."

"Nah, come on, Jake." At that moment, he pulled the towel off his face and saw the three deep scratches and said, "Some filly got hold of you, Jake?"

Jake, seeing nothing funny in this, said, "What's so *fuckin' funny,* Jeffcoat!" He pushed Jeffcoat backward a couple feet. Allen Jeffcoat had been out that evening drinking and playing pool in La Pine. He snickered and said, "Hey Jake, you gotta admit, it's really kind of humorous. Don't you think?" At that moment, Jake whipped out his deer knife and plunged it into the abdomen of Allen Jeffcoat. He moaned and his eyes turned glassy as Jake turned the knife and withdrew it. Allen Jeffcoat slumped to the floor—dead.

* * *

He left her at her office and said, "I'm going home to change and I'll see you at the funeral. Valley Memorial Chapel at one o'clock?"

"Yes. Do you know where it is?"

"I think so. On Franklin, right?"

He leaned over to kiss her and saw someone get out of their car. He winked at her and said, "See you, *beautiful.*"

She smiled and waved goodbye.

David Long saw Susan. He asked, "Do you want to ride over with me?"

"I think I'm riding with Joanne. Thanks, David." She looked around and didn't see any sign of Joanne. *I hope she's all right,* she thought. She was about to tell David Long she would ride with him when Joanne came huffing and puffing in the door. "Sorry, I'm late, everyone. My car had a dead battery. Good ol' AAA came through."

Susan looked at Joanne and said, "You had me worried for a moment. Are you ready to go?"

Joanne said she was. She and Susan got in her car and were off to the chapel. They entered in the front door and were on their way to their seats when she was bumped by someone. She looked over and it was Lieutenant Santorini. He said, "I'm so sorry." At that point, he came a step closer and said, "I shouldn't be so clumsy." Simultaneously, he slipped in her hand a note. She looked at him and said, "That's quite all right." When they got to their seats in the third row, she made a point to sit on the aisle, leaned over into the aisle and read the note. MEET ME AT BROKEN TOP IN THE DOWNSTAIRS LOUNGE AT 2:30 P.M. IMPORTANT.

After the services at the chapel, she and Joanne made it to the cemetery out on Skyline Road. Standing there while the minister gave his eulogy, across the way and up the hill, was Bob. He smiled at her. After the services at the cemetery, they drove on back to Gibraltor Realty. There was lots of food and refreshments, care of Irene. It was 2:05 P.M. and Susan didn't know what she was going to do. She went outside and called Bob, hoping he could assist her.

"Hello, Bob?"

"One and only."

"No time to be kidding. Could you meet me up at Broken Top? Do you know how to get there?"

"Yes."

"I'm leaving right away."

"Is everything all right, Susan?"

"Uh . . . Yes."

Susan left immediately, after telling Joanne and Irene she had to leave, and was in the parking lot at 2:20 P.M. She looked over and saw Bob's Jeep and waved him over. She looked him in the eyes and said, "I hope I'm doing the right thing."

"What's that?"

She showed him the note. He paused for a second or two, took a deep breath and said, "Now is as good as time as ever to get this over with. Let's go."

They walked into the lounge, which was practically empty. A woman said, "have a seat, someone will take your order." They sat there for a few minutes, no one came to take their order. A woman came out and said, "Is your name Susan Woodson?"

She said, "Yes."

The waitress brought the phone over to the table and Susan picked it up. "Hello."

"Susan, this is Lieutenant Santorini. I'm being followed by the FBI, two people. I'm less than one minute from the parking lot. I'd advise you to get out of there."

Susan looked at Bob and told him that the FBI were coming in less than a minute; that they followed Santorini. Bob stood up and said, "Stand up easy and follow . . . here . . . this way." He led her through the back door out into the golf course area. He took a few steps toward a boy with a golf cart and said, "I'm from Broken Top Realty. I'm here to show this young lady some property. The pro inside told us we could have a cart for a few minutes."

The boy looked quizzically at Bob and said, "Well, I guess it's . . . all . . . right." He looked in the pro shop, with his arms outstretched, and no one looked his way. "Go ahead."

Bob and Susan jumped in the cart and took off down the side road toward some houses. They made a left at the first street, which turned into a dead end. He looked and saw a cart path out towards some trees and followed it for a way, when the path started to sway back and forth. He stopped the cart and looked at Susan and said, "We're having another tremor; it's lasting a lot longer." They sat in the golf cart and eventually there was calm. He came to a golf green, behind which was a street, Broken Top Trails. He let Susan off on the street and said he was going to return the cart and would pick her up in a few minutes.

* * *

Lieutenant Santorini exited his car in the parking lot, followed by Agent Olsen and his partner, Agent Kelly Hamlin. Agent Olsen said, "Lieutenant Santorini, we have reason to believe you were meeting Susan Woodson here; is that correct?

"I don't know what your talking about, Agent Olsen. I just came up for a late lunch."

"Well, that's a very good excuse. Let's go inside, Kelly."

The three of them entered the lounge and Agent Olsen pulled out a photograph of Susan Woodson and showed it to the waitress. "Have you seen this woman in here in the last thirty minutes or so?"

"Yes, but she left about five or ten minutes ago."

"Where did she go, do you know?"

"I didn't see where she went."

"Was she alone?"

"No, she was with a young man."

Agent Olsen took Lieutenant Santorini off to the side and said, *"Now, Lieutenant,* my patience is wearing thin. Who is this *young man?"*

"I have no idea, Olsen. Now, if you'll excuse me I'm going upstairs to the restaurant."

Kelly Hamlin went into the pro shop, there was a girl behind the counter. She approached her with a photograph. "Have you seen this woman in the last thirty minutes or so?"

"No, I sure haven't. I just took over five minutes or so ago. The pro was here before that, he's on the lesson tee now."

As Kelly Hamlin was talking to this woman downstairs, Bob Hoaglund arrived with the golf cart. He saw the woman being shown a photograph and the woman shaking her head back and forth. He looked for the young boy from whom he received the cart and he was nowhere to be seen. He slinked around the corner of the building and into the parking lot, where he got in his car and proceeded to pick up Susan. He went out the driveway, turned right, to find Broken Top Trails. A young teen was out in front of his house, in the driveway. "Can you tell me the way to Broken Top Trails?"

The young boy said, "Just go down two blocks and turn right, you'll run into it."

"Thanks." When he arrived, Susan was sitting on the curb. He said, "Well, you could at least have your thumb out or something."

"Always looking for a laugh, aren't you?"

"Reminded me of *It Happened One Night*."

"Well, I'm not in the mood for reminiscing."

She got in the Jeep and asked, "What now, Sherlock?"

"*Sherlock,* yet. Well, there apparently were *two* FBI agents. We must thank Lieutenant Santorini for the heads up on this. We can go back and try to get your car and go from there, or we can wait until later. What do you think?"

"I think we ought to wait until later, but we must try to see Lieutenant Santorini pretty soon."

"I agree. Do you have his card?"

"Yes. Somewhere in here. *Yes, here it is.*"

"Well, we'll give him a call tomorrow. I'm sure he won't be working, but we can leave a message for him to get in touch."

*   *   *

Jake Hanson gathered up Allen Jeffcoat's body, put the body in a tarp, and loaded it in the back of Jeffcoat's blue pickup. He loaded his motorcycle in the bed and drove down 97 South towards Klammath Falls, past Beaver Marsh, where he turned off a forest road and drove to the Williamson River. He took out some rope and fastened Jeffcoat's body to a large piece of metal that was at Jeffcoat's house, and lifting the body onto a small log, shoved it out into the river where the body eventually sunk to the bottom. He took out a flashlight and looked for any blood. Having found none, he rolled up the tarp and tossed it into the river. He took his motorcycle from the rear end of the truck and made his way back toward La Pine.

17

The lead story in the morning *Bulletin* was the tremor under Mt. Bachelor the day before. The headline read: MT. BACHELOR SHAKES VIOLENTLY. the article read in part:

> Yesterday, at 2:34 P.M., a violent tremor, measuring 4.9 on the Richter Scale, shook the City of Bend. It lasted thirty-four seconds. "The earth seemed to sway back and forth" said one person. The community remains on edge as to what the future will bring.

Bob looked at Susan and said, "This is really getting serious. The turbulence is quickening, and the mood of the city is becoming dire."

"Was there anything in there about volcanic activity?"

He read on down, almost in a scrolling manner. "Um . . . no."

"We were pretty lucky to get out of there yesterday, Bob. I think we ought to call Lieutenant Santorini this morning, first thing."

"I agree. We've got to agree on a meeting place. What do you think?"

"Well, the business is out. I would think they might be watching my house by now. How about . . . how about on the river next to the Old Mill District?"

"Good idea. What time?"

"Oh, maybe—how about six o'clock?"

"Let's do it. You better call because . . ."

She looked at him with a perturbed smirk and said, "I know *because.*" She looked at his card and dialed his number. Five rings and no answer. Then a message. "This is Lieutenant Santorini of the Deschutes County Sheriff's Office. I'm not available at the moment, but leave a message and I'll return your call shortly."

"Yes. This is Susan Woodson. I know it's Sunday, and you're not working. I hope you call in to get your messages. I will be down at the river in the Old Mill District at six o'clock sitting on a bench at the river. Bye."

*   *   *

The telephone rang in Brian McCartney's residence. He answered with, "Hello, this is Mayor McCartney."

"This is Richard Thomas, Brian. How are you this morning?"

"Fine, Governor. Nice to hear from you."

"Listen, I heard the news about the activity you had yesterday. I'm calling to see what the mood of the community is. Do you have a feel for it?"

"I think I do, yes. This last one was a little more severe and has the community real jumpy right now. We have no further news as to geological findings or anything of that nature, but we have everything in place. We had a meeting two days ago as to the responsibilities within the community and delegation of such. Have you any further news?"

"No. I wanted to tell you that Charles Warren is bringing a team up there within the next few days. He's getting mixed signals as to the size and scope of activity. He'll be in touch early in the week. Everything else okay?"

"Yes."
"I'll keep in touch then, Brian."
"Thanks, Governor. Good bye."

* * *

It was early afternoon and Lieutenant Santorini called in to get his messages. He had a hunch; lo and behold there was a message from Susan Woodson to meet her at 6:00 that night. *Maybe, just maybe this is what I'm looking for?*

He drove downtown at about 5:30, looking all the while in his rearview mirror for some tail, there was none. To be on the safe side, he parked over by Mirror Pond. As he got out of his car, he looked across the street and recognized Kelly Hamlin. *I knew that Olsen, that . . .* he locked his car and proceeded across the parking lot and into a little café, and immediately moved quickly through the front door and onto Wall Street. He made a left and crossed the street into an alley and onto Bond Street. He zigzagged his way over to Industrial way and into the *Old Mill District*. It was 5:45 and he had a few minutes to kill, so he walked into a couple shops, all the while wary that Ms. Hamlin had picked up his tail.

He moved along the river until he came upon a bench with two young people sitting on it. He walked up behind them and said in a low voice, "Hello, Susan. It's Lieutenant Santorini."

She turned around and said, "Hi, Lieutenant. Have a seat."

He sat down next to her and she introduced Bob. "Lieutenant Santorini, this is Bob Hoaglund."

"Hello, Bob. You must be the missing puzzle."

"You think so, Lieutenant?"

"I do. Do you want to stay here or go somewhere else?"

Bob said, "No, this will be fine. What did you want to know?"

Lieutenant Santorini took out his notebook with some notes already prepared. "First of all, how do you know each other?"

Susan said, "I live here in Bend, Bob is from San Diego. We met on Highway 40 by the Deschutes River."

"How did that meeting take place?"

Bob chimed in and said, "It's a long—well, not *long* story, but a complicated one. I was fishing on the east side of the Deschutes when I ran into a clearing. In that clearing was what I perceived to be a boot of some kind. As I proceeded further, it was indeed a boot within a six-by-six square, with four round silver, jade-like pieces facing north, east, west and south. I started back to the car when someone shot an arrow a foot above my head into a tree. I turned and didn't see who shot it. I hoofed it back to the car, where I observed my tires slashed and my cell phone gone. I started to panic and flagged down the first car coming my way, which was Susan. I commandeered her Explorer, despite her protestations, and we drove over to the Crane Prairie Store, where Mr. Jensen, the forest ranger, ultimately arrived. Mr. Jensen and I went back to the spot where this ceremonial display was and there was nothing there. It was all cleaned up. We went back to the store and he wrote up a report, which I signed. He left, and I got a tow truck and went back to Bend."

So, there was a report after all, Lt. Santorini thought. *Should I pressure him as to why he didn't report this or—no, not now.* "So, Susan you obviously left. Did Mr. Jensen call you?"

"Yes, he did. I wasn't home and he left a message asking if I wanted to follow through with any charges. I never returned his call."

"So, where are we in all this?"

"Oh, I'm not done just yet, Lieutenant. You'll probably want to hear more."

"Sure."

"Then two days later, on the middle Deschutes, down near Terrebonne, there was another incident with this same person, I assume. Another boot in a clearing, with only one silver piece. This time I was shot at from the bluff up above. I scrambled amongst the shrubs to hide. There was some movement and rustling of dirt and shrubs. When I surfaced, the same thing. Everything was gone. I went back to my car, drove up the hill to where he was, which was fenced off, and determined that he had driven a motorcycle in there and had left that way."

"Did you get a look at this person?"

"Yes I did. I recognized him as being the person that I had also caught a glimpse of on Highway 40."

"Can you describe him?"

"Only that he had a very evil grin, and reddish-orange colored eyes."

It is him, Lt. Santorini thought.

"You left for San Francisco, Susan?"

"Yes, I did. Before we get to that, I must tell you that I have had two run-ins with the very same person. Both times at The Roundup."

"The western dance place?"

"That's right. The first time I danced with him, and after I rebuffed his advances, he mentioned that he was going to get me. He had such an evil way about him. The second time was when I got back from San Francisco."

"We know you didn't go to San Francisco, but we won't go any further."

"The second time I was at the same place and I went to check to see if my car was locked and he surprised me from behind with a knife on my neck. I wheeled around, caught him off guard and scratched the left side of his face."

"From where to where?"

"Just above his left eye, I believe, down to the middle of his cheek. I don't know how severe the scratches were, but . . ."

"You know, I think I'm going to—hold on just a second." He dialed Joe Stacy's number. "Hello, Joe? This is Al Santorini. Listen, I've got an emergency right now and I need a sketch. Are you busy? Well, if you could be here in a half hour I'd . . . where? Oh, down by the river in the Old Mill District. Thanks a lot, Joe. Bye.

"That was the person who does sketches; artistic renderings. He'll be here in a half hour. So, Bob, you and Susan . . ."

"And, Lieutenant, there's one further incident that we haven't talked about yet. Susan and I were fishing one day—after the first two incidents—on Lake Paulina. We had been out on the lake for a couple hours or so, when a man in a motorboat—*the man*—buzzed our boat. He swamped our boat, we both dove overboard and swam to shore, all the while he was shooting at us. We met a man who took us back to the restaurant and we drove home."

"Anything else I should know about?"

Bob said, "Yes, one further thing. After the incident where Susan scratched his face, he apparently now knows where she lives, because written on her bathroom window, in lipstick, was the words YOU DIE, CUNT."

They sat there for about twenty minutes discussing everything but the purpose of their meeting when the artist approached them. Lieutenant Santorini said, "Joe

Stacy, this is Susan Woodson and Bob Hoaglund." Joe Stacy shook their hands and brought out his sketch pad. "Are we going to do this here, Lieutenant?"

"Is that all right, Joe?"

"Sure. We have enough light left."

Bob and Susan took turns with the sketch, adding and subtracting to the chin cleft, the mouth, cheekbones, eyes and eyelids, the hair and hairline. When they got done they looked at each other and said with a smile, "That's *him.*"

Lieutenant Santorini thought to himself, *That is indeed him.*

Joe Stacy pulled out some plastic to superimpose over the sketch and asked Susan to show where the scratch marks might have been. When he was done, Susan said, "That's what I remember."

"Thanks a lot for coming, Joe," Lieutenant Santorini said. "If you can get that to me early tomorrow, I'd appreciate it."

"You're welcome, Lieutenant. Glad I could be of help. Bye everyone."

"Well, I don't know what to say to you two, except thanks for coming forward. I must advise you also that the FBI is involved in this case and may ask you some questions."

As Lieutenant Santorini began to walk away, Bob said, "You don't have jurisdiction, do you, Lieutenant?"

"What was that?"

"I think you heard what I said. The FBI wouldn't be involved except Jensen was a federal employee. You don't have jurisdiction."

"Pretty smart for a court reporter, aren't you? You're right, I don't. But there's a personal reason for this and . . ."

"Your best friend was Red Jensen; is that right?"

"You're pretty perceptive, Mr. Hoaglund."

"You want to solve this case yourself and hence the FBI is in your way. Well, Susan and I want to help in any way we can. Here's where I can be reached and I know you have Susan's number."

"Thanks a lot, you two."

It was about 8:00 and Lieutenant Santorini was making his way back to his car in Bend proper. As he was walking he was thinking, *It's beginning to fit.* He decided to make one more visit to Josh over at Crane Prairie, because he thought a key element to the puzzle may be over there. As he walked to his car, a familiar voice came from his left. *"Lieutenant Santorini, have a nice night on the town?"*

"It's a lovely evening, isn't it, Agent Olsen? The nights are starting to become a little warmer. Summer will be here before you know it. Evening, Agent Hamlin."

"Your sense of humor, Lieutenant is *always* refreshing. Agent Hamlin started to come over for a nice evening greeting, and *whoosh,* you were gone."

"Pity I didn't see you, Kelly."

"Don't placate us, Lieutenant."

"What do you want, Agent Olsen?"

"You know, I lost my train of thought, Lieutenant. Maybe I'll remember it tomorrow. If so, I'll give you a call."

"I'll be looking forward to hearing from you, Agent Olsen."

*   *   *

The phone rang and Josh Rollins picked it up. "Hello?" he said.

"This is Jake."

"What do you want, Jake?"

"You know that cabin on the other side of the highway, the one over by Little Cultus Lake?"

"Yes."

"I wonder if I could stay there for a few days."

"How about your job?"

"Well, they don't need me anymore so I need a place to hole up for a few days."

"Sure. Come by and get the keys."

"Thanks, Uncle Josh."

*   *   *

"Do you want to go home tonight or . . ."

"Do you think they'd mind if I stayed another night? I mean . . . it's just that I don't feel . . ."

"I know *I* don't mind."

"Come on, Bob. Get serious, would you? I mean, you just . . ."

"They won't mind. Besides, we'll just steal away up the stairs if we have to. In fact, they'll probably have some muffins out just for *us*."

She laughed and said, "You're impossible."

They drove over to her house and picked up some odds and ends, then drove back to the Inn. As they lay in bed contemplating their next move, the radio was on and an old Tommy Dorsey song was playing, *Robins and Roses*. The last verse ended with the words ". . . *a poem by Kipling while troubles go rippling by.*" They looked at each other, squeezed each other's hand, and fell off to sleep.

18

Lieutenant Santorini arrived in the office and immediately called Wally Berger. "Wally, could you get a car for us? We're going up to Lake Paulina."

"Okay, Skip. Will do."

He made sure that he had his briefcase with the sketches and they set out for the lake. When they arrived they both exited the car and entered the restaurant/store. Lieutenant Santorini walked up to the counter, there was an older gentleman there, and asked, "Are you the owner or manager of the store?"

"Yes, I sure am. The owner."

"I'm Lieutenant Santorini, and this is deputy Wally Berger from the Deschutes County Sheriff's Office. We'd like to ask you a few questions."

"Certainly."

"What's your name, sir?"

"I'm Jigs. Jigs Arnold."

"Mr. Arnold, I'm going to show you two sketches and I wonder if you could tell me if you have seen this person before."

"Yes. The one on the right, that's Billy Hanson. I've never seen him with scratches."

"How do you know Mr. Hanson?"

"Oh, he works for me, or at least he did until yesterday. He called in and said he wouldn't be working for me anymore. To bad, too, because he was a good worker."

"What did he do here for you?"

"Oh, you know, sort of a *jack of all trades.*"

"Did he leave a number or an address where you can get in touch with him?"

"No. I told him I'll have a check waiting for him when he comes by."

"Well, thank you, Mr. Arnold, for everything."

"You're welcome, Lieutenant. Glad I could help."

On the way back through La Pine, Lieutenant Santorini thought to himself, *That's our boy.* Lieutenant Santorini said, "Wally, let's stop in La Pine at a few places and see if we can get identification."

They stopped at a restaurant, a pizza parlor, a gas station. Nothing. Nobody recognized him. On their last stop, a Dairy Queen, he was showing the sketches to the manager, who could make no identification, when a young man, seeing what was happening, came by and looked at the sketch and said, "Yeah, I've seen him around."

"Does this person visit here often?"

"That, I don't know. I only work three days a week and it's usually on the weekend when I see him. He usually hangs outside and waits for other bikers to come by."

"Do you know his name?"

"No, never did get his name."

Lieutenant Santorini told Deputy Berger to get the young man's name, address and telephone number for future reference.

They got in the car and Wally said, "What exactly has this guy done. Lieutenant?"

"I'm not exactly sure, but we're soon going to find out."

*　　*　　*

Bob and Susan were at the bakery on Wall Street having a danish and coffee. Susan looked at Bob and said, "I think I'm going to stay at home tonight, Bob."

"We can do that, if you like."

"Not *we,* Bob. *Me.*"

"Susan, do you really think . . ."

"Look Bob, *I've decided.*"

Another side I haven't seen, he thought. *Pretty stubborn.* "Well . . . OK then."

"I have a very important two o'clock appointment today, then afterwards I'll call you and make a special dinner for us."

"Sounds like a great idea to me."

"But I have to get my things and get in a little early today."

"We can go back and get them and let you get along."

As they were driving back to the *Inn,* Bob thought to himself that he'd better check in with the judge. He hoped that she remembered to tell the coordinator that he wouldn't be in, that he'd taken another week off.

They went up to the room and Susan said, "You know, Bob, under all this chaos this has been the most exciting time in my life." She rushed to him, put her arms around him and said, "I hope you feel *somewhat* the same way I do."

Somewhat? he thought. "Everything's going to be fine, Susan. It seems like we've known each other for a long time, doesn't it?"

She nodded her head up and down.

They walked outside, loaded her things in the car, and she was gone.

Bob noticed that it was a little cool today, that the clouds were forming early over the mountains. Could be a wet day, he thought.

* * *

Philip Ross is a world renowned anthropologist and professor of psychology at The University of Oregon. Whenever Lieutenant Santorini had a serious problem, he called Dr. Ross, for he knew he'd get an answer.

"Hello, Dr. Ross?"

"Yes."

"This is Al Santorini."

"Al, how are you. Are you still in Bend with the Sheriff's Office?"

"Yes, I am. They'll probably have to haul me out of here."

Dr. Ross laughed and said, "Me too."

"Philip, I've got a problem that I hope you can solve, which revolves around a possible serial killer in Oregon."

"*Oh?* I don't think I'm familiar with that one."

"Well, I'll give you a synopsis of the facts. A gentleman was fishing and came upon a six-by-six clearing. Inside the clearing was a boot with some bone protruding from the boot was centered perfectly. On the outer fringes of the square, at ninety degree angles, were four round, jade, silver-like adornments, like on a belt."

"Is there anything symbolic about that array?"

"Well, there certainly could be. It sounds very much like an Egyptian pagan ritual. The four pieces of silver could connote—tell me, Al. How many murders has the person perpetrated?"

"Five that we know of. A family of four and a forest ranger. The family of four were shot through the head, and on two of the bodies, hands were cut off; two of the bodies had the bottom of their leg amputated."

"That narrows it somewhat. It's coming on the summer solstice, and as I said, an Egyptian ritual, such as the

Four Sons of Horus. Four people, in Egyptian, *Oebhsennuf,* designating East; *Duamutef,* South; *Imsety,* West, and *Hapi,* North. In the center, instead of a boot, would have been two candles, unlit, and incense, unlit. Presiding over this ritual is *Ra,* a self-appointed god who created himself; is all powerful.

"Now, this gentleman who apparently arranged this demonstration, is psychotic. He suffers from what I call *socius exspecture,* or a perceived, *his* perceived expectation of society. He's extremely dangerous in that the only way he knows how to communicate that desire is through violent, deadly means. He's an extremely vile and base man."

"Can you tell if he suffers from schizophrenia, Doctor?"

"Probably not. He's aware of what he's doing, he just doesn't want to stop it."

"Well, Dr. Ross, it's always a pleasure talking with you. Thanks again."

"Anytime, Al."

Just as I thought. This man has to be stopped, and now.

Sandy, his secretary, said, "Lieutenant, Evan Giles, the Sheriff from Klamath County, is on the phone; line four."

"Hello, Evan. This is Al Santorini."

"Hi, Al. Good to talk to you."

"What's up?"

"We're down here just outside of Beaver Marsh on the Williamson River. We've got a pickup truck down here that we've run through the DMV, that is registered to an Allen Jeffcoat from La Pine. The doors were open the keys were inside. We think there might be foul play."

"Has anyone been inside yet?"

"Just a cursory search—with gloves . . . plastic gloves."

"Listen, Evan, I want you to dust for prints on the truck. Don't let anyone in there without *protection* and I'll be down as soon as I can."

He thought about calling Wally to get a car, and then he figured he'd get a chopper. "Sandy, could you get Charlie Tucker on the phone for me?"

"His number at the airport?"

"Yes. Hello, Charlie, this is Lieutenant Santorini."

"Hi, Lieutenant."

"Charlie, I need your help. Are you flying today?"

"No. Just on call, you know."

"Well, I'm coming over in ten minutes and I want you to take me down to Beaver Marsh, just below Chemult. How long will that take?"

"Twenty-five, thirty minutes, I suppose."

"Get her warmed up."

Wally Berger drove Lieutenant Santorini over to the Bend airport and the Lieutenant boarded the Sheriff's helicopter, which is only supposed to be used in an emergency. Lieutenant Santorini considered this *an emergency*. They flew down to Beaver Marsh and over to the Williamson River. Charlie spotted a clearing and said, "We're going down right over there. Hang on, Lieutenant."

As he exited the helicopter, Sheriff Giles said, "*Boy,* this really must be important for you to take *that* taxi."

"Evan, it is. Is this the truck?"

"Yes."

"Has the evidence team arrived yet?"

"Not yet."

"Well, I'm going to do something a little irregular. I'm going to request to enter that truck and dust for prints myself." He took out a *print-a-kit,* and asked the sheriff for permission to enter the truck. "I know this truck is in your jurisdiction, but this is really important, Evan. I won't do it if you think . ."

"You obviously think this truck is pretty important. Do you have a line on it or anything?"

"No, it's just that I have a hunch, as you do, that there is foul play here and I want to make sure I get something started as soon as possible."

"Do you think this person, Allen Jeffcoat, may be involved in something?"

"I'm not sure, Evan. But things are happening fast in Deschutes County right now and I just want to make sure I get some fresh prints in the mill as soon as possible. You heard about Red Jensen, I assume."

"Yes, we all heard about Red. He was a fine man."

"Well, he was a very good friend of mine and just want to make sure I make every effort to . . ."

"Go ahead, Al. Just be careful."

Lieutenant Santorini smiled at Sheriff Giles and said, "I owe you one."

After he lifted some prints, he carefully put them in plastic bags. He told Sheriff Giles, "I have reason to believe that the person who is the owner of that truck is somewhere nearby in the bottom of that river."

Sheriff Giles said he thought so, too, and that they were preparing to drag portions of the river nearby.

Lieutenant Santorini boarded the helicopter and they took off for the return flight to Bend. On the way, Lieutenant Santorini called Wally Berger to meet him at the airport. It was raining as they set the helicopter down.

"Thanks a lot, Charlie. If the Sheriff gives you any

business about your log, you have him get in touch with me. Okay?"

"All right, Lieutenant. It's been so long since I've been up, it was a pleasure."

When they got back to the sheriff's office, Lieutenant Santorini told Wally to get those prints to evidence and see if they could get some identification.

*   *   *

It was around noon and raining at the Redmond Airport. Mayor McCartney was there to meet Charles Warren, the seismologist, and his crew. As Charles Warren came to baggage, Mayor McCartney greeted him and said, "Hello, Mr. Warren. I'm Brian McCartney, the Mayor of Bend. Nice to meet you. Did you have a good flight?"

"It was a little rough over the Cascades, but, yes."

As they drove into Bend, Mr. Warren asked what the weather forecast was to be. They told him it had been raining for about an hour and was expected to rain the rest of the day and into the night.

"How much snow do you think Mt. Bachelor will receive from this storm, Mayor McCartney?"

"Well, it's expected to drop close to a foot of new snow."

"If that's the case, we're going to have to shut down the mountain to skiing or hiking of any kind. Any sort of tremor could set off an avalanche on the mountain."

"Mr. Warren, this will be good for spring skiing."

"*Mr. McCartney,* I'm here to tell you there could be a disaster up there. Many people would be killed. This is *serious business.*"

At that point, the mayor started to grasp the gravity of what Mr. Warren was trying to say.

Mr. Warren said, "One foot of new fallen snow, in an avalanche, could cause a catastrophe."

"I understand, Mr. Warren. When do you think the cut-off time is?"

"Well, if it snows six to eight inches, they should shut down the mountain."

Mayor McCartney went in the next room and told one of his aides to call Mt. Bachelor and tell them to monitor the amount of snow; soon as it reaches six to eight inches, to shut the operation down.

* * *

Ben Olsen saw Lieutenant Santorini and said, "Lieutenant, I understand you took a little hop today in your chopper."

"That's right, Agent Olsen. *Sheriff business.*"

"Combined with?"

"*Sheriff business, Mr. Olsen.*"

"How are we doing with the murder investigation, Lieutenant?"

"You tell me, Agent Olsen. It's your jurisdiction."

"Well, we've sort of run into a dead end. I wondered whether you had anything to share with us."

"Nothing. The sheriff's office keeps me more than busy. Besides, I'm surprised the *FBI* hasn't cracked this case yet."

"We will, Lieutenant. We will."

"I know you will. I'm pretty busy, Agent Olsen. Goodbye."

He could see that Agent Olsen was really upset as he left the building, and didn't know what he would do next.

"Randy, this is Al here."

"Oh, hi, Al."

"Listen, I've got a favor to ask of you. Do you have access to the FBI computer with regards to fingerprints?"

"Well, I'd have to go through Ben Olsen."

"I thought so. If I send some fingerprints over, do you think you could run them through the computer? Agent Olsen and I are at, you might say, *cross purposes.*"

"That's understandable. Sure, send them over."

"Thanks, Randy. I owe you one. Oh, and the name I'm looking for is Billy Hanson, or *any Hanson.*

"Wally, when those prints come back, could you run those over to Lieutenant Randy Rivers at the police department?"

"I'll get on it, Skip."

"Sandy, do you have Sheriff Giles on the phone?"

"Evan, this is Al Santorini again. What did the registration reveal about the owner of the truck?"

"Let's see. Allen Jeffcoat. The address is Post Office Box 27, South River Road."

"Was there anything else of interest in that car?"

"Nothing of interest, Al. By the way, we've begun a sweep of the river, and as of yet, have come up with nothing."

"Thanks, Evan. I'll be in touch."

He went over to Wally's desk and gave him the information of Allen Jeffcoat. Hopefully, he could get an address or identity of the house from the post office box.

19

The day was turning ugly as Bob decided to take a trip out to Prineville to do some fishing. He arrived in Prineville and noticed that the sky was dark to the west and it was probably raining. The weather was starting to deteriorate here also. There were only three other fishermen on the river. Sometimes *weather* can cause the fish to feed because some flies hatch that otherwise would not. He tied on a golden stone and cast it into a pool where he saw a fish feeding. *Boom,* he hit it. A nice rainbow, maybe twelve, fourteen inches. He must have been the only fish in that pool; for the next ten minutes, no action. He moved upstream a little further and resorted to a baetis nymph, which resulted in some small fish. The fish were here, but he wasn't, he was worrying about Susan going home tonight, *alone. I mean, this guy is a psycho, totally evil. Who knows what he may do next.*

After another hour or so of fishing, he sat down to eat a sandwich he picked up in Prineville, and felt a few drops. It was also getting colder. He decided to call it a day and make his way back to Bend.

He arrived in Bend and it was raining as hard as he had ever seen it. *This must be a strong weather front,* he thought. After entering his room, he looked at his watch and saw the time at 2:00 P.M. The judge would be back from lunch.

"Hello, Judge Ruiz?"

"Oh, hi, Bob."

"Are you busy?"

"Well, I'm going back into court in ten minutes or so. When are you coming back down?"

"I'll be back by next Monday, for sure."

"How are things between you and that *classy* girl you brought down here?"

"I'm sure she'd love that compliment, coming from you. Real well."

"What's up, then?"

"Well, I think he's stalking her and . . . I just had to talk to someone about it."

"*Stalking her?* How?"

"She stayed with me at the *inn* a couple nights because *he* was there, at her house. He wrote a nasty note on her window that she was *to die.*"

"And you want to do what?"

"There's not a lot I can do. She wants to go home tonight—alone. I don't think it's a good idea, but she's pretty stubborn in that way, and that's the way it's going to be."

"Well, you can get law enforcement involved."

"No, I can't. *We* can't. If we do, then the FBI gets involved and it becomes a *house of cards.* Believe me, we have a lieutenant in the shcriff's office here who would love to help us out, but his hands are tied because he doesn't have jurisdiction. The man who was killed was a federal employee. It's real complicated."

"I've got to go, Bob. You take care of yourself . . . *and her* . . . and we'll see you next week. If I can be of any help, give me a call."

"I will, Judge. Thanks for everything. Bye." *That was the best thing I did so far today. I feel a lot better.*

Mayor McCartney got the call at 2:30 in the afternoon that six inches of snow had fallen. He still secretly hoped it wouldn't reach eight, but told them to shut down the mountain at eight inches.

He got on his computer to get the weather forecast and learned that it was to snow tonight; that it would not let up until later the next day. *Why did this have to happen on my watch?*

* * *

It was 1:30 in the afternoon when Joanne Behler walked into Susan's office. There she sat with a dour look. "How come the *hang dog face*, Susan?"

"This may be one of the biggest days in my sales life and look at the weather. I mean, can you believe it? It's supposed to go on like this the rest of the day."

"Have you got a showing this afternoon?"

"*Yes.* Two o'clock. You know that house out at Broken Top, the 2.5 million?"

"Of course."

"Well, the Sutherlands are supposed to come in this afternoon. They've been over to look at it today and now, *this*" as she pointed out the window.

"By the way, how's Irene doing?"

"You wouldn't believe it. She's been very calm and asking questions of everyone to see how she can manage this office in an effective manner. Temporarily, that is."

"That's good news. We all expected the worst. Let's go down the hall and get a coke."

They walked down the hall together. Susan's spirits seemed to buoy as they discussed Joanne's newest flame. "What's his name?" Susan said.

"How come we're always talking about *my* dating activities, Susan, and never *yours?*"

"Oh, I have a feeling we will, Joanne. We will."

David Long spotted the two of them down at the coke machine. He said, "Susan, you're wanted at the front."

She looked at her watch, it said 1:45. *They must be early,* she thought. "Hello, Mr. Sutherland, Mrs. Sutherland."

"Hi, Susan," Mr. Sutherland stated.

"Well, as you two can see, it's not the best of days. But I'll get my coat and keys and . . ."

"There'll be no need for that, Susan. We've decided to take the house."

Susan turned in her tracks and with a look of shock said, *"You want the house?"*

"We sure do."

Joanne and David both looked at each other, smiled and in a low tone of voice said, *"Yes!"*

Susan stood there aghast for a moment, then said, "Well, let's have a seat and get this thing in motion." The credit reports were all done, it was to be a cash transaction, so there wasn't a lot of paperwork to be done. They took about two hours to get everything assembled; then the Sutherlands left and Susan let out a shout, *"Can you believe it?"*

She walked out into the hall and told everyone she was treating today, that it would be champagne for everyone. She grabbed Joanne and they took off down the street to get some champagne, some brie and French bread. When they returned, there was four or five other employees and they began to celebrate Susan's big sale, for she had *cut her teeth* in the bigtime.

It was 7:00 P.M. and Susan remembered Bob. *Oh my gosh, I forgot to call him.* She rang his cell and he answered.

"Hello."

"Bob, this is Susan. I'm sorry I didn't call earlier, but I just made the biggest sale of my life and we're over here at the office celebrating. Could we make it tomorrow night?"

"Well, sure. Are you still planning on going home tonight?"

"*Yes, I am.*"

He could tell she was having one too many. He said, "Why don't you have a cup of . . . ?"

"Coffee, right?"

"Right."

"I'm way ahead of you, *dear.*"

Bob smiled and shook his head. "OK, Susan. Congratulations on your big day. I'll talk to you tomorrow."

She hung up the phone, paused, smiled for a moment and said to herself, *I wish I could be that understanding.*

After they cleaned up, it was 8:15 or so and starting to get dark. "Thanks, you all, for staying around. You're the greatest." She looked at Joanne and said, "I hope I'm doing the right thing by going home tonight."

Joanne looked at her, with a certain concern in her eyes. "I hope you are too, Susan."

They both went to their cars. Susan said, "The rain's stopped, but it looks like we could get a thunderstorm or something. Look at those black clouds. Bye, Joanne. Thanks."

As she turned down her street, there was a clap of thunder in the distance. She drove into the garage, opened the door into the house and hauled her luggage into the bedroom. She went into the kitchen to get a glass of water when suddenly a bolt of lightening and a clap of thunder hit. *It's getting closer,* she thought. She walked back into the bedroom and she was about to turn on the light when she heard this muffled sound of a motorcycle outside. She looked outside. It was too dark, she could see nothing. She began to unload her suitcase when she heard a jiggle of the front door. *What was that?* she thought. She stood frozen in her bedroom for a minute or two when she heard a jiggle of the back door, the sound of glass being broken and the back door being yanked open. *Oh my God. He's here.*

She had to get out of there. She looked at the window when she heard a voice: "You little bitch. Where are you? I'm going to cut your ass into little pieces." A light came on in the hall. All of a sudden a bolt of lightning, an immediate clap of thunder and the lights went out. "That's not going to help you, my little princess. Your ass is mine."

She fumbled in her purse for her phone and ran into the bathroom where she locked the door.

The phone rang and he picked it up. "Bob, he's here."

He dropped the phone, put on some pants and shirt, some sandals, grabbed his keys, and made a beeline out the door, slamming it on his way. On his way over to Susan's, he kept thinking to himself, *This is my fault.*

She cowered behind the shower curtain in the shower, knowing full well he'd find the door locked and try to enter. A few minutes went by and she could hear him fumbling around in the living room and bedroom. Suddenly, the door was violently shook. *"I know you're in there. Get your pretty little ass out here."*

How much longer do I have to live? she thought. He was still pushing at the door and making no headway. "*Shit!*" she heard. All of the sudden, the door gave way and she could see his shadow start to enter. At the same time, she heard a voice from downstairs. "Susan? Susan? Where are you?"

The man wheeled and turned his attention to the

voice. He took a few steps out into the hall and started toward the back door.

"Look out, Bob."

Bob saw his shadow and saw he had a pistol pointed at him. He ducked just before the gun went off, hitting the back door. "You're not going to get away with this, you son of a bitch!" He moved toward the living room and heard another shot, ducking behind a couch. He saw the shadow move toward the kitchen, got up and dove at him. They both went down, the gun clanging on the floor. The man kicked at Bob's head, temporarily dazing him. Bob grabbed for his leg, catching onto his boot . . . a motorcycle boot. The man yanked his leg a couple times, the third time, the boot came off. He rose and ran out the back door. Bob, still dazed and groggy, rose and opened the door. He heard the motorcycle start up and leave the driveway. He stood there for a minute, clearing his head, and thinking, *Shit, I had him.*

He turned his attention to Susan. "*Susan, where are you? He's gone.*"

She ran out of the bathroom and into his arms in tears. "I thought I was going to die, Bob."

"Do you have Lieutenant Santorini's number, his home number, Susan?"

"Yes. He gave it to me." She went into the bedroom and got her book and gave the number to Bob.

"Hello Lieutenant Santorini? This is Bob Hoaglund. I'm over at Susan Woodson's house. *That man* has been here. He almost killed Susan."

Lieutenant Santorini was extremely anxious. He said, "I'll be right over, Bob. What's the address?"

"What's the address, Susan? . . . 2422 Dunhill Road."

It was about twenty minutes later when Lieutenant

Santorini arrived. He came in the front door and noticed that Bob and Susan were both extremely shaken, Susan was almost in a trance. "Are you both all right?"

"Yes, we're both OK. I almost had him, but he got away."

Lieutenant Santorini began to investigate the house, seeing the door to the bathroom pushed in, seeing the door was yanked open in the rear. At that moment Bob said, "He had a pistol, it's right over here." Lieutenant Santorini walked over to where the pistol lay and, with his pen, picked it up by the trigger guard. *A .22-caliber,* he thought.

"I'm really sorry about what happened tonight. We're getting close to this guy, I can call the police in and get them involved."

Bob and Susan looked at each other, knowing that would open up the case to an uncertainty. Susan shook her head back and forth toward Bob, and said, "No, I don't think so, Lieutenant. We know the consequences of that, and we trust your judgment."

Lieutenant Santorini looked at both of them and said, "Thanks, to both of you. I'm going to take this pistol back to the sheriff's office. I think you ought not stay here tonight. I'll be in touch to see how you are tomorrow."

Bob looked at Susan and said, "Come on, *we're* staying at the inn tonight."

She looked at him and said, "I'm so sorry to put you . . ."

He put his finger on her lips and said, "Ssh." She smiled.

"Besides, you can tell me all about your big day today."

20

Lieutenant Santorini arrived in the office early in the morning, he transferred the pistol to a plastic evidence bag. He wanted to get those things analyzed as soon as possible. When Wally arrived, he wanted to go to La Pine. He noticed that the weather was still iffy, but he wanted to go out there anyway. He still was puzzled by this *man*, this person who was causing all this difficulty in the state—and *where* he was.

It was 9:00 A.M. when Wally came in, and Lt. Santorini said, "Wally, get a black and white, I want to go out to La Pine today."

"Sandy, could you get the La Pine Post Office on the line?"

"Hello. I'm Lieutenant Santorini from the Deschutes County Sheriff's Office. I wonder if I could ask a few questions. Do you have a Post Office Box 27 on West River Road?"

"Let me check. Yes, we do. However, there's a mail box out there now."

"Could you tell me who that mail is delivered to?"

"Well, Lieutenant, we don't usually do this over the phone. If you could maybe come on over, then . . ."

"Very well, then. Thank you. We'll be out."

Wally Berger brought the car around and they made their way out to La Pine to the post office. He entered and asked, "Hello. I'm Lieutenant Santorini from the DCSO. Could you tell me who's in charge here today?"

The postal clerk said, "Sure, Lieutenant."

"Hello, Lieutenant, I'm Lars Owens."

"Yes. I'm looking for the person who's registered to Post Office Box 27 out on West River Road."

"Well, you understand, Lieutenant, we usually don't . . ."

"Mr. Owens, you can do this now or we can go get a warrant and I won't be in such a good mood."

"Very well. The name is Margaret Jeffcoat."

"*Margaret?*"

"Yes. Oh, also an Allen Jeffcoat."

"Thank you very much, Mr. Owens." They drove out on the West River Road, where the residences seemed to stop. They looked around and saw nothing until they arrived at a mail box on the side of the road. Wally Berger read the lettering, BOX 27, MARGARET AND ALLEN JEFFCOAT. They took the road about a quarter of a mile back into the forest where they arrived at a run down house; almost a shack. They exited the car and knocked on the front door. No answer. They separated and went around to the back and saw no vehicle of any kind. Deputy Berger saw a window that was open and said, "Lieutenant, here's a window with a screen on it that's open."

"I'll be right there." The lieutenant took off the screen and entered the residence. It was a bedroom that appeared to be occupied, because men's clothes were hanging in the closet, and there was fishing gear inside the room. He made his way into the hall and into the living room, or rec room, where he found a potato chip wrapper and a cola can. He went into the bathroom where he found some toothpaste, a toothbrush and some shaving materials. There appeared to be two razors. *Two razors?* he thought. *Maybe two people were living here.* He went back into the living room, around the couch, and checked the couch. As he picked up one of the couch pillows, he spotted something in the crevice. He reached down and pulled up a patch of some kind. He turned it over and read CRANE PRAIRIE GENERAL STORE and the name JOSH ROLLINS. He put the patch in his pocket, and after a cursory search of the kitchen, told Wally, "We'd better go." After putting the screen on, they went back to Bend.

* * *

Susan told Bob, "Instead of the bakery this morning, I need some high octane at Starbucks."

"What? Like a double latte?"

"How'd you know?"

"Prescient, I guess."

They drove over to Starbucks and both consumed a scone and a latte. Bob picked up the *Bulletin* and the headline read: BEND STRUCK BY FREAK JUNE STORM.

> A freak June storm dropped over one foot of new snow on Mt. Bachelor yesterday and through last night. The seismologists monitoring the mountain were forced to withdraw for fear of an avalanche. Remnants of the storm are to linger throughout the day.

Bob looked at Susan and said, "I guess we weren't the only people affected by the storm last night."

"Not very funny, Bob."

"I know, Susan. But if this wasn't so tragic . . . well, you understand what I mean. My attempt at levity is just . . ."

"I understand, Bob," she said, grabbing his hand.

"Are you going to make another sale today so you can take the rest of the year off?"

"If I did, you would have to come to Hawaii to see me." Both began laughing. "But seriously, *one of us has to work.*"

"Ooh, you really know how to hurt a guy."

"I told you I'd make that *special* dinner, and tonight I will."

"I don't think so, Susan. You're not going back there tonight. Not this time. I'll take you out for that *special* dinner tonight."

"But *my treat,* Mr. Hoaglund."

"Well, if you insist. One doesn't argue with one who's *standing in tall cotton.*"

She looked at him and said, "*Yeah, ain't it great?*"

On the way out he said, "Where do you want to go?"

"This is *my bailiwick,* isn't it. I'll think about it."

He kissed her and they went their separate ways.

* * *

One of Mayor McCartney's aides said, "Mr. Mayor, the governor is on the phone."

Brian McCartney picked up the phone and said, "Hello, Governor. How are things this morning?"

"Hello, Brian. I understand you had a pretty big storm come through there yesterday and last night, and it dumped a lot of snow on Mt. Bachelor."

"Yes, it did. Over a foot."

"I just called to get an update on the conditions. Is Mr. Warren there?"

"Well, yes . . . he is." *Why doesn't he want to talk to me about it?*

"Hello, Governor Thomas."

"Hello, Charles. What can you tell me about your readings?"

"Yes. We set up some sensors on the mountain, but we haven't had much luck because we had to close the mountain yesterday afternoon due to the possibility of an avalanche. There was over a foot of newly fallen snow, and maybe some expected today."

"Yes, I know. The weather forecast is a bit iffy right now. Well, I just wanted to check in and see where we are on this. I'll talk to you later, Charles."

"Goodbye, Governor Thomas."

Mayor McCartney sat over in the corner fuming. *Why doesn't he want to talk to me about it? It's my city, for God's sake.*

* * *

Lieutenant Santorini got back to the office and there was a message to call Lieutenant Rivers over at Bend City Police. He got on the phone. "Hello, Randy? This is Al here."

"Hi, Al. Pretty rough storm last night, huh?"

"I guess so. Say, I got a note that you called."

"Oh, yes. I got your results off the FBI computer for those prints you sent over."

"Great. What's it show?"

"They came back Michael Hanson, also known as Jake Hanson, from Toledo Ohio."

"Did you say *Toledo*?"

"Yes. He has a rap. . . ."

"Hold on just a moment, Randy." He shuffled through his papers real quietly, until he came up with some notes from a conversation with Rollins' parole officer. *There it was, C.J. Josh Rollins, Toledo, Ohio.* He picked up the phone and said, "Go ahead, Randy. Sorry."

"I was going to say that he has a juvenile rap sheet a mile long, everything from burglary to assault with dangerous weapon, to attempted murder."

"Anything else?"

"No, that's it."

Lieutenant Santorini immediately wanted the number of the Department of Corrections—Parole Division of Ohio. Sandy got it for him and he called. "Hello, my name is Al Santorini, I'm a lieutenant at the Deschutes County Sheriff's Office in Bend, Oregon. I was wondering if I could talk to the person in charge of parolees for Ohio."

"Yes, this is Walter Beachum."

"My name is Al Santorini, I'm a lieutenant from the Deschutes County Sheriff's Office in Bend, Oregon. I'm looking for a parolee from your juvenile or adult supervision by the name of Michael Hanson, also known as Jake Hanson."

"Let me check real quick, Lieutenant. I've checked in the computer for the names you gave me and it shows Whereabouts Unknown."

"Thank you very much, Mr. Beachum." *Just as I thought,* "Sandy, I'll be out of the office for a few hours." It was 11:00 in the morning when he started up toward Mt. Bachelor and around to Crane Prairie Reservoir. *That bastard Rollins. He knew about this kid all the time.* He received a call on his radio from Sandy.

"Lieutenant, Agent Ben Olsen is here to see you. What should I tell him?"

"Tell him I'm running some personal errands right now and I'll get in touch with him later."

"All right, Lieutenant."

He drove into a parking lot, hopped out of his car and

entered the store. There were three people in there, but no sign of Rollins. "Hello, anybody here?" Josh Rollins came out of the back room and said, "Oh hello, Lieutenant. What can I do for you?"

"Where is *he?*"

"Where is *who?*"

"You know *damn well* who I'm talking about. What is it, Michael or Jake Hanson?"

"I don't know who you're talking about, Lieutenant."

Lieutenant Santorini walked over to Josh Rollins, grabbed onto the front of the shirt with both hands and said, *"Don't play with me, you piece of shit.* If you don't tell me where he is, you're going back to prison for the rest of your life. *You understand?"* There was no answer from Josh Rollins.

"You understand, Rollins?"

Josh Rollins knew that something bad must have happened with his nephew, but he didn't know what. Lieutenant Santorini *did.* "Yeah, I'll tell you, Lieutenant. He's up at a cabin by Little Cultus Lake."

"What's it look like? *Come on, Rollins. I haven't got much time."*

"It's over by the boat ramp, a little black shack."

Lieutenant Santorini looked over at the three people who were standing, agape, and said, "Sorry for that outburst and demonstration, good people."

He got in his car and headed for the lake, which was just up Deer Creek. As he was rolling past the boat ramp, he noticed a black shack. He slowed and parked his car. He jumped out and slowly took the strap off his weapon. There appeared to be no movement anywhere outside, so he went to the front door and knocked. "Anybody home?" No answer. He knocked a little louder. *"Anybody home?"* He went around the back and noticed a storage shed of some kind, and opened the door. There was nothing but firewood and a saw. At that moment, he turned around and saw a shadow pushing something through the brush . . . *a motorcycle.* "Hey! Stop there!" The man looked at Lieutenant Santorini, jumped on the motorcycle and took off. Lieutenant Santorini ran to his car and began to follow him. They went back to the highway and the motorcycle turned left . . . Lieutenant Santorini followed.

He noticed that the motorcycle rider had a pack on the rear of his motorcycle, and something hanging over. He got on the phone and called the sheriff's office. "Wally? This is Al. I think we've got *our man* going north on Cascade Lakes Highway toward Mt. Bachelor. I want you to call Lieutenant Randy Rivers from the Bend Police Department to dispatch some cars to Mt. Bachelor, along with some of ours. Also, call Charlie down at the airport and see if he can get aloft over Mt. Bachelor. Give me a call back once you've contacted everyone."

"Get right on it, Skip."

The man on the motorcycle was ripping down the highway at ninety–one-hundred miles an hour. The clouds were lifting so the visibility was good.

"Hey Skip, this is Wally. I've contacted everyone, and they are en route."

"Thanks, Wally." As they passed Devils Lake, the Lieutenant thought, *Why doesn't he just stop here and jump in?* They continued around the turn on the highway, around Sparks Lake, and toward Mt. Bachelor. *About five more minutes, buddy, and you're toast.*

Lieutenant Santorini was following about one-hundred yards behind the motorcycle when he saw an array of law enforcement, with lights on, around the entrance to Mt. Bachelor. The motorcycle slowed, then took a running start and jumped a small barrier into the parking lot of the ski area. The motorcycle wavered as it hit the ground, but he saved it. He drove the motorcycle up toward the north side, took his pack off, and started toward the mountain. Someone opened one of the gates and they all followed toward the motorcycle.

There was a mist, a light fog that started to envelop the mountain and, although the visibility was good at the lower levels, it was only about fifty yards or so at this level. They exited their cars and began to follow the person. He appeared to be bending down as if he was tying his shoes, with a pack on his back and a *rifle*. Al shouted, "Hanson, stop!" He turned around and looked at Al with that most unusual grin and said, "Not this time, Lieutenant." He raised his rifle, pointed and fired; just missing. Everyone ducked. When they stood up they could see he was starting up the mountain. He was walking easy, as if he had *snow shoes on. That's what those were on the rear of his motorcycle.*

"Does anybody have any snow shoes or skis; anything of that nature?" There was no response. "Well, break into one of the shops there and get some snow shoes." Al looked up and saw he was slogging up the mountain. The fog was getting thicker and the kid was starting to disappear from view.

In about five minutes, some officers came back with a few sets of shoes. Al moved closer to the snow and could not see Hanson anymore. "We might as well wait until the fog lifts a little. There's no sense chasing him in the blind."

Charlie called down and said that the fog was too thick and that he would be unable to fly.

They waited for fifteen minutes when the fog suddenly began to lift. "There he is," somebody said. "OK, let's get someone after him."

There was a violent shake of the mountain for about five to seven seconds, and it was over. Lieutenant Rivers and Al looked at each other, and Rivers said, "Come on guys, let's . . ."

Just then, they heard a mighty roar and looked up and saw the start of an avalanche. It was rolling right toward where Hanson was. As it picked up steam, it was the most amazing sight they had ever seen. The sound was like that of a locomotive running through a house. *It seemed like five minutes, but I know it was less than that, and it was over. Dead silence. It was as if time stood still,* Al thought.

Lieutenant Rivers and Al looked at each other and Rivers said, "What was that all about, Al?"

"Randy, I'll tell you about it over a beer . . . or *two*."

* * *

Susan had decided to go into Sunriver to a special place on the river where they had great seafood. They had a nice bottle of wine, some wonderful fish and basked in the fondness for each other. After dinner, they went back to her place and he stayed the night—discovering each other all over again.

The next day, Bob went out and got the paper. There on the front page was the headline: AVALANCHE ON MT. BACHELOR KILLS SERIAL KILLER.

> An avalanche, on Mt. Bachelor, buried a serial killer alive as he was evading law enforcement. At approximately 1:33 P.M. a tremor, measuring 4.3, set off an avalanche, the first since 1934. Michael "Jake" Hanson, thought to have killed a family of four, and a forest ranger, Red Jensen, was killed when the avalanche struck.

"Susan, *he's dead*. His name was Michael Hanson and he was killed in the avalanche yesterday on Mt. Bachelor." They hugged each other and smiled. "It's over," Bob said.

* * *

When the lieutenant got back to his office, he saw one message on his phone. "Al, this is Evan Giles. You were right. We found the body of Allen Jeffcoat this morning in the river."

* * *

It was two days after the avalanche on Mount Bachelor. Lieutenant Santorini was sitting in his office when Ben Olsen and Kelly Hamlin entered. "Agent Olsen and Agent Hamlin, good to see both of you."

"I wanted to come by and congratulate you for solving the case."

"Well, thank you, *Ben*. A few lucky tips and it all came together."

"You obviously were working much harder than I thought."

"But tell me, Ben. There was one piece of evidence you had that may have helped me. Were those twenty-two shell casings?"

"You're a genius, Al. They certainly were. But obviously you didn't need them anyway. How did you figure that out, if I may ask?"

"Well, I came across the gun during my investigation and realized there were two casings missing. Must have been in your pocket."

"You're too good for me, Lieutenant. Until next time."

He sat back in his chair, propped his feet up on the desk and enjoyed a Hershey bar.

* * *

Charles Warren was in the mayor's office. Mayor McCartney entered the office and said, "Mr. Warren, good to see you."

Warren thought to himself, *This guy is too much.* "Doing fine, Mayor. I just wanted to let you in on the latest. That last jolt we had two days ago may be the last one we have. It seems that it relieved most, if not all, of the pressure in the fissure down below. So, you may be in the clear."

"That's the best news we've had. You did a great job, Mr. Warren. Thank you. I'll tell the governor and let him know that news."

"Thank you, Mayor McCartney."

* * *

Bob and Susan had just dined at *Lucia's* and were walking down by the river when they came to the bench they had sat before. It was a balmy evening, a little on the cool side. Bob said, "Let's have a seat for a while. You know, this is our last evening together, Susan." She cuddled up beside him and said, "I know."

He said, "Best interpretation of Rocky's Third?"

"Horowitz recording with Bernstein."

"Ashkenazy's with the London Symphony, Anatole Fistourlari conducting."

She looked at him and said, "I've never heard that one before."

He looked down at her and smiled, "You will sometime. It's one of my favorite recordings."

Just then, she pulled an envelope out of her purse and told him to open it. He opened the envelope and there was a roundtrip ticket to San Diego for the last week in June. "You don't think I'm going to let you have a *whole* month with all those California girls, do you?" Just then, someone came up behind them and said, "Hello, you two. Can I join you?"

They both turned around and there stood Lieutenant Santorini. They both slid over and Bob said, "So you got that man, huh?"

"Well, we haven't found his body yet, but there's an enormous amount of snow covering him. We may have to wait for it to melt to actually find the body."

Susan said, "We both want to thank you for everything you did for us. You really stuck your neck out on a limb."

"Thank you both. This was for my good friend Red, may he rest in peace."

They sat there as the sun was beginning to set, a halo around Mt. Bachelor . . . *a devil's graveyard.*

* * *

Two fishermen were almost at the end of a BLM road in a remote section when one of the fishermen said, "You can park it right here. It's only a small hike down to the river from here." They parked their truck and started to walk and came upon a clearing where they saw something peculiar. "Let's go check this out." As they approached, they noticed a doe strung up on a tree limb, gutted, and a recent campfire. "Boy, you know, some people just don't get it, do they?"

They walked on down towards the river. One of the

fishermen said, "Right over here is a good entry. Last time, the fishing was really good." They turned left past a boulder and there sitting right next to the entry to the river, was a pair of snowshoes.

21

Jake Hanson sat on the bank, spent from his ordeal in the Deschutes River. He thought about how he had missed the avalanche by a matter of feet, how lucky he was to be alive. How loud the avalanche was coming down at him, rumbling like a freight train. Running down the mountain for two days, not knowing exactly where he was. He had floated for about half a mile downstream on a log, the water temperature around forty-eight degrees. He took off his shoes, wrung out his socks, pants and shirt, and lay in the filtered sun until his body began to warm. He was able to keep his backpack and rifle relatively dry on top of the log. After about an hour, his clothes semi-dry, he dressed and surveyed the terrain. There was a road just up the hill that led away from the river. He grabbed his pack and rifle and began to walk and saw a sign that said FR 9790 ROAD. He walked a little ways and turned right on another road that soon said N. CASCADE RD. There was a development, which he wanted to avoid, and skirted along the back of it until he reached a general store and gas station. It was beginning to get dark and he felt more comfortable. He entered the restroom and cleaned himself up, exited the restroom and contemplated his next move, which was to get to Highway 97.

* * *

George Rawlins was filling his pickup truck with gasoline. The kid there asked, "George, where you off to tonight?"

"I'm taking some chemicals down to Lakeview and won't return until tomorrow morning."

"Well, have a good trip then."

"Oh, you know, I need some cigarettes. Be back in a flash."

The pickup, a Dodge, had a tarp that covered the bed. The gas station was empty but for George's truck, and Jake moved stealthily toward the rear. He unsnapped a couple snaps, peeled back the tarp, threw his backpack and rifle in, jumped up, and slithered down into the bed.

George came out of the store and noticed some of the snaps were undone. *I must not be so careless,* he thought. He got in the truck and was off to Lakeview, which was about a three-hour drive.

It was dark underneath the tarp. Jake was trying to survey the surroundings, but could only see some five-gallon drums. The bed apparently was used to haul some manure and the stench was almost overwhelming. *That son of a bitch had to resnap them,* he thought.

When George arrived in Lakeview, it was going on midnight; the town was dead. He stopped in the only gas station that was open. It was convenient because he knew the owner. The owner, Heber, came out and greeted him. "Hey, George. Good to see ya. What ya got in the back tonight?"

"Oh, just some chemicals, Heber. They are pretty heavy, though. Could you give me a hand?"

"Sure."

They started to approach the back of the pickup when Heber tripped and let out a groan. George looked over and said, "Heber, you all right?"

"Yeah. I just tripped and sprained my ankle a little."

Jake didn't know where the two of them were, but he had to think of something, and fast. He reached around and attempted to unsnap the tarp, but was unsuccessful. He tried once more and was able to get the rear corner unsnapped. He stuck his head out and unsnapped another, got his backpack and rifle, and leapt from the truck, taking off running.

"*George, did you see that?*" Heber said.

George said, "Yeah, I don't know how he got in." *Yeah, I do. In Sunriver at the gas station.* "Hey, you! Stop!"

Jake Hanson went around the corner and was gone.

They unloaded the rear of George's pickup and he drove back to Bend, all the while wondering, *Who was he? What did he want with a ride to Lakeview?*

* * *

Lieutenant Al Santorini arrived a little late in the morning. He asked his secretary, Sandy, where Wally Berger was. She said he'd be in shortly, that he was up at Mt. Bachelor where the recovery of Jake Hanson was taking place.

A half hour later, Wally walked in and said, "Lieutenant Santorini, we've gone over every inch of the mountain where Jake Hanson was, and still no sign of him."

"What's the weather forecast for the next few days?"

"Still pretty cool, but a warming trend on the weekend. We should know pretty soon, Skip."

The snow was pretty deep at the site and it was of no surprise to Lieutenant Santorini that they had not found him yet. But he had this feeling, this feeling that maybe he wasn't there; that he had escaped somehow. *No, there's no way,* he thought. *No way.*

The phone rang and Sandy, the receptionist for Lieutenant Santorini, answered.

"Lieutenant, it's Mayor McCartney on line two."

"Thanks, Sandy. Hello, Mayor McCartney."

"Hello, Al. It's been a while. I just wanted to touch base with you on Mt. Bachelor. First off, the scientists have said that the chances of the mountain *blowing its top* have abated, so that's one less worry. The other thing I wanted to know is: How are we doing with the fugitive? It's been four days now and . . ."

"Well, not as I had hoped. We've combed every inch of the terrain where he was last seen and as of yet, no such luck. Our only hope now is that when the snow melts—and the bulk of the snow wound up down the mountain—we'll find him."

"I talked to Agent Olsen and he's agreed not to press charges, Lieutenant."

Press charges? he thought. *What the hell is that all about?* "That's very gracious of him, Mr. Mayor. But had he done *his job* we'd have had him a whole lot sooner. It wasn't my case and my jurisdiction but . . ."

"I understand, Al, and we're all grateful to you for everything you've done. Anyway, keep looking and good luck. Bye."

Keep looking and good luck? What an asshole! He thought about how crucial it was they find Jake Hanson, for if he was to have gotten away, who knows how many more people he would kill. He also thought about calling Susan Woodson and informing her they had not yet unearthed Jake Hanson from the snow, but thought better of it. She didn't need to know about it.

*   *   *

The phone rang. Josh leaned over and looked at the clock; it said 1:20. *Who in the world could that be?* "Hello?"

"You dirty bastard, you turned me in."

"Jake?"

"Who else did you think it would be, *Unc*?"

"I-I-I thought you were dead?"

"You know, Josh, you think way too much. Why did you turn me in? I thought blood was thicker than water, didn't *you*? I trusted you, *you dirty, lousy son of a bitch*, and this is the thanks I get. On the lam because of *good ole Unc*. Well, I just wanted to call and tell you that I'm gonna be your worst nightmare. Whenever you go, *Ra* will be looking over your shoulder. One day—one day you won't feel a thing; it'll be over (snap), just like that. So long, *asshole*."

He sat up in bed and thought, *He's alive. How'd that little creep do it? Where is he? Should I contact Lieutenant Santorini or Agent Olsen? No, I don't think so. Obviously they don't know where he is—or even if he's alive, so no. It could only bring me trouble, and trouble is Jake's middle name.*

* * *

Jake stood alongside the road just outside of Lakeview, Oregon. It was approximately two in the morning. He contemplated his next move, which was to get as far away from Bend as he could. Probably south on 395 is the safest bet. After fifteen minutes or so, a flat bed truck came slowly down the highway and stopped. The driver, an elderly man in his seventies, stuck his head out the window and said, "Where you going, son?"

"Just south to . . . to er . . ."

"I'm going as far south as Susanville. Is that all right?"

Jake didn't know where Susanville was, but he said, "Yeah, that's all right." He jumped in the passenger seat with his pack and rifle, sat his pack on the floor and rifle between the seat and the passenger door. The older gentleman looked over and said, "What ya got there son, a rifle?"

"Uh, no, it's part of a musical instrument."

"Boy, ya coulda fooled me. Sure looks like a rifle."

Jake knew he couldn't tell for sure because it was wrapped up in a towel. Hopefully, he would drop it.

"Where ya comin' from, son?"

Boy, he thought, *this guy better shut up.* He thought for a few seconds and said, "Burns. Burns, Oregon."

"That's a nice ole town, isn't it? Gets kinda hot in the summer though."

"Look, mister, you mind if I get some sleep? I'm kind of tired."

"No, go ahead, son. Just trying to be social."

Jake turned his head toward the passenger door and pretended to sleep, but couldn't. He apparently had dozed off when he heard a voice, "Well, son, here we are."

He woke up with a jolt and said, "Where? How long have we been driving?"

"About two and half hours, I'd say. Where you want to go?"

He surveyed the town and said, "Over there, by that gas station is okay."

The old man turned at the stop sign and dropped him off in front of the gas station.

"By the way, what time is it?"

"About quarter of five, I reckon."

"Thanks a lot for the lift."

"Glad I could be of service, son. You and that *rifle* take care of yourself." The old man smiled and drove away.

Jake walked into the service area and saw a man behind the counter. He asked, "Do you have a map of any kind?"

The man looked warily at him and said, *"What kind of map?"*

Jake thought hesitatingly, "A map of California, I guess."

The man pointed over at the wall, his eyes all the time on Jake, and walked behind the counter where the pistol was.

Jake knew what was going on, *Two minds similar think alike.* "Thanks." He walked over to the map and saw that 395 continued south on into Reno, Nevada. He didn't have much money left and said to himself, *That's where I'll go then.* He pointed to Reno. "Anywhere I can get some coffee?"

"Easiest place is right there in the machine," and he pointed over to the side wall.

Jake got some coffee and made his way out to the road. It was getting on after 5:00 and it was getting lighter in the eastern sky beyond the mountains. After a few minutes, a pickup truck came by and stopped. He was a younger gentleman, about thirty-five or so, with a cowboy hat on. "Where you going to?"

"Well, I was hoping to get to Reno."

"That's where I'm going. Hop in."

Jake started to open the passenger door when the gentleman stopped him and said, "No, no. I mean *hop in there.*" He pointed to the bed of the pickup truck which had some hale bales in the front part near the cab, and a few feet of open bed in the rear. "Sorry," as he looked Jake right in the eyes. "But I think you understand."

As he loaded his backpack and rifle in the rear, he looked at the driver with those evil eyes of his and said, "Sure, whatever you say." *What an asshole,* he thought. They rambled down 395 by Honey Lake, Milford, and just before they got to Hallelujah Junction, Jake got up in the back of the truck and knocked on the rear window and shouted, "I've got to use the bathroom."

The gentleman rolled down the window and said, "You can wait. It's only twenty-five miles to Reno."

I'm gonna kill that son of a bitch, Jake thought. He reached for his rifle, unrolled the wrapping and started back to the cab. There was no one on the road at the time. He was about ready to knock when he heard a honk behind the truck. He immediately put down the rifle, turned around, and saw a car menacingly close. The truck slowed down, over to the right shoulder, and let the car go around. Jake decided against any action and went over and sat down.

The driver of the truck heard the honk from the car in back of him and looked in his driver's rearview mirror and then his rearview mirror in the cab. At that point, he noticed a figure and glint from what looked like a rifle barrel raised at the rear window. *The SOB's got a gun,* he thought. *I'm not stopping until I get to Reno and then he's gone.*

When they got to a cross-section of the two highways in Reno, 395 and 80, the driver got off and proceeded to the parking lot of the Reno Super Motel. He made sure there were enough people around to feel safe. When he rolled down the window, Jake Hanson was right there in front of him, smiling that frightful grin. "Thanks a lot for the lift, man. I'm just sorry you weren't going further."

"Yeah, well, good luck to you." *I'm just sorry I picked you up in the first place.* He rolled up the window and took off on South 4th Street to South Wells and was gone.

*   *   *

Joseph Buchanan, his wife and four children were preceding east on 80 when they saw a person sitting along side the road with a backpack. He said to his wife, "That boy there looks like he needs a ride, Elsie?"

"You know we don't pick up hitchhikers, Joseph."

"Well, he looks pretty low, with his head in his lap there. Wouldn't hurt just this one time."

"Oh, all right."

Joseph stopped his car, which was towing a trailer. Jake looked up and was shocked that someone would stop with a trailer. He ran up to the car and said to Joseph, "How far are you going?"

"The family and I are going to Salt Lake, that's where we live. Care for a lift?"

"Oh, that'd be great. Thanks."

"Elsie, you take the kids and get in the trailer."

"But Joseph, we usually don't ride . . ."

"Just do as I say, Elsie."

Jake jumped in the passenger side door and they took off. "I'm Michael Hanson. You're Joseph, I guess."

"Yes. Sure am. Joseph Buchanan."

"Are you all Mormon?"

"Sure are."

"Well, I'm grateful for you taking me to Salt Lake. Have you been in the temple?"

"We were married in the temple nine years ago."

Jake noticed it was a young family and Joseph had started real young. He couldn't be more than twenty-five or twenty six. "Once we get to Salt Lake, is it pretty easy to get to Denver?"

"Oh well, you've got to go down through Orem, Provo and Price and then onto 70. You got family in Denver?"

"No, I don't. They just say you can get work in Denver pretty easy."

"What kind of work do you do?"

"Well, I work as a mechanic, mostly. But a lot of odd jobs."

"I've got a cousin down in Richfield who's looking for a mechanic. His name is Chuck Mason and he owns *Chuck's Auto Repair*. I can give him a call if you'd be interested."

Jake thought about it for a few moments and said, "Where is Richfield?"

"Richfield is one-hundred-sixty miles south of Salt Lake on Highway 70 about a two and one half hour drive."

"How big is Richfield, Joseph?"

"Oh, I'd say about 7,000 or so. A real small town. Pretty, though."

That just might be the place to lay low for a while, Jake thought. *Just might be.*

They drove for about four hours and arrived in Elko, Nevada. Joseph pulled over to the side of the road and said, "Care to join us for lunch, Michael?" "Sure," he said. As he lay back in the trailer eating a sandwich and drinking a cola, he said to himself: *How good could it be?*

They drove on and after another four hours or so arrived in Salt Lake City and the home of the Buchanans. After unloading the trailer, Joseph said to Jake, "I'm going to give Chuck a call and see if he still needs someone."

"Boy, that'd be great, Joseph." *Boy is this guy a sucker!* Jake thought.

"Hello, Chuck? This is Joseph. Say, I was . . . did we

have a good time? You bet. Say, what I was calling about was I have a gentleman here who's looking for a job; he's a mechanic. How good is he? Heck, I don't know. Sounds competent, though. Is it OK if I send him on down? You said you needed—you do? Great, I'll tell him."

He hung up the phone and went out to the trailer where Jake was. "I just got done talking to Chuck and he says he still needs someone. You can take the bus tomorrow morning."

"No, no buses. I'll just hitchhike on down. How do I get there?"

"Well, you just take 15 down to Nephi, then 28 on down to Richfield. Did you want to come up to the house for a little while?"

"No, that's all right, Joseph. Thanks."

"OK, Michael. We'll check on you in the morning. Elsie will fix you a nice breakfast before you go."

"Fine, Joseph."

The next morning Joseph went out to the trailer. He opened the door and said, "Michael, Elsie's got breakfast ready. Michael? You there?"

He went back in the house and told Elsie to hold the plate for Michael. He was gone.

22

Jake rolled over and looked at the alarm clock. It said 5:15. He rose and went into the bathroom to wash his face and shave. After cleaning up, he packed his backpack, picked up his rifle and left the trailer. He had about a mile walk to the center of Salt Lake City. When he arrived in Center City, he asked a cabbie where he might catch a ride on 15 South towards Richfield. The cabbie told him to go down about four blocks to the intersection of 15 and someone might pick him up, but to watch out for the police because they could be downright mean. *I must be careful,* he thought, *because if they catch me with this rifle, I'm sunk.*

He stuck close to the businesses with his rifle up against his right side as he headed south. When he arrived at the intersection, there was a bus bench with a skirt that went down to the ground. He put his rifle underneath and began the risky venture of catching a ride.

About ten minutes went by when a police officer stopped, rolled his window down and asked, "Are you waiting for a bus?"

"Yes I am."

"Where to?"

Jake looked over and caught a glimpse of the sign and recognized the word Provo. He made eye contact with the police officer and said, "Provo."

"Well, if you'll look at the sign more carefully, it says that the first bus is at seven-thirty A.M."

"Oh, I didn't know that. Thanks a lot, officer."

The police officer went onto the north onramp of 15 and sped away. *Should I stay here or move?* he thought. *I'll chance it and stay here.* About fifteen minutes went by when an older woman stopped and said, "Are you waiting for the bus?"

"No, I'm trying to get down to Nephi."

"I'm going that way. Hop in."

She looked like she'd lived a little, and was pretty gruff sounding. *But whatever will get me there.* "Where you headed?" he asked.

"I'm going down to Beaver, but I can drop you off in Nephi. How about yourself?"

"Well, eventually I want to get to Richfield. Do you know anything about the town of Richfield?"

"Yeah, I do, as a matter of fact. My daughter runs a drive-in there named Molly's. When you get there, just tell her that Martha wants to hear from her. Will you do that?"

"Sure."

"I can't ever seem to get a hold of her so . . ."

"I'll tell her."

They drove for an hour and a half or so and she dropped him off in Nephi. He immediately went over to Highway 98 and got a ride by a farmer from Richfield. They were there in an hour and a half.

"Where do you want me to drop you off?"

"*Chuck's Auto Repair.* It's on . . ."

"I know where it is." They drove up to the shop and the farmer let him off. He walked in the shop and saw someone sitting behind the counter. Is Chuck around?"

"I'm Chuck. What can I do for you?"

"My name is Michael Hanson, your cousin Joseph Buchanan called you. . . ."

"Oh, hi, Michael. I'm Chuck Mason. Glad you could make it. I forgot to tell Joseph that what I really need right now is a tow truck driver. Have you ever done that?"

"Uh, no. I was under the impression that . . ."

"Look, I'm sorry about the misunderstanding, but that's what I need."

"Yeah, I'll take it." *Damn it. Joseph did look like an imbecile.*

Chuck Mason looked Jake up and down and thought, *This guy looks kind of flaky, but I really need someone now.* "The pay's not great; we start you off at five hundred a week. You are on call for twelve hours at a time. Have you got a place to stay?"

"No, I don't. Just arrived in town and . . ."

"Well, we've got a place over the garage, a room with a private bath, ten bucks a day."

Jake thought for a minute. *He's got me up the wazoo.* "Yeah, I'll take it. When do I start?"

"We need you from twelve midnight to twelve noon. You can start tonight."

He followed Chuck back to the garage and up the back stairs. Chuck opened the door and showed him the room, which all and all wasn't too bad. *Yeah, this will do just fine,* he thought. "Where's the best place to get some breakfast and dinner, cheap, in this town?"

"Well, a few blocks down in *Molly's Drive-In.* You can get breakfast there for two-fifty to four dollars and around the block to the right is a diner that has some cheap eats; pretty good. What brought you to Richfield Michael? Not too many young men wind up in this town."

"As I said, your cousin Joseph recommended your business and I thought I could fit in. It's kind of hard to find work nowadays, if you know what I mean. There's not too many private businesses that need mechanics. I really appreciate your offering me a job, though."

"I can tell you that there isn't much need for tow trucks during the morning hours, but it's pretty competitive, and when you get the call, *you must respond immediately.*"

"Sure, I understand."

"There is a special phone jack for the room and I will get you a phone to put in the room. You won't have to be in the office all morning hours."

They both left the room and returned to the office where another driver, Ron Terry, was seated. Chuck said, "Ron Terry, this is Michael Hanson. He'll be driving the morning hours."

"Nice to meet you, Michael."

Ron Terry was a stocky man, early thirties, with a receding hairline, 5'8"–5'9", 200 pounds, and seemed awkward in appearance. He walked with a slight limp in his right leg.

Chuck looked at the clock and said, "Well guys, it's after noon and I've got to look in on the wife and kids. I'll leave it all to you."

Jake looked at Ron, sizing him up, and said, "How long have you been working for Chuck, Ron?"

"Oh, probably four or four and half months."

"All driving the tow truck?"

"Yep. Chuck doesn't want anyone hornin' in on his mechanic business. He wants it all to hisself."

Just as I thought. Cheap bastard. "If I wanted some transportation, such as a motorcycle or something, how would I go about acquiring one?"

"The town has a paper called the *Richfield Reaper* which has all sorts of want ads. There's motorcycles available all the time from Richfield, Monroe and Glenwood, which are small towns a few miles away. You without wheels?"

"At the present I am, yeah."

"Where'd you come from?"

"Oh, just south. You know, New Mexico, Arizona."

"Well, this is a pretty quiet town, Michael. If you're looking for excitement, this ain't the place. You shoulda stayed in St. George or Cedar City."

"Do they have any country-western dances or anything of that sort?"

"Oh, sure. Usually it's at the Stake a couple times a month."

"The Stake?"

"Yeah, sure. Are you familiar with the Mormons at all?"

"No, not really."

"You know they don't have any bars or anything like that. You gotta buy your booze from state liquor stores, and only at certain times. And the LDS churches have what they call Stakes. They oversee Wards, which they have about four or five in the area. So they're sorta like socials, but they're really dances. You understand?"

He was really getting impatient. "Not really, but maybe you can educate me."

Just then the phone rang and Ron answered, "*Chuck's Auto Repair.* You need a truck on I-70 just south of Salina? I'll be right up." He hung up the phone, looked at Jake and said, "They've had an accident, with fatalities, just south of Salina. You want to see how it's done?"

He thought about it for a second and said, "Yeah, why not. Let's go."

* * *

Molly Ryerson was a young, vivacious, pretty woman, twenty-five years old, who grew up in Richfield and was the owner of *Molly's Drive-In*. She graduated from BYU four years ago with a degree in economics and a minor in sociology. She was a devout Mormon who taught Sunday School and counseled parishioners at her Ward. She was, quite simply, the *Star of Richfield.*

Since taking over the drive-in six months ago, she's turned a business that was deep in the red to a successful eating establishment; as some people say in the community, *The place to be.*

She was a 5'6" blonde who was the most eligible lady in Richfield. However, since she arrived from Provo and took over the drive-in, there's been no time for men of any kind; all her energy has gone into church work and the business. One of her duties in town was to organize semi-monthly country-western dances at the Stake: organize the bands, the beverages, eats, etc. Her life has been hectic, but self-satisfying. Soon that life would change; *very soon.*

* * *

Ron and Jake arrived at the scene of the accident. It was a head-on between a Chevrolet/Suburban and a Honda sedan. The scene was not pretty. They were wheeling a couple from the Honda into the ambulance. It was obvious they were both dead. Ron said, "You never know what you'll see, and that's why my stomach churns every time I come upon one of these scenes." For Jake, the scene was not so revolting; it seemed to stir the juices in his evil soul.

When they arrived at the garage, they put the Honda in the compound and made their way into the office. Ron looked at Jake and said, "Well, it looks like it's your turn for awhile. You put that Honda on the bed just like you've been doing it all your life."

"Never had a problem with mechanical things." *It's people things that causes a lot of problems,* he thought.

23

Bob returned to work on Monday morning. However, the *Parade of Horribles* continued. He left his house in Fallbrook at 6:00 in the morning for the fifty-minute drive down to San Diego. An accident occurred on Highway 15 southbound near Escondido, fifteen minutes away, that snarled traffic for three or four miles. He was unable to arrive at the courthouse until well after 8:00 A.M. Normally, court is in session at 9:00 A.M. However, the judge wanted to hear a motion to dismiss in a protracted medical malpractice case at 8:00. So there he was, a half hour late and no one to take his place. He set up his stenograph machine in the courtroom, and gave his apologies, afraid to lift his head for fear the glowering of the lawyers would make him feel worse.

He walked into the back room where Judge Ruiz greeted him with a smile and, "Is it getting any better, Bob?"

"We'll see at the end of the day."

Jeri, the clerk, moseyed over and said, "Did you have a good time in Oregon?"

Bob looked at her and said, "Let's just say it was the most exciting time in my life, Jeri." He needed to change the subject real fast and said, "And look what kind of welcome you have for me: A med-mal with six lawyers. I suppose you've got a neurosurgeon as an expert today."

Jeri said, "You're extremely prescient, Bob."

"An expert something awful and it's bound to be worse." Everyone laughed.

Judge Ruiz looked at everyone and said, "Well, we might as well get on with it then." The hearing took an hour and a half and was a court reporter's nightmare, much less when he hadn't reported in court for *three weeks*. They took a recess of ten minutes before the jury was to assemble and return. Judge Ruiz looked at him and said, "Which is worse: A bad hangover or *that* hearing we just had?"

"Right now, I think I'd opt for the bad hangover."

"Are you up for lunch today, Bob? I'd love to hear about you and Susan."

"Sure. Just tell those lawyers to take it easy on me in there." They both laughed.

They recessed for lunch and the judge and Bob went up the street a few blocks to a local spot. "Well, tell me the *gory bits and the love notes.*"

"One really doesn't know where to start, Judge Ruiz. Not only did this man try to kill me, he tried to kill Susan, too. He found out where she lived and stalked her to an inch of her life. We are lucky she's alive; *very lucky*. I'd go into the details, Judge, but right now I just don't want to revisit any of it. *However,* with regard to the *love notes,* well, things are just about as good as—she's coming down this Sunday for a week, and so I'll be asking for another week off, my last week."

"You know, I could tell that one night I spent with both of you, there was a special spark and that it could develop into something special. I wish you the best. But could I ask you one question about this man. Did they find him?"

"They did. He was killed in an avalanche on Mt.

Bachelor a few days ago. They haven't uncovered him yet, but the snow will melt shortly and they will."

"So what are you two going to do for a week?"

He smiled and said, "We won't be involved with any medical malpractice cases, I can assure you of that." They both laughed and had a nice lunch.

The nightmare of the case extended into the afternoon. All Bob could think of was Susan and the next week. They agreed not to have any contact in the meantime and he hoped she was as miserable as he was, but knew she wasn't. At the end of the day, Terry O'Reilly, one of the defense lawyers, looked at him and shook his head and said, "I bet you were hoping for a nice little promissory note case when you returned, weren't you?"

He looked at Terry and said, "Now you're reading my mind, Terry. What else did I wish for?"

"You look positively exhausted. Better go home and get some rest because it won't get any easier tomorrow."

"Thanks, Terry. You've made me feel a whole lot better." They both laughed.

Bob left the courthouse and began the long trek home, all the while thinking of Susan and an itinerary for next week. The cell phone was only inches away and a call would help the day immeasurably. *But no, an agreement is an agreement.*

* * *

Joyce Gilmore was in Bend and gave Susan a call. "Susan, this is Joyce. I'm in Bend and looking for a lunch partner. You busy?"

"So, are you a frequent visitor now, or are you permanently entrenched in your new shop?"

"Oh no, not for a few weeks. But I'll be in and out, so I'll be bugging you."

"Great. How about *Heidi's Bakery?* They've got good salads."

"Sounds fine to me. What time?"

"I've got a meeting at eleven-thirty could run about an hour. How about one o'clock?"

"See you there."

Susan walked in and saw Joyce. They greeted each other, sat down, and ordered lunch. Joyce looked at Susan and said, "So, how's everything going? We were worried about you."

"Thank you for that. Fine. You heard the news about that killer, I suppose."

"No. Fill me in."

"They found him and he was killed in an avalanche on Mt. Bachelor. They haven't found his body, they're waiting for all the snow to melt, which should be in a couple days."

"How's Bob?"

"Oh, he's back at work down in San Diego."

"You say that without much sentiment. Or is there a touch of *melancholy, my dear?*"

Susan laughed and said, "No, Joyce, not at all. Sunday, I'm going down to San Diego for a week. We made an agreement not to talk to each other until then."

"Here, you want my cell phone?"

"Don't you dare give that to me, Joyce. You are an instigator, you know that?"

"I've been told that."

They finished their lunch and were walking outside. Susan said, "Don't tell me you've bought some new boots," which brought a smile to Joyce.

"I can buy a pair a day, if I want to. Talk to you later, girl."

"Bye, Joyce." *What a neat friend she is,* Susan thought. *Just what I needed, a little levity.*

* * *

The report came in from Mt. Bachelor. They were unable to find the body of Jake Hanson. Lieutenant Santorini pounded his fist on the table, in a rare show of temper, and he cursed the bad luck. "Sandy, would you get the mayor's office on the phone for me."

"Sure, Lieutenant."

"Mayor McCartney, this is Al Santorini."

"Oh hello, Al. Have you got anything new on this fugitive?"

"That's what I wanted to talk to you about. We've got the report from the people on the mountain and they say he's not there. This matter is case sensitive and I really don't think . . ."

"Al, this is very serious, having a serial killer running around in the Bend area."

"I *know* that, Brian. But we have to handle this very carefully and not call undue attention to his being missing. I suggest that we give the *Bulletin* a heads up, *right now,* that he's most likely escaped and . . ."

"Most likely escaped? For God's sake, Al, *he's gone."*

What does it take to get through to this knucklehead? "I understand, Brian, but we have to handle this very carefully. The town has been on pins and needles for a few weeks, now, and we have to give them a break. So I ask of you to call the *Bulletin* and tell them to run a story that centers on Mt. Bachelor, and skim over the fugitive, killer, serial murderer, however you want to describe it. We'll find him, Brian."

Lieutenant Santorini hung up the phone and contemplated his next move. *Should I call Bud Olsen? He'll think I'm desperate and need his help. Well, I do.* "Hello, Bud? This is Al Santorini. How are you doing?"

"Just fine, Al. I heard the news, *our boy has flown the coup.* Is that right?"

"You're absolutely right, Bud. Do you have any suggestions?"

"Sure. Get an APB out on the *bastard* and pick him up."

"Is that how the FBI does things nowadays? It's your case. Do *you have an APB* out for Mr. Hanson? I shouldn't think so, that's not like *you.*"

"Didn't take much to get your dander up, did it?"

"Not with you, Bud. Thanks for the help." *Now there's a real SOB I can do without.*

At that moment, Deputy Berger came into the office and told Al that Sheriff Malone wanted to see him. He knocked on his door, he looked up and saw Al and said, "Oh hi, Al. Have a seat." Sheriff Byron Malone had been Sheriff of Deschutes County for going on twelve years, and by this time, was a pretty easygoing guy. Nothing really bothered him—except when his image in the community came into play.

"Al, I got a call from the mayor this morning and he says you're trying to—how should I put it—*convince* him that we ought to push this maniac into the back pages."

It didn't take him long to get hold of the sheriff, did it? "Well, Byron, that's not exactly the way . . ."

"That we'd be better off if there was no mention at all of Mr. Hanson."

"Look Byron, I told him that we might want to lay low

on the news about Jake Hanson because the town's been through a lot and . . ."

"I understand, Al. But when it comes to the mayor, *You let me handle him from now on.*"

Al looked at him and reluctantly agreed.

"How's Jennifer and the kids doing?"

"As good as can be expected."

"And *you?* I know you want this son of a bitch, but if he's gone he's gone."

"Yes, I know. Is that all, Byron?"

"Just watch yourself, Al. You're too good a man to be roped into all this. Watch your back."

"I will, Byron. Thanks."

24

It was the middle of the morning and Jake Hanson was getting bored. He walked down the street looking for a coffee shop or something to pass the time, figuring a half hour away from the shop wouldn't hurt anything. A couple blocks down, there was a gas station with a little diner inside and he entered. There were two other people in the station: a clerk and an old man, maybe seventy or so. He sat down with the old man and said, "Howdy. You want some company?"

The old man looked at him and said, "Sure. Gets mighty lonely in here this early in the morning—except when people are going hunting or fishing. How about you? How come you're up at this time of the morning?"

"I work a tow truck and I'm just killing some time."

"Pretty quiet, huh?" The old man stuck out his hand and said, "I'm James Francis Tyler. Most people call me Jimmie."

"Glad to know you, Jimmie. I'm Michael. Do you fish?"

"I run the fish hatchery out of town, and I still fish a little."

"Where abouts you live?"

"Oh, just out of town toward Glenwood. Probably three miles."

The two sat and chatted for twenty minutes or so and

then Jake said, "Maybe I"ll see you around sometime, Jimmie."

"Look forward to it, son."

Jake walked back to the shop and noticed a message on the answering machine. He pushed the button and the message said: "This is *Chuck's Auto Repair.* We had a car out on Annabella Road that needed a tow. No one answered, so we'll find someone else." He looked for the delete key and pushed it, the message was gone.

* * *

It was after 9:00 A.M. when Chuck arrived at his repair shop. Jake was sitting on the counter talking to someone when Chuck asked, "How'd it go last night, Michael?"

"Pretty slow, Chuck. Not a call."

"Not a call?"

"Nope, as slow as it gets."

"What a great way to break in. Here, I thought you'd break your teeth on a juicy one or something."

"Oh, that happened last night with Ron. Bad accident, two people killed."

"Well, I didn't really mean . . ."

Jake gave that smirk of his and said, "I know what you mean, Chuck." The gentleman Jake was talking to left and he approached Chuck with, "Say, Chuck, listen. I'm a little short now. Could you maybe advance me a hundred or so. I need to get some clothes and . . ."

He looked at Jake, went over to the till, took out a hundred and said, "Sure, Michael. Let's just *hope* that it picks up this morning."

"Yeah, let's hope."

Chuck went back to the garage to do some automobile repair. Jake went up to his room. At 11:15, the phone rang and it was a request for a tow truck. He went down the stairs and told Chuck that he was on a run; that he'd be back in a little while.

*   *   *

When Jake got back, it was afternoon and he was off duty. It was time to go into town and check out some duds. As he was walking around, he noticed a sign in a shop that said, WESTERN DANCE SATURDAY NIGHT FROM 7:00 TO 11:00 AT THE 4TH WARD. He needed a new pair of Levis and a western shirt of some kind. He could probably do without the hat, he didn't have enough money anyway. After he found the shop and made his purchase, he wandered around town and said to himself, *So this is what Mormon life is all about.*

It was after 6:00 and Jake thought he'd check out Molly's. He found out it was a little more of a hike than Chuck originally said. As he walked in, he noticed the place was practically full. He walked up to the counter and found a place. He picked up a menu and ordered some meatloaf. He asked the waitress, "Is Molly here tonight?"

"She sure is. Who should I say is here?"

"Oh no, I didn't want to see her, but just to know if she was here."

As he was eating his dinner, he noticed a pretty blonde girl, dressed in all red come out from the back. He said to himself, *Oh yes. I shall meet this girl Saturday night.*

The next three days were uneventful for Jake, although one night he had a tow for a police vehicle. The officer kept looking at him with inquisitive eyes that made him uncomfortable. "Is there anything bothering you, officer?"

"Oh no. You just look familiar, that's all. Are you from Salina?"

"No. I work here in Richfield."

* * *

Saturday night brought the dance, and an eclectic group was there; everyone from six to sixty, as they say—and older. Jake surveyed the hall and noticed plenty of single women to choose from. He asked one girl to dance, doing the *Texas Two-Step,* and by the end of the dance, she complained to him of dancing too rough. He went up and tried a line dance and had trouble keeping up, which prompted some snickers from some participants. *I wish I had a fuckin' beer,* he thought. Right then his emotions got the better of him and he went to ask a girl to dance. Right in the middle of the dance, she looked at him and said, "What are you doing? Keep your hands to yourself, Dude."

At that moment, Molly came up and asked the girl what happened. She pointed at Jake and told Molly about the incident. Molly walked up to Jake and said, "Sir, you're new to these dances. We don't comport ourselves that way and I think you should leave right now."

Jake looked at her and said, "Well my hand wandered and it won't happen again, Miss."

"*She* said your hand didn't wander, *you put it there.* I think you should leave right now, sir."

"Well, I'm not going to leave. It was . . ."

Just then a hand appeared on his shoulder and it was the police officer from last night's tow. "The woman said to leave, and we're going to leave." They walked outside and the officer stopped and looked at Jake. "What's your name, cowboy?"

"Allen . . . Allen Jeffcoat."

"Let's see some ID, mister."

Jake pulled out his wallet and pulled out a card.

"This is a Costco card."

"Well, that's the only thing I brought with me tonight, officer."

The police officer looked at Jake rather skeptically and said, "You know, if I was on duty, we'd go further with this. But I'm having a good time in there, and you better get your *little ass* out of here before I make you my quest."

Jake walked away, steaming. *Somebody's going to pay for this little escapade,* he thought.

* * *

It was early in the morning and Jake couldn't sleep. The clock said 3:00, and he thought he'd go over to the gas station and see if Jimmie was there. He walked in, and sure enough, in the corner, was Jimmie drinking his coffee.

"Hi, Jimmie."

"Hey, Michael. You can't sleep either?"

"No, I got enough sleep to last for the night. What's happening with the fishery?"

"It just runs itself, there's nothing to it. Getting some big German Browns in there."

"Say, Jimmie. I'm looking for a motorcycle . . . a used motorcycle. You know anyone who wants to sell one?"

"You came to the right place, Michael. My grandson's got one over at the place he doesn't ride anymore, a BMW."

"How much he want for it?"

"Gee, I don't know. Why don't you come look at it?"

"You got time this morning?"

"Sure. Hop in the truck."

They drove out for a couple miles to Jimmie's house, a little rundown farmhouse. They went in the living room and Jimmie got the keys. "It's out here in the garage." They went in the garage and Jimmie showed Jake the bike. "Hey, this is real nice. What year?"

"A ninety six, I think."

"How much he want for it?"

"Ten thousand."

Ten thousand? Jake thought. "Well, how about I take it for a spin a little later and let you know."

"Sure. When the sun comes up."

"You got change for a twenty, Jimmie?" It was an old ploy to see where the money was.

"I got change, Michael." Jake gave him the twenty and Jimmie went over to a can and got a ten and two fives. "How's that?"

"That'll do."

They sat and chatted for a few minutes and Jimmie said he had to use the restroom. He got up and left the room. Jake wandered over to the can, opened it up and his jaw opened. *There must be a few thousand dollars in here,* Jake thought. When Jimmie came back in the room, Jake said, "I think I'll get back, Jimmie. I'll think on that motorcycle."

"Let me give you a ride back to town, Michael."

Jake went up to his room and began to set the wheels in motion. He had to have that bike. Unfortunately, there was only one way to get it.

It was 4:00 in the afternoon. He had just walked the two-plus miles to get to Jimmie's place. He knocked on the door and Jimmie said, "Who is it?"

"It's me, Michael."

"Oh, Michael, come in. Nice to see you. Did you want something to drink; a beer or something?"

"No, that'll be fine. Does anyone live here with you, Jimmie?"

"Just myself. Don't need anybody else."

"Can I see the BMW back in the garage, Jimmie?"

"Yeah, let's go take a look at it."

Jimmie got the key and they went back to the garage, opened the door and there was the motorcycle sitting right in front. Jake got the key and started it up the first time, w-h-o-o-o-m, just like all BMW's sound. He looked at the gas gauge which said *full*.

"Do you want to take it for a spin, Michael?"

"Don't think I need to, purrs like a cat."

Jake looked around the garage and spotted a jack handle. He saw that Jimmie had turned to go out. He grabbed the jack handle, made three quick steps and struck a blow to the head. Jimmie crumpled to the ground. Jake left him laying on the garage floor and went in the house in search for the keys to the truck. First, the living room, then the bedroom and there on the kitchen table were what looked like keys to a truck. He grabbed them, went to the front door, looked both ways, saw nobody, went out to the truck and started it. *Now I've got to get the money,* he said to himself.

As he entered the house the phone rang, and rang three more times until he heard, "Jimmie, this is Ralph. Sorry I missed you, but I'll check back later." He went over to the can and grabbed all of the money. Not bothering to count it, he picked up his rifle, which he brought, went out front, got in the truck and brought it around back. He lifted Jimmie up, put him down in the front seat, covered him up with a blanket he found in the garage, loaded the motorcycle in the rear bed of the truck, and contemplated where to go. He knew there was forest land to the east. He drove to Highway 119, turned south on 24 and drove for a few miles until he came upon FR 058, a forest road. He turned left and drove a few miles into a deserted area where he parked the car off in a secluded spot.

As he dragged Jimmie from the vehicle, he noticed that there was a low, painful groan and he wasn't dead after all. *Most people would have died,* he thought. He dragged him over to a tree, face down, pulled out his rifle and said, "Sorry, old man. You seemed like a good egg," and fired one shot into the back of his head. He rummaged in his pack and found his fishing knife, which he had used before to make the offering.

Once back on Highway 24 he stopped to think. *Which way? Better go right back where I came from.* He came to a cross street that he recognized from walking in Richfield, Annabella County Road, and turned left. It wasn't dark yet, so he thought he'd stop somewhere and get a beer until dark and proceed to *Chuck's Auto Repair.* It was pitch dark when he walked his motorcycle back behind the garage and then went up to his room.

* * *

Jake figured it would be a few days before anyone found the truck, but that he'd better leave soon. No one had seen him with Jimmie except the clerk in the gas station serving coffee, and Jake didn't think he'd paid much attention to him.

He told Chuck that Monday morning that he's sorry to leave him in the lurch, but that it hadn't worked out as a driver, that he hoped he'd find someone else.

Chuck asked him, "Where you off to, Michael?"

"Back to Arizona or New Mexico."

"You hitchhiking all the way back?"

Good. He hadn't found the bike yet. "I guess so."

"Well, good luck to you. Ron said you'd have made a good driver."

"Good of him to say." But before he left, he had some unfinished business. Chuck was in the office when Jake went up to retrieve his belongings. He went down the back stairs to his bike and walked it quietly past the outer side of the shop where there were no windows. He got on the bike and turned south on Main Street toward Molly's. As he got off his bike, he noticed Molly walking to her car in a workout outfit. She got in her car and headed south to Carpenter Road, over to Monroe Mount Road where she pulled off on a private road and got out of her car. She did a few exercises and began to run off the road. He followed her. She had run about a mile and turned around. There standing in front of her was Jake, smiling as only he could.

"Who are you?"

"Don't you remember, *Molly?*"

"You're the one that we . . ."

". . . kicked out of the dance. Yes."

"What do you want?"

"*You, Molly.* No one embarrasses me like that and gets away with it." He approached her. She was shaking and pleading with him with her eyes. He pulled out his fishing knife and got up next to her and said, "What do you think I ought to do with you, *Molly? Let you go?* I don't think so."

"Look, mister, whoever you are . . ."

"You don't have a right to know my name." At that moment, he put the knife in the middle of her chest and cut the middle of her sports bra. "Take if off now, Molly."

She stood there terrified, and reached over and pulled it over her shoulders to the ground.

"My, My, what lovely *tits* you have, *Molly.*" He reached over and fondled her left breast and kissed it. She shuddered with fear. He did the same with the right breast. At this time, she could feel the cold steel blade on her hip as he ran it down the leg: first on one side, then the other. He backed off as her shorts fell to the ground.

At this point, Molly knew she was about to be raped and probably killed. She went to her knees and shouted, "Oh, God, no. Our Father, which art in Heaven. Hallowed be thy name. Thy Kingdom come, Thy will be . . ."

"Don't fear, *Hathor,* my Goddess of Fertility, for you are the eye of *Ra,* and I mean you no harm."

She raised her head slowly and looked at him. The look of evil was gone. He was a different person. She took a chance and said, "Don't you think it's time to go, *Ra?*"

Suddenly he looked at her with disdain again and said, "Yes, but you never speak of this, *Hathor,* or I will seek you out and destroy you." He walked back to his motorcycle, got on and was gone.

Molly Ryerson stood there shaking and crying, having no time to appreciate her mortality. She walked the mile back to her car, completely naked, opened the car, found a sweatshirt and towel to cover herself and drove back to Richfield, all the while thanking God for sparing her life.

25

Susan Woodson and Joanne Behler were driving to the Redmond airport. It was 1:00 in the afternoon. Joanne looked at Susan and said, "I'll bet you're really excited, aren't you, Susan?"

"Joanne, this is the most nervous I've ever been in my life. I don't know how I feel. When I see him, I don't know how . . . I just don't know." She shook her head back and forth and almost started to cry.

"It's only been a week, for cripes sake. You two have gone through so much emotion it's hard to tell where you are. But I'd trade places with you in a minute."

Susan looked at Joanne and said, "You always know how to make me feel better, you know that? You're a true friend."

"See, you're making a big deal out of nothing."

"Well, it's hardly nothing, Joanne. I mean, I'm going down to see a man that was involved in a surreal episode. I don't know how he feels about me."

"I just wish I was a fly on the wall."

Susan looked at Joanne and smiled. "I'll just bet you do."

They arrived at the airport, unloaded Susan's bags, and Joanne said to Susan, "Now if you need my help in this, you give me a call," and Joanne gave her a wink.

"Oh, you know I will. Yes, ma'am."

"Have a good trip, girl."

"Next Sunday at noon—unless you hear otherwise."

*   *   *

Bob looked at his watch, it said 5:45. *Her plane should be touching down at any moment.* He told himself he wouldn't get excited about this, but there he was, like a little kid in a candy store. The passengers were coming toward him. A dozen, two dozen, three dozen, no Susan. Then shuffling along, pulling her carry-on, and looking left and right, was his girl. "Susan, Susan, over here!" She stopped, looked up and saw him, and ran into his arms. "Bob! God, I missed you so much." They kissed and hugged each other, and Bob said, "And I worried about this moment all week, Ms. Woodson."

Susan looked at him and said, "Piece of cake." They both laughed, collected her bag and proceeded to baggage. As they were walking, she looked at him and said, "You haven't aged a bit."

"Thanks a lot. You look like you have a little . . ."

"Don't say it. Leave it alone." Again, they both laughed.

After they collected her baggage and proceeded to the car, she asked him how the week was at work. He told her the first day was the worst day of his work life. It was a difficult case, and with the stress of the three prior weeks, left him emotionally exhausted.

"Well, you'll just have to get into real estate. We don't have those kinds of days."

"Right. A little more of that and your nose will grow."

It was almost an hour to Bob's home in Fallbrook. The music was turned up and Susan said, "That's music from the second act of *La Boheme.*"

"Geez, Susan. Isn't there anything you don't know about opera?"

"Not much."

"You probably know more than I do."

"Probably."

"Boy, you're a cocky little thing."

She reached over and kissed him on the cheek and said, "Oh, don't take it personally, Sir Robert."

They arrived at his house and unloaded the Jeep. He told her that he had a couple steaks in the fridge and that he'd get on them in a moment. She looked at him with bedroom eyes and said, "Oh, there's no hurry. Just get us some wine and we can contemplate dinner."

They sat out on the veranda watching the light grow dim, never for a moment considering steaks, dinner, wine, but only each other. They kissed one another and suddenly two chaise lounges became one. "Make love to me out here, Bob."

"But people can see on this veranda."

"It's getting dark and we'll be quiet as a mouse."

They both undressed and he kissed her neck, her shoulder, her breasts, and ran his hand down her waist to her thigh, where he removed her panties and found her wet. He aroused her to the point of ecstasy and then he entered, probing for utter fulfillment. They both arrived at once and then lay naked, together as one.

"Is there anything you don't do well, Mr. Hoaglund?"

"Not really." And they both laughed.

Susan told Bob that they were unable to find Jake Hanson, that he had gotten away. Where, they knew not. That the threat of an eruption from Mt. Bachelor was gone, for the moment.

"I've got these steaks. Don't you think we ought to get back to them?"

"Well, I just had *my* desert, and now you want the main meal?"

"Wait a while for that. Do you want to eat or not?"

"You know I do. But I just wanted to make sure that..."

"You made sure, Susan. You *always* do."

"Thank you," and she smiled.

They fixed dinner and watched a movie and then retired to bed. Bob said, "I didn't think that movie would ever end."

"Why?" She asked.

"No reason."

"Then why are we going to bed?"

"Oh . . . no reason." They looked at each other, gave thumbs up and went to bed, sort of.

The next morning, when they awoke, she asked: "What do you have for me this morning, my dear knight?"

"My dear knight? Get off it. It's too hot to wear armor. Seriously, though. I thought we'd take a ride up to Julian and show you this neat little town."

"Julian. Has a nice sound to it."

"You'll like it."

They drove up to Julian, spent the better part of a day there, and drove down to the desert, to Borrego Springs. Bob explained that in the early spring there are some wonderful desert blooms worth seeing. When they got home, it was overcast and a bit cold. Bob explained that this is what they call June gloom, a phenomenon that happens almost every year. "You mean you need a sweater to sit out here every night?"

"Yes, you do, my dear. In the morning there's a mist, almost like sprinkles. It's air conditioning for an early summer. Do you want some Mexican food tonight?"

"Oh, that sounds great. But maybe some wine and . . ."

"Come on, Susan. Let's have the Mexican food first."

"Oh, all right. It's your venue. Can't argue with Rome."

"Good thinking, my dear. You'll make someone a good wife."

"Is that a proposition?"

"As a matter of fact, it is." He got down on one knee and said, "Susan, will you marry me?"

She didn't even have to mull it over. "*Yes!*" and she jumped in his arms. "Right here, right now?"

"Well, can you wait until . . . it'll take a couple days to . . ."

"I know, Bob. But I just . . ."

"Let's go get some dinner, what do you say?"

"Can you believe you asked, and can you believe I said *yes?*"

"On both counts . . . yes."

"Pretty sure of yourself."

"Right now I am."

"And so am I. I love you, Bob."

"And I you, Susan."

They went into Fallbrook and had some tasty Mexican food. When they got back to Bob's home, they both agreed that Judge Ruiz could marry them, that Joanne would fly down to be the maid of honor and that Terry Jacobson, an old friend of Bob's, would be best man. "Hello, Judge Ruiz, this is Bob."

"Hi, Bob. Did Susan get down on time?"

"Yes, she did." Susan grabbed the phone and said, "Judge Ruiz, this is Susan. Bob has asked me to marry him, I said yes, and we would be honored to have you marry us, if you would."

"Oh, for gosh sakes. Congratulations. I would be so honored. When is this going to take place?"

Bob retrieved the phone and said, "Hopefully, day after tomorrow. We'll plan on it. OK?"

"You are an adventuresome pair, I must tell you. Let me know tomorrow what the schedule is."

"I will."

Susan dialed up Joanne; she answered, and Susan said, "Joanne, do you have a busy week?"

"Not really. Why?"

"Would you be my maid of honor?"

"*I knew it! I knew it!* Boy, you two don't waste any time, do you. Wouldn't miss it for the world. When and where?"

"Day after tomorrow. I'll call you and make reservations for your flight in."

"I can't wait."

Bob called Terry Jacobson, who lived just up the road in Newport Beach and told him he'd call him at work tomorrow with all the details.

The next day they went down and got blood tests and the marriage license. As they were driving home Bob said, "It's getting late, Susan. You still want to go through with it?"

"I won't let you out of it."

"Didn't think you would." They both laughed.

But as they drove back to Fallbrook from San Diego, Bob said, "Susan, you know, there's two questions that we haven't . . ."

"I know. K&K. Kids and 'Kareer.' "

"You always surprise me how quick you are. And how do you feel about it?"

"The kids? That's easy. As long as they're yours. The career?"

"I'll answer that. You are obviously happier in your career than I am in mine."

"That's not . . ."

"Hold on and hear me out. So when we get back from our honeymoon . . ."

"Oh, we're going on a honeymoon?"

"You know damn well we are. And quit changing the subject. We'll work it out. *I'll make sure we work it out."*

"I know you will, Sir Robert."

* * *

The wedding was held on Thursday, June 21st at 6:00 P.M. in Judge Ruiz' chambers. After the ceremony, they all went to a steak house on Shelter Island and celebrated. Judge Ruiz looked at Joanne and Terry and said, "Did you ever think this would happen with these two?"

Joanne said she wasn't sure and Terry said he gave up on Bob years ago. Bob told the judge he didn't know if he'd ever be back to work, the way things were going. He couldn't take the hectic pace.

Susan said, "You ain't seen nothing yet." Everyone laughed. When the party was over, Joanne went back to her hotel, and Terry had gone home, on the way to their cars, the judge said, "You two make a lovely couple and I wish you all the best."

"Thanks, Judge."

Susan and Bob had agreed to wait until Monday to start their official honeymoon activities, but would begin the preliminaries immediately.

* * *

Jake Hanson, on his BMW, whizzed along I-70 toward Grand Junction, Colorado. He needed a place to stay the night and stopped at a Quality Inn. He had to decide where his destination was going to be. It was the start of summer so he needed to find some work like he had in Bend, fixing motors at a lake resort or something like that. He pulled out a map of Colorado from the room and decided that he would go on to the town of Dillon, and the lake there.

In the morning, he drove the three hours to the town of Dillon. As he came upon the ramp to Dillon he noticed the lake was on his right and decided to exit there. While riding around he noticed a sign that said Marina. He drove out to the end where there was a building. He got off his motorcycle and wandered into the building. It was a nice day, a lot of people were on vacation and wanted to go boating. *A good sign,* he thought. He approached the desk and asked who to see about a job. The clerk at the desk said, "You want to see Dave. Dave Pollack."

The clerk went to the office and said, "Dave, there's someone here to see you."

Dave came out of the office and saw Jake. "Could I help you?"

"Yes. My name is Michael Hanson, I'm looking for a job."

"What kind of work do you do?"

"I'm a mechanic, specializing in boat motors."

"Well, I'll be darned. You're in luck. My mechanic left just yesterday and you can start today, if you want. I have some motors in back that are in need of repair. I'll start you at eight bucks an hour for the first three weeks, then ten to twelve dollars an hour if you work out."

"Sounds fair to me. Is there anywhere I can find some accommodations"

"Well, down the street and to your left three blocks is

a rental office. I'm sure you can find some low cost rentals across the lake."

"Thanks a lot, Dave. I'll be back in a couple hours"

Jake went over to the rental office and found a rental across the lake for $150 a week. Normally, during the ski season, they rent for $800 to $1200 a week. He went over and checked it out. A one room, with a TV and a small kitchen. *Couldn't be better,* he thought.

When he arrived back at the marina, he went in the building and Dave showed him the shop in the back. There were seven or eight motors up on a bench that needed attention. He got four of them running in the afternoon and thought, *Maybe I better not show my abilities here, they'll ask me to do more.* He stopped, put a motor on one of the boats and took it out for a test run. As he approached the beach on a finger island, he saw a beautiful girl with no top on; no one around. *This is my lucky day.* He started toward the girl when a guy came toward her. He looked at Jake and gave him the finger.

"In your dreams, asshole."

Jake pulled the boat around, thought to himself, *I'm not going to let that bother me. I just got here. But next time, you prick, I'll . . .*

A clap of thunder came from the south and Jake thought it best to get back. When he arrived at the marina, the sky was very dark, a bolt of lightning and clap of thunder only a mile away, and the sky opened up. *This is gonna work out just fine,* he thought.

26

Bob and Susan both called their mothers to give them the good news about their wedding. Bob told Susan his mother would only be concerned because she wasn't invited to the wedding, and he was right. That's all she did was complain; although she did wish them well. Susan, on the other hand, was very nervous about telling her mother because she was a very controlling individual and would go off on a tirade that she was just like her father, irresponsible; that she didn't have the courtesy to tell her she was dating some man, much less got married within three weeks. She told her mother that there is more to the story than just a cavalier dating frenzy, and that when she met him she would understand. That didn't seem to sit well with her mother, and Susan told her that would just have to do.

They didn't get away on their honeymoon until a day later, on a Tuesday, and made it as far as Cedar City in Utah. "Where are we going, Bob? What's our final destination?" He looked at her and said, "That's for me to know and you to find out."

"Boy, you're like an elephant, you don't forget anything, do you?"

"Nope."

When they awoke in the morning, they dressed and went over to a little café for breakfast. Bob brought a *Salt Lake Tribune* and went through the first section haphazardly before getting to the sports section. He gave the first section to Susan and she read with a little more thoroughness. Suddenly, Susan gasped and said, "Oh no. My God, no!"

Bob looked up and said, "What's wrong, Susan?"

She gave him the section of the paper back and pointed to a blurb in the upper right-hand corner. It read:

> Richfield—The body of a man was found in the upper reaches of a forest road, apparently the victim of a homicide. The scene was colored by the fact it was done in a ritualistic setting. The name of the victim is being withheld pending notification of relatives.

Bob looked at Susan and said, "He's here in Utah. We better notify Lieutenant Santorini about this."

He took out his cell phone and rang the number of the Deschutes Sheriff's Office.

"Deschutes County Sheriff's Office. How may I direct your call?"

"Lieutenant Al Santorini, please."

"Who should I say is calling?"

"Bob Hoaglund, please."

"Just a moment."

"Hello?"

"Lieutenant Santorini, this is Bob Hoaglund."

"How are you, Bob? Good to hear from you."

"Doing well, Lieutenant. Let me turn you over to Mrs. Hoaglund."

"Hello, Lieutenant."

"Did I hear that right—*Mrs. Hoaglund?*"

"You did. We work fast, us two. Just wanted to say hi. I'll give you back to Bob."

"Lieutenant, I want you to listen to this." Bob read

the blurb from the paper to Lieutenant Santorini over the phone. When he was done Lieutenant Santorini said, "I . . . I can't believe it. He's struck. Where are you two?"

"We're in Cedar City, Utah, on our honeymoon, and on our way to . . ."

Susan grabbed the phone and said, "He won't tell me, Lieutenant."

Lieutenant Santorini laughed and said, "I'm going to get a plane down to Salt Lake as soon as I can, and then drive over to Richfield. That's on I-70, isn't it?"

"Yes, it is. We're only a little ways away and we'll meet you there."

"You needn't do that, kids. Go enjoy yourselves."

"We're in this as much as you are, Lieutenant."

"Yes, I understand. I'll see you there, then. Bye."

* * *

Lieutenant Santorini walked over to see Sheriff Malone. His secretary said that he was down in Grants Pass at a conference and wouldn't be back for a couple of days. She said that Captain Smith was in his office if he wanted to see him. He knocked on his door, Captain Jim Smith saw who it was and greeted Lieutenant Santorini. "Well, hello, Al. Nice to see you."

"You, too, Jim. We don't see each other often enough, much less get together. Listen, Jim. Byron's gone to a conference and I need a real favor of you. You know the murder of Red Jensen that I was involved in?"

"Of course. We all know about that, Al."

"Well, you know that he did not turn up after scouring Mt. Bachelor. I got a call this morning from a friend of mine who read in a Salt Lake newspaper about a similar murder in Richfield, Utah; the ceremonial trappings and all. I was wondering if I could take a few days and go over . . ."

"Of course, Al. We all now what Red meant to you and no one would deny you this request."

"Thanks, Jim. And when I get back . . ."

"We'll get together, I know. And we will."

Lieutenant Santorini walked out of the captain's office and back to his. He got on the phone to Richard Allenson, who lived in Sunriver. Mr. Allenson was a retired CEO from Pfizer who had a jet parked at the Sunriver Airport.

"Hello, Richard? This is Al Santorini."

"Al, nice to hear from you. How are things in Bend?"

"Well, right now chaotic. I suppose you heard about the killing of Red."

"Yes, I did. Red was a fine man; an institution in the county and your best friend. We were all saddened to hear about it."

"I've got a favor to ask of you, Richard."

"After all you did for my son, you name it."

Richard Allenson's son was involved heavily in narcotics, and Lieutenant Santorini did all he could to help him out, eventually getting him to a successful recovery.

"We think that the murderer of Red has surfaced in a little town of Richfield, Utah. I was wondering if I could impose on you to fly me there or . . ."

"Of course we can. I'll call my pilot, Murray Schaefer, and he can run you over there. I don't need the plane until next week."

"I'll pay for all the gas and his flight time."

"Nonsense. For all you did for me? Are you kidding? What's your number? Murray will give you a call. Nice hearing from you, Al."

Lieutenant Santorini told Sandy, his secretary, that

he would be away from the office for a few days, that he would be checking in periodically, to reach him on his cell phone. He went home to pack. On the way, he got a call from the pilot, Murray Schaefer, that it would be a couple hours; they could leave about 2:00. When he got home, he gave Deputy Berger a call, and for him to pick him up at 1:00.

When they got to Sunriver Airport, Murray was waiting for him on the tarmac. He took his suitcase out of the car and said, "Thanks a lot, Wally."

"Happy hunting, Lieutenant. See you soon, I hope."

The jet was a Citation Encore, and cruised at 500 mph. The flight from Sunriver to Richfield, which was only 520 miles, took only an hour and a half. For such a small community, Richfield Airport has a 6,600 foot runway, long enough to accommodate jet aircraft. As they landed, the sheriff of Sevier County, Hal Emerson, was waiting with a sheriff vehicle. As Lieutenant Santorini stepped off the plane, Sheriff Emerson extended his hand. "Hi, I'm Sheriff Emerson."

"Glad to meet you, Sheriff. I'm Lieutenant Al Santorini."

"I hope you can shed some light on this, Lieutenant, because we're at a loss here."

"*Hopefully,* Sheriff. *Hopefully.*"

Lieutenant Santorini introduced the sheriff to Murray, and then said, "Sheriff, I need to make a call for a second."

"Sure. Take your time."

He dialed Bob Hoaglund's cell phone and said, "Hello, Bob? This is Al Santorini."

"Where are you, Lieutenant?"

"We just touched down at the Richfield Airport. Where are you?"

"We're at the Quality Inn on Main Street. We just arrived about a half hour ago."

"We'll get our bags and meet you there. Bye."

The sheriff, Lieutenant Santorini and Murray Schaefer all went to the Quality Inn where the lieutenant and Murray Schaefer got their respective rooms. Bob and Susan Hoaglund met them downstairs.

"So, you two are married, huh? Congratulations."

"Thanks, Lieutenant."

They all stood around exchanging pleasantries, stories about the wedding and all. Lieutenant Santorini said that he'd meet them at 7:00 down in the lobby for dinner that he was going over to the sheriff's department to look at some evidence and reports.

When they arrived at the sheriff's department, Sheriff Emerson brought out the report and some pictures of the scene. In looking at the scene, from the pictures, Lieutenant Santorini said, "Could you orient me on this photo as to which way is north, south, etc."

Sheriff Emerson put a visquine overlay on the photo and oriented directions for the lieutenant.

"So, this silver piece here is what, facing south?"

"No. It looks like—maybe east, if I've got my bearings straight."

After reading the report, Lieutenant Santorini said, "Did you find any evidence of a vehicle of any kind, other than the pickup? I know it's a long way to the main road from there; a good hike."

"We looked all around and were unable to pick up any tracks at all."

"Is there anybody else that may have noticed any of the victim's habits?"

"Well, the only person we've come up with is a grandson named Ralph, who called and left a message on the answering machine."

"What did it say?"

The sheriff ruffled through some reports and said, "It said, 'Jimmie, this is Ralph. Sorry I missed you, but I'll check back later.' Ralph is coming into town tomorrow morning." He looked at Lieutenant Santorini and said, "You apparently know a little bit about this person who killed Jimmie. Is he some psychopath, or what is his motive behind all this?"

"You now, Sheriff, I hope we get to find out."

* * *

The three of them met in the lobby and proceeded over to Dan's Steakhouse for dinner. Lieutenant Santorini wanted to know about the wedding, and then asked, "So, have you decided where you're going to live?"

The two looked at each other and Susan Hoaglund responded, "*N-o-o,* but Mr. Hoaglund here says it will be no problem."

Bob Hoaglund said, "It won't be a problem until we address it. Right now, we're on a very important case."

Susan looked at Bob quizzically, and just laughed. "You see, Lieutenant, he's shrewd that way, isn't he?"

"Too much for me."

Bob Hoaglund looked at the lieutenant and asked, "Is it the same guy?"

"It sure looks that way."

"Which way do you think he's gone?"

"Well, it's either south or east. Let's hope east. Are you kids sticking around tomorrow?"

"We thought we would. Besides, Susan thinks our

reservations, wherever we're going—that we're going to be late."

"*Really. How would I know that if I don't know where we're going?*"

"See how fast she's learning, Lieutenant?"

They all laughed, finished their dinner and said goodnight.

*   *   *

The next morning Lieutenant Santorini arrived at the sheriff's department office and met Sheriff Emerson, who told him that Ralph Stowers would be in around 1:00; that he could run him up to the murder scene. When they arrived at the murder scene, with the reports, evidence and photos, Lieutenant Santorini got out of the car and asked, "Where exactly was the pickup parked?"

Sheriff Emerson responded, "Right over there by those trees."

"Can I see the autopsy report? Is that done yet?"

"It just came in this morning. It's preliminary."

Preliminary? That's something for my benefit. "It shows he was hit with some kind of blunt instrument and then shot in the head? I can't make out . . ."

"Apparently that's what it says. *Blunt instrument to the left side of the skull, causing massive trauma with subsequent gunshot wound to the Occiput.* There apparently was no struggle, no overt injuries to any other part of the body."

"Is there any sign of . . . was he dragged anywhere?"

"Just over here."

The lieutenant walked around the scene, looking at the pictures, and said, "What is that in the rear of the pickup? There."

"That was determined to be oil."

"*Oil?* Looks pretty light and pretty fresh, wouldn't you say?"

"Yes, I would."

"Like something maybe used in a *motorcycle?*"

"Yes." The sheriff thought a moment to himself. *Why didn't they pick up on that? It's right there in front of their faces.*

"You know, Sheriff, it's a trick I've heard before. A person can lead you off track by moving a motorcycle away from the scene, without any tire marks, for some fifty feet or so, and nobody knows the difference."

"Lieutenant, I'm sure glad you came. I'm certain you've got a few more pearls for me."

They both laughed and proceeded back to the sheriff's department office. When they got there, Ralph Stowers was waiting.

"You must be Ralph Stowers. I'm Sheriff Emerson, and this here is Lieutenant Santorini."

"Glad to meet you both."

"We're both very sorry about your grandfather. Everybody loved him in this town."

They drove out to Jimmie Tyler's house, got out of the car and opened the door. Upon entering, Lieutenant Santorini said, "Ralph, can you tell me a little about your grandfather?"

"Oh, well, he was a nice little old man who ran a fish hatchery. He didn't have many friends."

"Was there any place in town he used to hang out?"

"Yeah, there was. There was a gas station with a little diner that he used to go to because he couldn't sleep. He'd go there at two or three in the morning."

"Do you know the name of it?"

"No, I don't. But I could show you where it was."

"Is there any reason, you know of, anyone would want to hurt your grandfather?"

"None that I could think of. He was a . . . just a moment." At that point Ralph walked over to the can on the shelf and opened it. *"It's gone. It's all gone."*

"What's that, Ralph?"

"He used to have money in this can. Lots of money."

"How much?"

"I don't know. Maybe well, *thousands of dollars.*"

"Thousands? Are you sure not *hundreds?"*

"No. Literally *thousands.*"

"Anything else missing?"

"Not that I can see in here. Let's go out to the back garage."

They walked out to the garage in the rear and opened the door. Ralph looked around and said, *"That's gone, too."*

"What's that, Ralph?"

"The motorcycle."

The motorcycle. Just as I thought. "What kind of motorcycle was it, Ralph?"

"A BMW. I left it here because I thought he might be able to sell it."

"Anything else missing?"

"Not that I can tell."

They locked up the house and proceeded over to the diner. They walked in and talked to the cook/waiter and asked him who worked the early morning shift. He said, "You know, he's right in the back. Denny."

Denny walked out, looked at the three people standing there, one dressed in a sheriff's outfit, and said, "Can I help you?"

Sheriff Emerson took out a photograph and showed it to Denny and asked, "Have you seen this person before?"

"Yeah. He comes in early in the morning sometimes, three or four in the morning."

"In the last few days, have you seen anyone with him?"

"Yeah. As a matter of fact, I have. A young man was talking with him a few days ago, although I couldn't tell you what he looked like because his back was to me."

"At that point, Lieutenant Santorini jumped in and said, "Was he tall or short? Heavy or skinny?"

"Yeah. He was kind of tall and thin."

"That's all you saw of him?"

"Yeah. At that time of the morning. I don't pay attention too much."

"Well, thanks a lot, Denny."

"Yeah, sure."

They walked out to the car and returned to the sheriff's office. Sheriff Emerson said, "Thanks, Ralph. That's all we need for now."

Lieutenant Santorini stopped Ralph and asked him, "Do you know the license number on the BMW?"

"Yes, I do. 15416."

"Thanks, Ralph." As Ralph walked away, Lieutenant Santorini looked at Sheriff Emerson and said, "There's your motive, Sheriff. *Money and transportation.*"

27

Lieutenant Santorini gathered his photos and began the process of visiting businesses to see if anyone had hired or recognized Jake Hanson. Knowing that Jake was a mechanic, he visited three or four garages before coming upon Chuck's Auto Repair. He walked in the office and sitting behind the desk was a young man. "Who is the owner of this garage?"

"He's not here right now. Can I help you?"

"Well, maybe. And your name, sir?"

"I'm Ron Terry."

"Have you been working here long?"

Ron Terry looked skeptically at Lieutenant Santorini and said, "A little while. Why?"

Lieutenant Santorini picked a photo out of his pocket and said, "Have you ever seen this man before?"

Ron Terry immediately recognized it as Michael Hanson and said, "Who wants to know? I mean, who are you?"

"My name is Lieutenant Santorini, I'm from the Deschutes County Sheriff's Office. I'm looking for this gentleman."

"What are you doing down in Richfield?"

At that moment Chuck Mason stepped into the office and said, "Can I help you?"

"Yes. I'm looking for the owner."

"That would be me, Chuck Mason."

"I was just talking to your assistant here. I'm Lieutenant Al Santorini from the Deschutes County Sheriff's Office. I wonder if you could tell me if you've seen this man before."

"Yes. That's Michael Hanson."

Lieutenant Santorini looked over at Ron Terry and said, "Do you mind if I talk to Chuck, Mr. Terry?"

Ron Terry looked over and smiled and took a seat up front. "No, not at all."

He looked over with stern eyes and said, "*Alone.*"

"Oh, I see. Yeah, sure." He left the office.

"Could you tell me how you know Mr. Hanson?"

"Well, he was recommended by my cousin in Salt Lake, Joseph Buchanan, as needing a job. So he came by about a week ago and I hired him as a truck driver."

"Truck driver?"

"Tow truck driver, from twelve in the morning until twelve noon. He worked a few days and quit, haven't seen him since. Still have his check here."

"Where did he stay?"

"He stayed over the garage."

"Did he have any transportation of any kind?"

"Not that I saw."

"Where would he eat?"

"That I don't know. When we get new employees like Mr. Hanson and Mr. Terry, we always give them the same recommendations. The diner around the corner and Molly's Drive-In a few blocks away. It's cheap."

"Did he ever say anything about eating at any of those places, or a gas station with a diner a few blocks away?"

"No."

"Well, thanks a lot, Mr. Mason."

"One other thing, Lieutenant. You know, there was

something about that boy. I don't think I trusted him. There was a way about him."

* * *

Lieutenant Santorini checked out the diner around the corner and nobody recognized him. He walked six or seven blocks down to Molly's Drive-In and entered the restaurant. There was a waitress at the counter and he showed the picture of Jake to her and she shook her head back and forth, she didn't recognize him. Another waitress was down at the other end of the counter. He approached her and showed her the photograph. At that moment, a woman came out of an office and said, "Excuse me, sir. What are you doing?"

"I was asking this woman if she recognized this photo."

"And *who* are you, sir?"

"My name is Lieutenant Al Santorini. Who am I speaking to?"

"Molly Ryerson. I'm the owner of this restaurant."

"Well, Ms. Ryerson, I will ask you. Have you ever seen this person before?"

Molly stepped back a step, her eyes got very big, she seemed to gasp a little. "No, I haven't seen him before."

Immediately Lieutenant Santorini knew that she *had* seen him, and pressed her further. "This is very important, Ms. Ryerson. Take a moment. Have you ever seen this person before?"

She looked at the lieutenant and said in a very stern manner, "*I told you, Lieutenant. No, I haven't seen him.*"

The restaurant and its patrons suddenly became very quiet. "OK, Ms. Ryerson, I understand. Thank you."

As he left the restaurant, he pulled out his phone and rang Bob and Susan. "Hello, Bob? Can I speak to Susan?"

"Yes, she's right here."

"Susan, I think I've got someone down here who knows Jake Hanson, but I need your help. Can you come down right away?"

"Yes, I can."

"I don't know the addresses very well, but it's somewhere in the seven-hundred block of Main Street. It's called Molly's Drive-In."

"I'll be there right away, about ten minutes."

Bob and Susan arrived at Molly's and met Lieutenant Santorini in the parking lot. Bob said that he was going to get a milkshake at the drive-in and would meet her there. Susan went inside and asked for Molly. "Hi, Molly. I'm Susan Hoaglund, a friend of Lieutenant Santorini's. Could I talk to you?"

"I've said everything I'm going to say about this, Ms. Hoaglund."

"No. I understand how you feel, and I'm sympathetic with you."

Molly turned toward Susan and said, "You don't know how I feel. Why would *you* make a statement like that?"

"Because this person almost killed me twice. I'm very lucky to be here today."

"You say that, but . . ."

"Look, Ms. Ryerson? It is Ms. Ryerson?"

"Yes, it is."

"We can do this here or in the office. I don't think your customers want to be a part of this conversation."

Molly motioned her in the office and walked to the back facing away from Susan, and said, "What do you want?"

253

"We want you to tell us about any encounter you had with this man, Michael Hanson, or Jake Hanson." Susan could see that Molly was beginning to cry, a tear was falling down her cheek.

She hadn't turned around, but said, "I met him while I was running on the road. He stopped me in a remote section, approached me with a knife and threatened me. He then cut my training bra off, exposing my breasts." At this point Molly was in total tears. "He then fondled my breasts and kis . . . kissed them, all the while cutting my shorts off so I was totally naked." Molly turned toward Susan with a pleading look, "I thought I was going to die. I started to quote the Lord's Prayer and all of the sudden, he looked at me and his whole attitude changed. He started to talk about *rah,* or *raw,* or something similar, that I was the goddess of fertility, *Heather*, something; and said something about an eye. He said he meant me no harm. It was horrible."

Susan approached Molly and comforted her. "It's all right, Molly. It's all right." She realized as a strict Mormon, she was ashamed of what had happened. "I know this is rough, and I'm sorry you had to divulge all of this. But we don't want this person to kill anyone else."

"I know. I'm sorry."

Susan left Molly's office and met Lieutenant Santorini and Bob in the drive-in. She told the lieutenant everything that Molly said. He wrote it all down, word for word. "I'll bet you guys had a milkshake and didn't leave any for me. Right?"

"Right, *Ms. Holmes,*" Bob said. They all laughed.

They drove the lieutenant back to the motel and he said that he had to meet Murray for dinner, that he would be leaving Richfield tomorrow. He shook hands with Bob and gave Susan a hug. "You guys have a nice vacation. At least you can start it now."

Bob said, "You know we wouldn't miss this. Besides, Susan may have found a new career." They all laughed and said goodbye.

Lieutenant Santorini met Murray Schaefer downstairs at quarter of seven and they went off to eat dinner. While at dinner, Lieutenant Santorini said, "I think we might want to go to Eagle tomorrow. How far is that, do you know, Murray?

"Well, it's about three-hundred miles or so. About forty to forty-five minutes flying time."

"Can I get a car at that airport?"

"Sure you can. It's the airport for the skiing mecca; for Vail, Breckenridge, etc."

"I think that's what I'll do then, and you can go home. Richfield makes for some exciting nights, don't you think?" They both laughed.

*   *   *

The lieutenant and Murray met in the lobby at eight the next morning and had a deputy sheriff drive them to the airport. Murray checked out the plane, determined it was ready to go and they were off to Eagle, Colorado. While en route Lieutenant Santorini decided to ring the Deschutes County Sheriff's Office. Sandy answered the phone and Lieutenant Santorini asked if he could speak to Wally. "Hello, Wally? How's things at the office? Anything I need to know about? . . . The sheriff wonders what I'm doing? Well, you tell him I've got a lead on our boy, hopefully we'll find him soon and I'll be home. Other than that, everything is okay? Great. See you in a few days."

They landed at the Eagle Airport and Murray taxied

the Citation to the terminal. He opened the door and Lieutenant Santorini made his way to the ramp. "Murray, I sure appreciate everything you've done. You tell Richard that I'll talk to him when I get back. Take care now." With that, he said goodbye and entered the terminal. He went over to the car rental agency and rented a car and was on the road toward I-70. He stopped at a couple gas stations along the way and showed the pictures of Jake to the attendants. No one seemed to recognize him except for a young man in the garage.

"Yeah, I saw him. He was on a BMW motorcycle."

"Why do you remember that?"

"Because we had words and he called me an *asshole*."

"Which way did he go?"

"He went toward Vail."

"How far is Vail from here?"

"Oh, maybe thirty miles or so."

Al got on I-70 and proceeded east to Vail. He got off the exit and looked for a café to get some coffee and call Phillip Ross. He stopped in the Vail Village at Charlie's Deli and grabbed a cup of coffee, a sandwich and called Phillip Ross.

"Hello, Phillip?"

"Yes."

"This is Al Santorini."

"Oh, Al. Nice to hear from you again. Did you ever get that man you were looking for?"

"No, Phillip. He got away from us, and that's what I'm calling about. He's struck again—this time in Utah. Do you have time for me to run a scenario by you?"

"Of course. You know *us* academics, our plate is always full. But I'll make time." They both laughed.

"Let me posit this scenario for you. Our predator has come upon a girl, jogging on a lonely road. He pulls up beside her on his motorcycle, parks it, gets off, and corners her. He pulls out a knife and cuts her training bra off, exposing her breasts.

"Further, as he's fondling her breasts, he cuts off her shorts and exposes her completely. She's terrified and starts reciting the Lord's Prayer, at which time his personality changes: He begins to tell her that he is *Ra,* that she is *Heather,* the Goddess of Fertility, something about an eye; that he means her no harm. He then mounts his motorcycle and leaves her.

"What do you make of that?"

"Well, obviously he's . . . a little further history. You remember that as *Ra,* he is a self-appointed god. When he speaks of Heather, it is actually *Hathor,* who is the Goddess of Fertility. When he speaks of an eye, *she* is the *eye of Ra,* and as such, a part of him. Also, when he says he means her no harm, well, that may well be his Achilles heel, for we now know that he feels some emotion toward something. However deep, we don't know. But this is a break for you, Al, because he's now thinking about her and his loyalty toward her, and might not be so reckless. Has he killed again?

"He has. Apparently just before this incident I'm describing."

"Well, that explains his rage, and why it came to an abrupt, however maybe temporary, stop."

"I asked you this once before. But with the information I gave you, can you rule out schizophrenia?"

"Rule it out?" Not entirely. However, if you're asking what do I think he suffers from? Probably an atypical psychosis. These are disorders which are marked with psychotic symptoms, such as marked loosening of associations, grossly, and I emphasize *grossly,* disorganized behavior that do not meet the criteria for any other nonorganic psychotic disorder.

"There simply is not enough evidence to come to a specific diagnosis without seeing this gentleman. That's my best guesstimate from the information I have. Does that help, Al?"

"It sure does, Phillip."

"Where are you now?"

"I'm in Vail, Colorado. It's a beautiful day. I want to thank you once again, Phillip."

"Well, *thank you*. It's always gratifying when I can use the *noodle* once in awhile. Bye, Al."

Lieutenant Santorini sat there eating his sandwich, thinking, *I can feel he's near. I'm going to get you, Jake Hanson. Soon.*

28

Lieutenant Santorini was on the road after lunch toward Breckenridge, Dillon and the Frisco area. He arrived in the town of Dillon in the late afternoon and took a room in the Super 8 Motel. He decided to go into the town of Breckenridge and look around. He hadn't been to a ski resort in a long time, not since his wife died, and he felt right at home. It was summer, so it felt a little different—people running around in summer clothes in the evening.

He found the Summit County Sheriff's Department and went inside. He asked for the duty officer, and a lieutenant came to the front counter.

"Hi. I'm Lieutenant Santorini from the Deschutes County Sheriff's Office in Bend, Oregon."

"Nice to meet you, Lieutenant. I'm Lieutenant Jack Halloran. What brings you up here?"

"I'm looking for a fugitive from Oregon." The lieutenant pulled out a picture of Jake. "His name is Michael Jake Hanson. We believe he committed a murder in Richfield, Utah, and may be in the area."

"Do you have any other photos?"

"I sure do. I'd appreciate it if you'd circulate them to the area law enforcement agencies. One other favor, Lieutenant. Could I look at your hot sheet for stolen cars or motorcycles in the last week or so?"

"Let me get the person in charge of that. Nice talking to you, Lieutenant."

"Same here, Lieutenant Halloran."

In a few minutes, a deputy came forward with a sheet, composed of two pages, of thefts in the area. "Here you are, Lieutenant."

Lieutenant Santorini started scanning the sheet for information. The first three were car thefts of the last few days. When he came to the fourth item, it piqued his interest, because it involved a motorcycle.

> Subject stated that when he came out of restaurant, he noticed different license plate on rear of motorcycle. Original license plate of A2213 was replaced with plate I5416.

There it is, he thought. *Just as I expected. He's a shrewd man; still in the area.* "Thank you, Deputy. You've been most helpful." *Most helpful indeed.*

The lieutenant walked out of the sheriff's department knowing that tomorrow could be an eventful day. He had to figure that he was working as a mechanic in some capacity. *And what might that be?* He worked as a boat mechanic in the Bend area. He apparently had that old man, that he killed, convinced that he was interested in something other than the fish hatchery. *We'll see about that tomorrow.*

He went back to his motel room and looked for some place to eat, someplace Jake might be. He came upon a place called the Snake-Eyes Saloon. He drove over and walked into the saloon. There weren't too many people inside, it was rather early. He walked up to the bar, the bartender said, "What can I get ya?"

"Oh, just a draft."

The bartender brought him the beer and the lieutenant said, "Say, have you ever seen this person before?"

The bartender looked at him and said, *"Who wants to know?"*

"Well, I'm just looking for . . ."

"Are you a private dick or something?"

"Well, sort of."

"We don't rat out on people for beating their wife or anything like that up here, Mister."

Lieutenant Santorini looked at the bartender, brought out his badge, and said, "Look, sir. You can either say *yes or no* here, or we can do it downtown. Now, have you ever seen this person before?"

"Well, ye . . . yeah, I've seen him."

"How often does he come in here?"

"Seen him a couple times. Ornery little cuss, always causing trouble."

"What kind of trouble?"

"Well, you know, hasslin' girls, threatening people. Just a no good. Hope he never comes back."

Lieutenant Santorini finished his beer, saluted the bartender, and left the bar. He went on into Breckenridge to get something to eat. He found a nice little café, went back to his motel and went to bed.

* * *

Bob and Susan were approaching Colorado Springs. Susan looked at Bob and said, "How much further to our *appointed destination?*"

"Not far, Susan. Not far." He reached over and pulled a black scarf from the back seat and told Susan to put it on.

"What do you mean, *put it on?*"

"I know it sounds funny, but could you put it on? It's a surprise and I want to . . ."

"Man, you are weird, Robert. You know that?"

"Maybe you won't think *so weird*."

They drove for twenty minutes or so, Susan all the while complaining about how people must be laughing at her. "At least I haven't heard a car honk its horn. I'm going to take this thing off."

"Ah, ah. Just a few more minutes." They drove a few more minutes, Bob stopped the car and Susan took her scarf off her eyes.

"Where are . . . The Broadmoor? We're staying at The Broadmoor?"

"You got it, beautiful."

She looked at him and said, "Sir Robert. You're the best."

* * *

The first place Lieutenant Santorini checked the next morning was the marina on Lake Dillon. He walked into the marina office and asked to speak to the manager. The gentleman at the counter said, "He's not here right now. Could I help you?"

"Well, maybe you can. I want to show you a photo and see if you recognize it."

"No, I don't. However, I don't work here full time, I'm just filling in today."

"Is there anyone out back I can talk to?"

"Yes, there is. He's right over there where they store the boats."

"Thank you very much."

The lieutenant walked out to the storage shed and

asked the young man sitting there. "Do you work with the boats?"

"Yes, I do. I'm Danny Rodgers."

"Hi, Danny. Have you worked here long?"

"Oh, about two weeks or so."

Lieutenant Santorini pulled out a photo of Jake and showed it to Danny. "Ever seen this man before?"

"Oh, sure. That's Michael."

"*Michael?*"

"Yeah. I don't know his last name."

"When's the last time you saw Michael?"

"Let's see. I didn't see him yesterday or day before yesterday."

"Is he due to come in today?"

"That, I don't know. You'd have to ask the manager. He should be here after one or two o'clock."

"Thanks, Danny."

Lieutenant Santorini thought to himself, *I hope I haven't missed him again.* He got in his car and made his way across I-70 to the town of Frisco, a town on the Blue River, hoping to maybe spot Jake somewhere. After driving around for an hour or two, and stopping at several places, there was no sign of Jake and so he went back to the motel, dispirited.

He lay down and drifted off to sleep for a couple hours, and when he looked at the clock it was around three in the afternoon. He arose from the bed, put on his shoes and made his way back to the marina. As he walked back into the office, he noticed a motorcycle parked off to the side of the shed out back. He approached it from the front and noticed that it was a BMW. When he went to the rear, there, plain as day, I5416. He saw a pack on the motorcycle and was about to remove it when he heard a

"Hey, you. What are you doing there?" The gentleman approached and said, "What's going on?"

Lieutenant Santorini flashed his badge and said, "I'm interested in knowing who owns this bike."

"What authority do you? . . . "

"Who owns the bike and where is he, goddamnit?"

The man was taken aback and said, "Michael Hanson and he's out on the lake right now testing a boat. What do you want with him?"

"Let's just say it's a police matter. Where can I get a boat here?"

"Look, Officer, whoever you are, I don't know . . ."

"Listen, *sir*. If you don't settle down I'm going to charge you with obstruction of justice. Do you want that?"

"No."

"Then fix me up with a boat and tell me which way he might have gone."

"Probably around the bend down there, in that fingerlet."

Lieutenant Santorini hopped in the boat, started the engine and began his way out into the water. He checked his weapon to make sure it was fully loaded and ready.

The manager ran into his office and called the Summit County Sheriff's Department and told them that there was a crazy police officer out here threatening him.

The lieutenant's boat wouldn't go very fast and so it seemed like a long time to reach the bend. Most of the boats were on the other side of the lake. As he approached the bend, the boat's engine began to sputter and spurt. "Come on, you SOB. Keep running." He rounded the bend into a small inlet with a piece of land like a finger that jutted out. There, down about a hundred yards, was a boat sitting in the water. As he approached the rear of the boat from fifty or so yards, he could see it was Jake Hanson.

Jake turned around and saw a boat coming toward him. He saw a figure in the boat he thought he recognized. The man shouted, "Jake! Jake Hanson!" He knew then who it was. At that time, Lieutenant Santorini's boat began to cough and quit. Jake started his boat, which was an older model speedboat, and turned around toward Lieutenant Santorini. The lieutenant was busy trying to start his boat. When he looked up he saw Jake had slowed his boat and was starting to rise with a rifle pointed right at him. He realized there was no time to pull his weapon and was awaiting the inevitable. At that moment, Jake took a step toward the front of the boat and a dock line, which was laying over the side, into the boat, wrapped around Jake's foot and pulled the lever down on the side of the boat. The boat lurched suddenly forward at a high rate of speed, pulling Jake into the water. The boat made a wide circle around the lieutenant's boat, pulling Jake behind it. The boat headed for shore on the finger side and beached itself with a forward lurch, and stalled. All was quiet.

Lieutenant Santorini started paddling with his hands toward where the boat was beached. On the way toward shore, he noticed a body floating near. He got out of the boat and pulled the body toward shore. When he got to the beach, with Jake's body, he noticed the dock line. On the end of the line was a tennis shoe with part of Jake's leg.

* * *

It was about fifteen minutes before a boat, with the Summit County Sheriff's Department, arrived on the scene. Lieutenant Halloran stepped off the boat and said, "Well, Lieutenant Santorini, what do we have here. Is this what you were after?"

"This is it, Lieutenant."

"You know, you're going to have to make a report about this."

"Gladly, Lieutenant. Gladly."

As they took the body of Jake back to the marina, Lieutenant Santorini sat back and reflected on the past month's events. He looked skyward and said, *"Red, wherever you are, you're in a better place. I'll miss you, buddy."*

Epilogue

After making out his report for Summit County, Lieutenant Santorini called the sheriff of Deschutes County, Byron Malone. "Hello, Byron?"

"Is this Al?"

"It sure is. I'm calling from Dillon, Colorado, and I just wanted to call and tell you that we got *our boy, Jake Hanson,* here in Dillon. *He's dead.* So you can call Mayor McCartney and tell him he can *breathe a sigh of relief.*"

Sheriff Malone laughed and said, "That's great news, Al. When are you coming back?"

"I'll be back tonight. See you tomorrow, Sheriff."

He had two more calls to make. "Hello, Jennifer? Al Santorini here."

"Oh hi, Al."

"I wanted to tell you that we found Jake Hanson."

"You—you found him?"

"Yes. And he'll no longer bother anyone. He's dead."

"Thank God."

Lieutenant Santorini heard her crying in the background and said, "I'll see you in a couple days. Take care, Jennifer."

"You too, Al. Thanks."

He hung up the phone and made one more phone call. "Hello. Susan?"

"Yes. Is this Lieutenant Santorini?"

"You can call me Al, Susan. Yes. I wanted to tell . . . is Bob around?"

"Yes. I'll give him to you. But first, do you know where we wound up?"

"No. That's another . . ."

"We're at the Broadmoor Hotel in Colorado Springs. Can you believe that stinker was able to keep that a secret?"

"Well, that's Bob, isn't it. But congratulations. Have a nice time. And have a glass of wine for me."

"Sure will, *Al*. Bye."

"Hello, Al?"

"Yes. Hi, Bob. I wanted to tell you that we found Jake Hanson in Dillon, Colorado, and he'll no longer be bothering anyone."

"That's great. *By bothering anyone?—*"

"He's dead. Well, you and Susan have a great time. When you're in Bend, dinner's on me."

"We'll take you up on that. Bye."

* * *

Bob and Susan walked down toward the lobby. Susan saw a grand piano sitting nearby and she said, "Hold on a sec, Bob." She sat down and began to play. Bob, feeling nervous, sat down and was in awe of how easy she made it seem, and how beautiful her playing was, far different than before. All the while she was playing, a group of elderly folks, who had gotten off a bus, mingled together, listening. When Susan completed the piece, they all applauded, and one woman said, "What's the name of that piece?"

Susan said, "A Chopin Waltz."

"Well, you play wonderfully, young lady. Did you ever think of becoming a concert pianist?"

Susan looked at Bob, his eyes beaming, then looked over at the woman and said, "Well, thank you for the compliment, but no."

As they were walking away, Bob looked at Susan and said, "How did you do that, Mrs. Hoaglund?"

"You remember those few days away from each other? Well, just between you and me, I practiced a little bit." They both laughed.

As they were walking down the hall, hand in hand, Susan said, "You remember that song about the birds and a poet?"

"Oh, you mean *'Robins and Roses?'* "

"Yes, that's it. How does that go?"

Robins and Roses, and maybe a tree; a few morning
glories, a cottage two stories high . . .
Robins and Roses, and then life will be, a poem by
Kipling while troubles go rippling by.